Disclaimer

Lakeside Bosses and Peons

Who Worked Where In 1969...

Crane Stables – on Fieldsburg Lake, WI:
Cal Masterson - Boss
Wyatt Moretti – Third Year Peon
Earl Thorne – Third Year Peon
Coolidge - First Year Peon

Hillcrest Stables - on Mt. Lewis Lake, WI:
Hank Nelson – Boss
Parker Moretti – Fourth Year Peon
Lenny White– First Year Peon

Dumped Off

June 5th 1969, thirteen-year old Michael Bentley, who did not know yet that his name would soon be Coolidge, was in his father's aging Buick station wagon inhaling second-hand Kent cigarette smoke as he had been for the last two hours during the mostly silent drive from Milwaukee. His neatly packed duffel and a rolled up, heavy cotton sleeping bag were in the back seat. He knew why he was here. His mother had arranged a summer stables job for him in the country through her German friend, Ma Nelson, whose college aged son was one of the owners. *A summer job at a camp? I know nothing about horses. Is this okay with mom? What about theater camp?* "Doesn't matter," Mrs. Nelson said. "They'll teach you everything you need to know. It's in the middle of Wisconsin – beautiful! Hank loves it there! It will be good for you to get away for a while."

Michael's father, Perry Bentley, was fine with the situation. His car wash business had fallen on hard times, and the arguments with Michael's mother about not being able to afford the price of theater or tennis camp, or even the cheaper price of the local racquet club where Michael could at least swim and hit tennis balls against a backboard, were getting old. *People would feed and house his son for a whole summer and put him to work too? Perfect. It's camp without the fees.*

But Mr. Bentley began to have second thoughts when he pulled the faded gold Buick station wagon off the two-lane highway and onto the dirt driveway that was almost completely hidden by overgrown grass and weeds. The driveway wound around an old red livestock barn and led to an infield-sized farmyard with a wooden grain shed on one side by the woods, and a tiny cabin not much bigger than the car he was driving on the other. The only sign of habitation was a late model green Mustang convertible parked by the white-boarded pasture fence that ran between the cabin and the granary. His dad shifted the lever on the steering wheel to park and said, "Stay here, Mikey. Let me see if anyone is around." He crushed his cigarette out in the filthy and overflowing dashboard ashtray and turned the engine off. He got out, shut the heavy car door tentatively, and threaded his way through the tall weeds to the cabin.

The owner of the Mustang, Cal Masterson, student of veterinary science, third year boss of the stables, had arrived before his partner Hank to spend a few days setting things up and relaxing with his steady girlfriend, Sam, before she left for the summer. (No girlfriends were allowed at the stables, even beautiful, blonde steady ones with masculine nicknames.) At the exact moment of Michael's and Perry's mid-afternoon arrival, however, after a day of beer drinking and flirtatious swimming at the local flooded quarry, Cal and Sam were relaxing (rather vigorously) in the boss's queen bed crammed in the corner of the tiny cabin. There was a smaller single cot in front of them and a tall metal bunk bed to the side that served as the less luxurious sleeping quarters for the yet to arrive workers, the "peons." At the stables, unless you were there alone, the only privacy one could find was among the hay bales in the barn or in the outhouse.

The sight of Cal and Sam's impressive lovemaking must have been immediate and stark for Perry because Michael watched him pause at the cabin steps and stare into the doorway for a long time. But from Michael's perspective, fifty feet away peering through the dirty windshield and residual smoke in the Buick, it just seemed like another mysteriously drawn-out adult greeting ritual and that he had been forgotten for the moment. He watched his dad linger at the door of the cabin puffing on a new cigarette, then step inside.

As Michael waited, the mid-morning early June sun baked the inside of the tank-like Buick to an intolerable temperature and forced Michael to seek air outside. *Dad's sure been in there a long time.* Outside the car, the bright June sun hurt his eyes. Waist high thistles and dandelions were everywhere, and his sneakers sank a bit in the soft sand that extended about the yard. *Where are the horses? The people?* The corral behind the cabin was empty save weeds even bigger and nastier looking than those about his feet, and the big wooden barn doors above the crumbling concrete entrance ramp were rolled shut as were the smaller doors on the side that the horses came in and out of.

Michael noticed a weird, red open-bedded trailer of some sort with spiny gears and levers sticking out of it parked next to the barn under one of its shuttered windows. It looked like some antique primordial farm robot that had seen better days.

Time passed, but after hours of putting up with his dad's cigarettes and the noisy snow tires on the neglected car, the slight breeze blowing outside felt relaxing. *Should I walk over to the cabin? No, better wait.* He wished he had a book to read. "Don't bother taking books, you'll be way too busy to read," Mrs. Nelson had said.

Michael put his hands in the pockets of his white tennis shorts, leaned on the front of the car and immediately burned his left thigh on the sun-scorched fender. "Shit!" he said, springing away from the car and right into a prickly thistle that scratched him painfully on the other thigh. As the red and purple weed bit into his skin, off jumped a huge grasshopper onto his arm. The startled prehistoric creature then dug its crusty back legs into his skin and sprung away with a buzzy flutter.

Michael shuddered and quickly brushed his legs and arms vigorously with both hands. When he was confident there were no more giant insects or plants attacking him, he took a deep breath and wiped his brow with the western looking red handkerchief that Mrs. Nelson had given to him as a going away present. He looked back toward the cabin near the pasture fence. *Why was this taking so long, anyway? Are there any snakes around here?*

It took until early July before Michael learned about the encounter between the copulating couple and his reluctantly voyeuristic father that morning. The older peons let it slip - they were under orders to keep the secret from him to allow it to fade away - mostly for Sam's comfort, who did manage to visit Cal at the beginning and end of summers despite the unspoken rule forbidding serious girlfriends from hanging around. Even when Michael found out about the incident from Earl and Wyatt on a rare day off when they snuck into the county fair, the full extent of its meaning took a while to sink in. *People actually have sex in the middle of the day? Did his father really witness Cal and Sam naked together in a bed and not get upset? So weird...*

Michael's naivety about his father that summer was not his fault. Michael was young, and despite Perry's worshipful love for his alcoholic dad, Perry Sr., Perry learned nothing about parenting from his deceased father or how to communicate and build trust with Michael or anyone else for that matter. Perry did learn to drink, though. Following enthusiastically in his father's vodka-infused footsteps, he was completely incapable of providing self-reflective paternal nurturing.

So, given his upbringing, how to court and love someone was an impenetrable social mystery beyond the realm of Michael's imagination and certainly a subject never spoken of with his father. He just assumed (incorrectly) that Perry would condemn any attraction to sex on Michael's part. Michael had no real evidence for this assumption, of course, other than adolescent fear of broaching such an uncomfortable subject matter with busy parents or other adults.

One thing for sure, was that his father was a businessman and not a hippie enamored with free love. When he thought back on that first day, after knowing what his dad had seen in the cabin, it amazed him that his dad didn't reject the place outright. When Michael himself was a father many decades later, he remembered how young he was when he was dropped off. He often wished his father had been sufficiently morally outraged enough to just put him back in the Buick and thereby spare him all the disturbing things that happened to him that summer. Had Perry even momentarily put on a lens with any label other than "get Mikey out of the house for the summer at all costs," he might have said no, or at least thought to call his wife to talk it over. His Mom, deeply intuitive despite her illness, might have saved Michael from the confusion, pain and grief of those three months. Or maybe not, since all Perry and his mom could focus on at that time was her own pain and failing health as well as vicious fights over money and his recent taste for weekend "business meetings," late nights and vodka. Probably what was mostly on Perry's mind when he, Cal and Sam ultimately walked from the cabin to the station wagon to welcome Michael to his new summer job was getting to a bar in Fieldsburg for a few martinis before heading back home to what he hoped would now be a slightly less complicated Gordian knot of domestic pain.

Cal spoke first: "Hi Michael. I'm Cal. I just had a nice visit with your dad showing him the cabin where you'll be living this summer. I'm glad you came early. You're the first to get here this year! Wyatt and Earl will pull in tomorrow. Welcome to Lakeside Stables! I am your boss. You'll meet Hank Nelson later - he's your other boss, as you know, the Hillcrest boss. And this is Sam." Sam smiled at him, and Michael smiled but kept his eyes on Cal. Perry stood with a nervous look on his face looking mostly at the ground.

The more Michael looked at Cal the more tension he felt in his spine. To his credit, he managed a whispered "hi" despite a creeping paralysis due to visual overload. From the moment he laid eyes on his new boss, every nerve fiber of his attention was riveted on the amazingly coarse and abundant black hair spilling from the upper lip of Cal's caucasian yet dark and scary face. He was big and strong, but the mustache carried his strength like the hair of Samson. This was a real man's mustache, a scary mustache with a matching scary unibrow, a mustache easily worthy of Iraqi dictators, an angry deep mustache flanked by an equally intimidating set of mutton chop sideburns above Cal's strong and assertive jawline.

"Want to bring your stuff into the cabin?" Michael heard the mustache say, but he was still transfixed. The unibrow lifted in anticipation of an answer, then gave up. "Anyway, the upper bunk is for you. I'll show you where you can unpack after your dad leaves. Mr. Bentley, we'll take good care of Michael here and make sure he writes home every once in a while." Cal subtly edged Perry toward his car. "The phone isn't hooked up yet but will be soon; it's the same number we've had since 1946." He wrote the number on a business card and handed it to Perry. "Call anytime, please. Michael can call collect once it's hooked up. It's been a pleasure meeting you. Give my regards to Mrs. Nelson, please!" Cal smiled and extended a hand toward Perry. Sweat dripped down his sideburns. Sam smiled at Perry briefly and then looked kindly at Michael.

"I'm sure this will be a great experience for him," Perry said meeting Cal's handshake and glancing briefly at Sam's chest. And so the transaction for his son was made.

Peon Punch

S am left late that very afternoon on a bus for points south. Cal dropped her off at the Fieldsburg Greyhound station in his convertible green mustang. Whatever relationship she had with Cal during the year at the University of Wisconsin Veterinary School at Green Bay was clearly put on hold for the summer. Presumably she went back to her parents' house to read books and suntan in the back yard or maybe by a glittering pool someplace. Michael, left behind to hack down weeds in the yard with an Active Andy, didn't have a clue. All he could think about was that when Cal came back he would be alone with him that night in the little cabin, and the prospect of sleeping in close proximity to that mustached face felt a little like bedding down with a Doberman in a junk yard. Although he didn't know Sam at all, she was beautiful, and he vaguely wished she would stick around, feeling that her presence might provide a tempering influence on Cal.

He learned much later that since the stable facilities (barn, granary, cabin, outhouse, mangers, pastures, and fences) were owned by Camp Crane, an episcopal organization run by the overtly moral and upright Father Able and overseen by the church diocese itself, any unmarried cohabitation on the property by stable bosses was sure to be detrimental to business. In point of fact, the stables would be out on its historical ass if Sam set up housekeeping with Cal at the stables, or if the stables otherwise brought any undue negative public attention to the camp. Married would be one thing, possibly, but harboring unmarried couples on church property was sure to rile up the Bishop if word got out, which it certainly would do. So Sam had to head south before the horses came and camp got started. There are, after all, some public relations protocols bosses cannot violate, even for the tempting delights of lovely, kind, sensible (and sexual) girlfriends. For the boss of the other stables location, also on a church property eight miles away, cohabiting with a steady girlfriend was not an issue – Hank's girlfriend lived a safe Harley ride away from the stables at her parents' vacation cabin on the nearby lake.

Lakeside Stables had survived since 1946 by providing horseback riding at a profit to campers at Camp Crane in Fieldsburg and also Camp Hillcrest eight country miles away because harried camp directors like Father Able simply did not want to deal with horses. Horses are scary, dangerous, mysterious to feed, psychologically complicated, and huge liabilities for men of the cloth already out of their element running camps for children. To be fair, it wasn't exactly the primo clergical assignment to be sent by a Bishop to rural Wisconsin to mold the moral fibers of youth dumped off by parents anxious to have their summers free for cocktail parties and, well, more cocktail parties. Father Able, and his counterpart at Camp Hillcrest would have preferred instead to lead the same flocks his luckier colleagues enjoyed in high-end suburban churches in Milwaukee where issues of hormonally-ridden camp counselors, nasty bugs in understaffed kitchens, and generally strangulated operating budgets were unheard of. No, the prospect of also managing a stable full of horses and the strange people capable of understanding them on top of everything else that needed to be managed at the God-forsaken camps was to be avoided at all costs. The decision to relinquish any and all restraints over movements and actions of the rather smelly horse boys and their smooth-talking, capable, but suspiciously young and virile bosses was worth it to preserve the popular attraction of horseback riding for the returning campers. Over the years the bosses had even talked the directors into feeding the horse boys as a perk for taking care of the messy business of providing rides. Their dirty boots and clothes lent a certain "tolerable country aura" to the dining room atmosphere even if they couldn't shower before meals or attend services on Sundays.

Cal returned at dusk carrying burgers and fries from the local drive-in, and a case of Old Milwaukee beer in bottles for the fridge. Michael's weed hacking had uncovered a huge wooden power company cable spool by the cabin that, lying on its side, made for a sturdy and decent-sized table. Cal pried open a beer on a nail sticking out of the spool, hopped on top of it and handed Michael a burger.

"Best part of the year being back here. Nothing beats the summers. Back at the stables! You have no idea how lucky you are to be here, Michael," said Cal. Michael noticed Cal's vocal enthusiasm dipped a little when he said Michael.

Michael had no reply to this unexpected expression of sentiment from his new boss. *Does Cal like me?* Chewing and looking off at the darkening skies seemed the safest and most reasonable response. There was certainly no basis yet to judge the merits of Cal's pronouncement, and he hoped things would improve from lonely weed cutting and deserted old farm buildings. He was willing to give it a chance, he guessed. *What choice do I have?*

"We believe in working hard and playing hard around here, Michael...God, we've got to get you a different name!" Cal scowled and shook his head after delivering this conversation-ending pronouncement. *What?*

The meal finished with the awkwardness of Michael wondering what was wrong with his name, and Cal frowning, chewing and tipping his beer to his mouth with one finger across the lip of his long-necked bottle. As they ate, Venus announced her shining presence above the barn to the west, followed shortly by the dramatic glory of a half-moon Milky Way. The night crickets and cicadas punctuated the sudden damp coolness of the falling night. Cars on the highway beyond the corral dopplered from high whines and bright headlights to low roars and red tail lights as they passed.

"Boys will be here in the morning...big day tomorrow." Cal shook the foam out of the bottom of his empty beer, climbed off the table slowly like dismounting a horse, and moved powerfully toward the cabin, fists clenched and arms stiff at his side as if he were ready at any moment to Kung Fu monstrous forest thugs jumping from the shadows of the pine trees next to the cabin. Michael followed meekly behind him.

"We piss outside through the fence into the corral. There's a sink with water behind the cabin," Cal said once the screen door banged behind them and Michael had rolled out his sleeping bag on the top bunk. He dug a down pillow from his duffel bag - a small reminder of his room at home - and went back outside to follow instructions and brush his teeth. There were thistles and nettles growing around the white enameled kitchen-type sink resting on posts by the fence behind the cabin. *Better whack those tomorrow.* He extended his toothbrush between ominous stalks of nettles to the cold flow of water. Somewhere nearby a water pump kicked on with a thump.

The cabin had an ornate metal floor lamp with a graduation tassel as a switch by Cal's bed and a bare bulb hanging on a wire overhead. Two small windows were screened and propped open. Cold air poured in as Michael climbed up top and pulled the red-checkered sleeping bag up to his chin.

"You are going to like Wyatt and Earl. They're both third year peons. Driving this year, thank God, although Wyatt will probably won't have a car since Earl's sure to bring some piece of shit."

Michael took this in staring up at the ceiling. Then his examination of the hundreds of dried bugs stuck to the hundred-watt bulb dangling near his head ended when Cal in his boxers flipped off the switch by the door and settled back onto his double bed with a book, some kind of treatment manual for horse medical emergencies. Michael looked down at him and thought of his books at home and about his mother. *How would she get along without him helping her in and out of the wheelchair?*

"We're going to get our horses in here any day now, so we'll be making do, but don't worry, camp meals start soon,"

Cal said over his book. "There's always cold water in a bottle in the fridge in the granary so be sure you drink often so you don't get dehydrated and sick, and fill it up outside when it gets low. We don't have any washing machines here, but you'll have time to catch a ride to town on the weekends on your Sunday off. Wash your clothes by hand if you want. Everyone does that a little bit. Sun dries things quick. If you have any questions don't hesitate to ask me, or anyone. There's a lot to learn here, but I hear you're smart so you'll do fine."

What prompted Michael to finally and impulsively utter his first complete sentence of the summer to Cal with a "Thanks, Mom" he never completely figured out, but certainly at the time he meant it lightly, not mockingly. The thought occurred to him many years later that the humor of it was primarily just for him, not Cal. It had been years since his mother or anyone else at home had provided any specific parenting directions for him, and it felt ironic at that moment while resting in that surprisingly comfortable bunk bed to be cared for in a quasi-motherly way by someone who could best be described as the quintessential hard-guy cowboy. Had Michael had the time or inclination to reveal to Cal at dinner about his mother's MS being at the seriously-paralyzed-wheel-chair stage, or about his father Perry's alcoholism and arguments with her, Cal might possibly have compassionately hesitated in his own emotional reaction to Michael's unfortunate utterance. But since Cal didn't know Michael or any of these things about him yet, and Michael's short sentence linked Cal, the tough-guy boss of Lakeside Stables, to possibly becoming an on-going maternal figure in

Michael's life, and that that was not even in the tiniest sense something Cal wanted to encourage, the "peon punch" to Michael's right thigh under the too thin sleeping bag was delivered with abruptness and wordless fury.

The extremely painful blow forever imbedded the following two conclusions in Michael's mind as he clutched his leg and cried: one, that the mustache, sideburns, cowboy boots, and all the other rough characteristics of Cal's appearance would forever be an image of terror in Michael's psyche, and, two, that he really *wanted to go home*, even if going home meant that he was a quitter and would miss out, even if home hadn't existed for him for years other than as a disturbing place to sleep between purposefully extended fourteen-hour days at school.

Going To Town

The next day a red 1960 convertible Chevrolet Impala roared around the barn and into the stables yard fast enough to skid sideways through the sand and send the gloved Michael with his Active Andy weed cutter scurrying for the safety of the concrete ramp leading to the barn. Pausing only to crank the front tires, Earl pressed the V-8 gas pedal hard and finished his entrance with four 360-degree donuts around the yard. It raised a cloud of dust into the air the size of a small blimp. Small rocks pinged like bursts from a Gatling gun across the side of the barn where Michael was cowering. *What the hell?*

As the dust settled around Michael, he looked out across the yard at the now parked Impala and saw Cal standing outside the cabin. Cal's fists were clenched at his side and his boots were spread apart in a strange dominating stance. Michael felt the still painful bruise on his thigh and assumed the short dark-haired teen jumping up from the white leather seat and stepping out of the vault-like door of the Impala was in for it, but Cal just kept standing there scowling. Maybe it was the second young man emerging from the passenger seat that made Cal pause. In a fight, two against one is never good odds, although the passenger with the prominent nose and curly dark hair was almost as small as the driver.

"Son of a bitch, Earl, you woke me up from my nap! God damn you! Glad to see you worthless peons decided to show up finally now that the horses are coming any minute. What's this piece of shit you're driving, Earl? I thought you were going to buy something that had at least a little power?" Cal was speaking loud enough that even across the barnyard, Michael could hear him distinctly.

"Hey Cal." Earl extended a three-fingered handshake, and received a shake and a firm slap on the shoulder. "Just a beater I picked up from Norm. Good stables car, eh?"

Cal turned to the passenger. "Welcome back, Wyatt. Your brother behind you?"

"Yep, He's going to the cabin first to drop off some stuff for my mom. How ya doing Cal?" said Wyatt. More handshakes and backslapping.

"Coolidge, get your ass over here and meet your fellow peons," yelled Cal.

The three turned to look back at the thin and lanky Michael who that morning had wisely ditched his tennis shorts and was working in a t-shirt, blue jeans, and laced hiking boots. Cal snorted a laugh again through his mustache, "Look at him, doesn't even know his name yet."

"Coolidge, yeah you, who else do you think is around here? Git over here and meet your fellow peons, Wyatt and Earl." Cal straightened his mustache with his thumb and forefinger.

Coolidge - *that's a name?* - took off his work gloves, leaned the Active Andy against the barn and walked tentatively across the yard avoiding the deep trenches in the sand left by the ticking Impala next to and dwarfing the green

Mustang. Intimidation fueled his awkward movements. *Cal doesn't like me - will Wyatt and Earl?*

"Coolidge, will you hurry up? Jeeezus, why are first year peons always so slow? When I call your name you come running, do you understand that, Coolidge? Fast! Coolidge, this is Earl and Wyatt. Earl and Wyatt, this is Coolidge. Coolidge doesn't know his name is Coolidge yet, but he does now, don't you, Coolidge?"

Coolidge looked from Cal to the two high schoolers in cowboy boots and collared shirts in front of him.

"Coolidge doesn't like to talk much, but he'll learn to say yes sir, ain't that right Coolidge? You're not scared of me are you, Coolidge? Is this any way to greet the people you'll be working with this summer?"

Coolidge didn't know whether to say no, or yes, or yes sir, or no sir. "Um..."

"Hey, Coolidge. Good to meet you," Earl said and extended his hand for a brief shake. Despite his relief at being rescued, Earl's quickly executed handshake surprised him. It felt physically incomplete, like shaking a couple of sticks for a microsecond. He learned later from Wyatt that Earl never lingered on handshakes since blowing off his little finger and half his ring finger while trying to hide a firecracker from a cop during a Fourth of July rampage in Milwaukee when he was in middle school. This was one of the only times Coolidge ever heard of an Earl failure.

With only that one glaring exception, Earl Thorne reveled in the thrills of risk-taking and escaped paying the consequences. Besides amazing physical coordination, ample brains, and spot on social instincts, he had a couple of crack

Thorne family lawyers in his back pocket to bail him out if he ever faltered. His father and Earl's older brother, Norman Jr., provided periodically needed pro-bono legal work for the stables, mainly because Norm had been a boss a decade ago and knew Hank Nelson's older brother, Burt (also a previous boss). If Burt and Hank Nelson were the Bush family legacy to the stables royalty, then Norm and Earl Thorne were the Kennedys. Parker and Wyatt Moretti were another legacy family, perhaps the Roosevelts, except that Parker and Wyatt were both working at the stables now at the same time instead of kicking back at the family cottage on the lake near the stables' other location, Hillcrest. Working at the stables was a family tradition for most of the peons. No one, of course, in Coolidge's family had even set eyes on the stables before his father dumped him off. He was here because his Aunt Alice knew Ma Nelson, who knew her son Hank was looking for new peons. Otherwise Coolidge might have been mowing lawns, caddying, or babysitting like everyone else his age in Coveside.

"Great to make your acquaintance. Where you from, Coolidge?" said Wyatt Moretti, also extending his hand, normal sized.

"Mwaahkee..."

"Ah another Milwaukean. Chicago is better. So you know Earl and the Thornes already?" Wyatt pronounced Chicago with truncated syllables, similar in some ways but different from Earl's Wisconsin accent.

"No, but Mrs. Nelson told me you go to my school?" Coolidge mumbled to Earl.

"Coolidge! Speak up! Jeezuz, how do you expect to carry on a conversation when you're whispering to your shoes? Horse boys know how to talk to people. Look Wyatt and Earl in the eyes and speak to them so they can hear you!" Cal looked frighteningly serious.

"Nice to meet you, Wyatt. I think we go to the same school, Earl," Coolidge said louder this time.

"Great to meet you, Coolidge. Looking forward to working with you," said Wyatt smiling then turning away. "So, Cal, what's this I hear about horses coming early?" he continued. Earl, ready to get to work, was already heading to his Impala to grab his bags from the back seat.

Cal finally stopped staring angrily at Coolidge and looked at Wyatt. "The damn phone company says the line would be activated yesterday, but it just came on this morning," said Cal. "Waiting for Marvin to confirm, but he's swinging by the farm to pick up the truck and should be here around dinnertime with his rip-off horses. Got to get the fence up and running - that's the first task for you and Earl. I've got to go into town and get provisions." He paused and stared again menacingly at Coolidge. "Coolidge where are your boots?"

Coolidge looked down at his feet.

"I mean your boots, your cowboy boots? You can't be a horse boy without a real pair of boots, can you?"

"Don't have any. Didn't know."

"Well we're going to have to buy you a pair. They're about $30 at the tack shop."

"I don't think I have thirty dollars," Coolidge said looking at the sand.

"Well that doesn't surprise me. Leave it to a first year peon to be totally unprepared, right Wyatt?" Cal just shook his head and looked put-upon, annoyed, and amused at the same time. Coolidge glanced up in time to catch Wyatt's quick wink.

"Are we going to get stuck with Big Brother and Little Brother again this year?" Wyatt asked, turning to Cal and smirking a bit.

"Yep. It's all or none of them as usual. Fucking Marvin. He's going to be here soon. You guys get the fence ready - there's some fresh wire and insulators in the tack room. I'll try to get back here as soon as I can so I can see him deliver his jackass excuses for horses. Got to pick up some new peon work boots to break in!"

"Will do. Sounds good, Cal. See you later, Coolidge."

"I expect Hank to get here soon too," Cal said to Wyatt's back.

Coolidge, still not sure how or why he was Coolidge, liked Wyatt's strength and the kind way he said goodbye. He really wanted to stay with Earl and Wyatt, work on the fence or maybe whack some more weeds rather than climb into a car with Cal, but Earl was already finished stashing his bags in the cabin and was heading to the barn. Wyatt opened the trunk to the Impala to grab his bags.

"All right Coolidge. Coolidge! God damn it. Don't be slow when I am in a hurry. Get in the car. So worthless!" Cal muttered and shook his head, thumb and forefinger again parting the shaggy curtain of his mustache. "You're going with me to town. We need to buy you some real work boots, deduct it from your paycheck. You ready? Get in!"

Back seat or front? Coolidge got the clue when Cal abruptly tossed some stuff off the passenger seat into the back and unlatched the canvas car top. The perfectly tuned Ford engine purred to life, and the power steering complained only briefly as Cal backed out of his prime parking spot by the cabin. He dropped the transmission into drive and spun away from the yard cruising around the barn to the highway. Sun and wind in their hair, Cal's left elbow rested on the Mustang's green door. He punched the gas and spun out onto the highway to get up to speed fast on the dangerous straightaway there. Cal was smiling, even relishing the moment, and Coolidge, for reasons he couldn't fathom, was suddenly relishing it as well. He felt his back relax into the passenger seat like he might belong there. After all, didn't he have *real business* to attend to with this scary person of ultra-seriousness and power? (He had rarely if ever been in a vehicle with anyone before who wasn't a parent or bus driver.) *I'm going into town for boots and provisions. In a convertible!* He didn't know why, but for the first time that day he could look at his boss with something beyond just fear and the memory of his sore right thigh.

"This is just the best, Coolidge," said Cal straight black hair fluttering and eyes protected from the wind behind aviator glasses. "Horses coming in this afternoon; it's all starting up again. Man! My seventh summer. You know, most people don't get to do this anymore in our world. They don't even know what it means to work. They think they know what work is, but they don't know work. We work hard around here, and that's because we're smart. People are stupid and lazy but not horse boys. You can't get ahead in this life unless you work hard, unless you're really smart and work damn hard, really damn hard. You're going to meet a lot of counselors and maintenance losers at this camp this summer who don't know how to work, but we're not losers. Remember that. We're horse boys. They're going to be jealous of you, Coolidge. Be ready." He pulled a toothpick out of his pocket and rolled it from one side of his mouth to the other.

Coolidge thought about this as Cal drove, apparently done with his pronouncements for the moment. The talk about work didn't scare him. He'd always been a hard worker, at least in school - good grades and all, lots of reading. He'd plowed through "War and Peace" that school year in his spare time just because someone said it was the longest and hardest novel ever written. He could hit a tennis ball against the backboard three hundred times without resting.

The hay fields along the highway gradually gave way to a few houses, a burger joint, a run-down motel, a laundry mat, and an outdoor theater all set back far from the highway. Then the pavement narrowed into the modest maze of two-story brick buildings that comprised the block and a half of "downtown" Fieldsburg. Cal angled into an open parking spot in front of "Benny's Bar and Grill."

"That's Garcia's Restaurant," Cal said gesturing across the street before putting on his hat. "Best Mexican food in the state." He hopped out and Coolidge followed Cal up a short flight of steps and into a farm and saddle shop a few doors down from Benny's.

The cool smell of tanned leather was strong as they left the radiating heat of the sidewalk. Ropes, saddles, buckles, gloves, salt licks and all manner of horse lineaments lined the walls and shelves. The elaborate cowboy boots in the back room underneath the rack of cowboy hats and fancy rodeo shirts had prices on them well above what Coolidge was told by Mrs. Nelson was to be his summer salary - $50 total for June, July, and August. He looked at Cal.

Cal spoke a few words to the aging cowgirl attending the register. "My eyeballs say his size is about an eight and a half," he said. Soon Coolidge was squeezing his sweaty feet into medieval torturing devices disguised as plain leather cowboy boots. "They're too small?" asked Coolidge, wincing.

"They are right now," Cal said smiling at the salesperson as if sharing a secret. "You want 'em tight so they don't fall off when you ride. Don't worry, they'll break in once we oil 'em up." Cal lifted two full gallon tins of Neatsfoot onto the counter, plucked a dozen red handkerchiefs off a display rack. "Neatsfoot oil - nature's best leather preservative. Don't you ever forget that, Coolidge. Only way our saddles have lasted for twenty-five years is 'cause we feed 'em Neatsfoot Oil. Can we start our summer tab, please, Mrs. Gossens?"

"Will you be needing a work hat for the young feller?" Mrs. Gossens smiled at Coolidge who was tenderly hobbling a few steps across the floor in his tight new boots.

"Yep, the usual."

The first few hats she handed Coolidge perched on his head like a roosting chicken and looked ridiculous. They finally found a straw one that was snug but comfortable.

Cal signed the credit slip.

"I hope you have a good summer, Cal," the Western matron said tucking the voucher into a small metal box by the register.

"You too, Mrs. Gossens. Thanks for keeping those boots in stock for me. We'll be back soon, I am sure, once we get the saddles fitted we'll need some more leather. See you around the barn."

"You know I don't just keep 'em in stock for you, Cal - they're popular with the pickers too. Cheap and durable, you know?"

"True. As long as you break 'em in right," winked Cal at the door. Coolidge hobbled after him carrying his old hiking boots in the new box and wondering if the dark leather boots, odd and weirdly handsome as they were, were now permanently stuck to his swelling feet.

"Stay by the car, Coolidge, and watch this stuff until I get back," said Cal when they reached the car and he had dumped his purchases. The hot sun glared off the metal of the Neatsfoot oil containers now in the back seat. Coolidge's new hat kept his face protected, but it was still hot. The traffic on Main Street was sparse, and he noticed a sheriff in a white patrol car parked by the only light in town. Three Mexican men in boots like his and wearing dusty t-shirts pulled open the screen door to Garcia's across the street. Looking at the neon sign advertising "Mexican Food," Coolidge remembered sharing a half a chicken and creamy rice with his mother at a fancy restaurant one time in Coveside many years ago when she could still walk. The memory was powerful in part due to his hunger - the last food he'd eaten was the burger Cal tossed him the night before.

Cal eyed the downtown scene too, and then, again swaggering like he dared someone to try and stop him, headed toward Benny's. The heavy bar door expelled a blast of air-conditioning and brief strains from a country jukebox. "Stay by the car," he said over his shoulder, as he disappeared inside.

Coolidge wondered when Cal would return. Some tourist girls his age in swimsuits on the sidewalk were holding ice cream cones and laughing. They ignored him and played nervously with the beach towels draped over their shoulders. He thought of the Brook and Court Tennis Club back in Milwaukee and the pool he used to sunbath next to in summers past. "It was either the club or school," his dad said when he announced that he had axed their longtime family membership to the small club by the Milwaukee River. A fierce argument ensued in the club parking lot between his mother and father. "You can't even walk from the parking lot to the pool anymore, and Mikey is getting too old for that crap," Perry had yelled at his wife, veins sticking out from his neck. Coolidge suspected his dad's sore back and failing tennis game had a lot to do with that unpopular family decision to quit the club last summer, that and the fact that he had just beaten his dad at tennis for the first time in his life and his dad had often jokingly promised to "stop playing tennis forever if that ever happened."

Cal eventually emerged from the bar with one hand wrapped over a huge case of bottled beer perched on his shoulder - Schlitz this time. The case bounced into the back seat with the Neatsfoot oil and Coolidge's shoebox. "One more quick stop. Let's go."

To Coolidge's relief, the stop was an A&P grocery store to pick up some food. Fish sticks, frozen burgers, hotdogs, buns, ketchup, some eggs and Wonder Bread came out with

Cal from the store. Cal put the paper grocery bags on the floor of the back seat. He pulled out two white-wrapped day-old deli sandwiches and a couple of cold cokes and handed one of each to Coolidge. The mayo, cold cuts, and wilted lettuce on a poppy seed white roll tasted like salvation.

"When everyone's here we'll all go to Garcia's for some real food. Clean out our sinuses!" said Cal, noticing Coolidge's appetite and munching on a sandwich of his own. Cal snorted at his own joke. Coolidge's didn't understand the reference. He'd find out later that Garcia's special extra hot pepper sauce was indeed a sinus cleaner. At that moment he only cared about his tortured feet and not wasting one bit of the soggy Bologna sandwich, or worse spilling it onto the front seat of Cal's Mustang.

Horseshit and Father Figures

The stables yard became significantly busier later that afternoon after Cal and Coolidge returned. As they drove in, Coolidge saw a balding middle-aged man in a white t-shirt with a significant potbelly climb out of a pickup truck that had obviously just left a cloud of dust on the dirt road coming from the pine forest behind the granary. Cal reached back and discretely draped his windbreaker and a towel over the case of Schlitz. "Coolidge, smile now. You're about to meet Tim Reinke. He's dangerous."

"Hey, Tim, long time no see," said Cal after he pulled into his parking spot by the shade of the pine trees around the cabin. "Have a good winter?" Cal was indeed smiling and extending a hand to Tim who crushed his smoke under his heel and, unsmiling, returned the proffered handshake.

"Oh, can't complain, I guess. Didn't think you guys were here yet, but I saw Wyatt and Earl in the pasture. You were supposed to let me know when you got here, Cal Masterson."

"Yeah, of course, Tim! We meant to come see you right away, but we found out the horses are arriving today ahead of schedule, and we didn't want them to get out of the pasture since the fence was down. Just coming to see you right now in fact, but here you are! Thanks for making the effort to stop by. How's the good Father Able?" Cal's dark eyes shined with friendliness and sincerity.

Tim shook a new Winston out the pack he had rolled in his t-shirt sleeve and lit it with a match. "He'll be here tomorrow." His eyes wandered with a frown to the donut marks in the horse yard.

"Great, well we'll look forward to seeing him. Want to stick around for the horses? They'll be here any minute." Cal knew Tim couldn't stand horses. Give him plumbing pipes to fix or simple holes to dig with a backhoe and he's happy. Complex personalities like humans and horses set him on edge.

In answer, Tim climbed back into his truck, his sweaty stomach grazing the steering wheel as he settled in. "You all let me know if the power is sketchy out here. Been having trouble with the company lately," he said.

"Diocese not paying the bills again?" Cal joked. "By the way, Tim, this is Coolidge, our new peon."

"Keep this guy out of trouble, Coolidge, will ya?" said Tim, taking the cigarette out of his mouth briefly. "It won't be easy." A wry smile curled about the corners of his mouth despite his best intentions to stay grouchy. Coolidge noticed little burn holes all over the front of his t-shirt.

"Nice seeing you again, Tim! Hope we have as much fun this summer as we did last," Cal said.

Tim grimaced. "Yeah, fun, my butt." His truck roared back to life. "So much friggin' work to do, and Able cut my crew by half this year, God Bless him and the Bishop."

Coolidge could tell that Tim was holding back and wanted to complain more vigorously, and he was right. Tim knew the church looked down on the curse words Tim preferred to use, and in fact did use most of the off season when no one was around and all he had to do was go deer hunting and snowmobiling with his beer drinking buddies. It was always a sort of game among the bosses to get Tim to open up and let loose with his profane mouth like they knew he wanted. There were usually plenty of frustrating issues to bait him with; trying to keep the camp running smoothly on a shoestring maintenance budget clearly tried his patience. The stables boys were just enough outside of the main stream of camp life that he could let his guard down sometimes. Conversely, of course, he could also dump on the horse boys with impunity as well, so it was a dicey political game dealing with Tim – a PR minefield dictated by his mood. Today, though, he was smiling. He put the cigarette back sloppily into his mouth, shifted the steering column arm to D, circled the yard slowly and made his way back down the primitive mile-long dirt road to camp.

"That's Tim Reinke. Maintenance King at camp. As far as you're concerned, Coolidge, if he asks you anything, you know nothing. You understand that? Nothing. Just say you don't know and refer him to me or to Hank, or to Wyatt or Earl if you have to. We can't afford any PR fuck-ups this year. We had enough last year – Father Able is out to get us. Everything has to go smoothly this summer or we're out of here."

"Okay, Cal," said Coolidge. *I don't want to talk to that guy anyway.*

"He's as two-faced as they come. You've just got to bullshit him."

Coolidge had no idea what *that* bit of advice meant, but they barely had time to unload the groceries into the ancient round-shouldered refrigerator in the granary - the beer took up most of room - before the deep-throated growl of a Harley motorcycle next announced itself in the yard.

"Hank Nelson!" said Cal, and right behind Hank a lumbering flatbed stake truck loaded with horses was visible behind the barn turning in off the highway.

"Hank, you son of a bitch," said Cal as Hank pulled in behind the Mustang. He was not wearing a helmet. His face was clean-shaven and his hair was long and dark but not as dark as Cal's. No mustache. "Did you see who is behind you? You even ready for this?"

Hank killed his engine and bear-hugged Cal. He was dressed in a leather jacket, leather chaps, cowboy boots, and a duffel bag strapped to the back of his hog.

"Horses here already, huh? Pasture ready?"

"I sure hope so," said Cal. Why don't you get back on that piece of shit you call a motorcycle and find Wyatt and Earl in the pasture – they've been there all day - see if they have the fence done. I'll bullshit Marvin until you get back."

"Who's that?" Hank smiled and pointed a gloved finger at Coolidge.

"This is Coolidge. Coolidge, meet Hank, Hank Nelson, your other boss."

Hank nodded curtly to Coolidge, unstrapped his duffel bag from the motorcycle, and tossed it onto the ground. He kicked the bike back to life, pushed open the corral gate and roared past the mangers and down the horse path to the hidden and expansive pasture. The stake truck slowly circled into the yard and backed itself up to the same open corral gate that had just swallowed Hank. A seething mass of horses shifted and stomped to keep their balance on the wet and rocking bed of the truck. The sight mesmerized Coolidge. *Those horses are huge.*

Why is the truck bed so wet? Coolidge approached the impressively filthy vehicle that had lumbered to a halt with its back end facing the pasture gate: *It's shit!* Horseshit, pure and simple, was on the truck's tires, falling out of the sides of the truck sticking everywhere. *Wet, piss-soaked horseshit.*

And did it stink! The fifteen horses packed into that mobile jail cell were covered in it up to their knees, or hocks, as Coolidge would later learn was the proper term. The stench rolled off the truck like a reportable weather front, slapping everyone in the stables yard across the nostrils and playing reveille to every dormant fly in the barnyard.

"Well, I'll be a cock-suckin' mother-humpin' piss drinkin' son of a bitch, look what the cat drugged in! Who was drunk enough to let you out of jail?" shouted a short, corpulent, older middle-aged man dressed in blue jeans and a blue-collared work shirt. The man descended with visible arthritic difficulty from the cab of the horse truck. *No boots?* His voice was high which for Coolidge somehow added to the stark surprise of the vile language he was smilingly directing toward Cal who had by that time taken his patented scowling stance in front of the cab of the truck.

"Jail! What do you mean, Marvin, you know you saw me there this morning – it's where *you* live. I'm just an occasional guest," retorted Cal, folding his arms across his chest.

"You *cock-sucker*, the only place you visit is pussy. How do you keep your hands smelling clean, anyway? I've always wondered. Oh, that's right. You don't 'cause you're always *sniffing* them all day long instead of doing any work." Marvin flashed a shit-eating smile as he wiggled his fingers under his nose. *Who is this guy?*

"Look, Marvin, what's this load of crap you're dropping off here? I thought I told you we wanted horses," said Cal taking a step toward the dark-haired, slightly balding, horse dealer.

"And horses you're getting, you imperceptive ingrate." Marvin swept his hand back toward the truck bed. "These are the finest examples of horse flesh in all of Barret County, maybe all of Wisconsin!" said Marvin.

Both men were shouting loud enough to be heard a mile away. Coolidge, behind Cal and still trying to draw in a breath of unpolluted air, listened to this exchange and saw Hank with Wyatt on the back of his motorcycle return from the pasture.

"Marvin, if these horses were whores and I was a John I would pay you just to take them away they are so mangy and disease ridden! Just look at these pathetic things!" continued Cal.

"Well, dribble dick, you should know about diseased whores, I guess, considering your pathetic symptomatic face!"

"Ha! You'd give your left nut just to set your cretin eyes on the quality pussy I've gone to bed with just in the last week, and you know it!"

Coolidge had heard a bit of locker room language in his day but nothing this impressive. *These were adults?*

"Well, goddammit I believe you, you crotch master," Marvin said, now close to Cal and for the first time not shouting. His smile became genuine and his handshake was warm.

"Coolidge!" Cal turned back to Coolidge. "Marvin, this is Coolidge, our new first year peon. What do you say, Coolidge?"

"Good to meet you, Marvin," Coolidge said, remembering to speak loudly. Marvin stared at him and seemed to forget to extend a hand, so Coolidge merely touched his hat and glanced at Cal.

"Get that corral gate open, Coolidge! God dammit. We got us some horses to unload!" said Cal.

Coolidge pulled the gate open just in time for Hank and Wyatt to ride through. Earl was jogging behind carrying a small spool of wire and an eagle claw.

Wyatt hopped off the moving bike and Hank pulled up next to Marvin and Cal cutting the engine. "Marvin, you dick-head. How the hell are you? You're looking good – what'd you do, find a pussy fountain of youth?"

"Nah, I've just been using your technique, Hank – my left hand. You riding that thing because you forgot how to ride a horse?"

"Got to wrap myself around something in the daytime to keep in practice for the night," retorted Hank.

"You, pussy master," said Marvin smiling.

"Fence looks solid, Cal, but we haven't tested it yet" said Earl. "Hey, Marvin."

"Earl! You cock. Where you got the pussy hiding? Don't tell me in that little cabin you sleep in, or do you have them stashed in the granary this summer?"

"Oh, you know me, Marvin, each summer it takes a day or two for them to find me," replied Earl.

"Well, that's a good thing, I guess, gives you a rest from all those city whores you chase around all winter long," Marvin smiled.

Coolidge wondered briefly if this were true. He knew Earl went to Varsity School, the best private school, he was told, in Milwaukee. Hell he went there too, on a scholarship, but he didn't know Earl. Earl was older, in high school already, hence unapproachable. Earl probably had girlfriends there, but he couldn't imagine sex happening for anyone at Varsity School, but he supposed it was possible. Earl wasn't denying it, but certainly *these people are just goofing around here?* He could tell from their tone that this was a verbal game of some sort, a teasing game, affectionate even in its imagistic harshness. A lot of conversational effort and energy was certainly being expended. The horses, massive and tightly packed in the truck, danced on their hooves and breathed loudly. Their eyes were on the pasture and their neighing was impatient. More urine flowed from between the stakes of the truck bed.

Later in the summer Wyatt and Earl filled Coolidge in about Marvin. Marvin's day job was as a petty bureaucrat, taking applications for fields to be left fallow and advising farmers how to navigate the tricky financial pitfalls of the Wisconsin Farm Bureau. It was boring, so bantering with and collecting under the table cash from the horse boys kept him entertained every summer. People often buy horses and then discover the commitment and hard work. Marvin takes them off their hands. Renting his ever-growing herd to the stables provided a business that was a mildly profitable and satisfyingly diverting for him. He relished locking his office at the end of the day, stopping at the burger place for a vanilla soft serve, and pulling his purple Ambassador sedan into the stables yard for off-color banter and a dose of contact high with youthful horse boy testosterone was well worth the cost of hay he had to shell out for his mangy horses all winter long.

Cal and Hank, as the latest pair of bosses in a long string, knew full well that the financial viability of the stables depended greatly on Marvin and his willingness to rent horses at a low cash-only rate. The relationship with Marvin was key to each summer's success at the stables, and the verbally pornographic "fun factor" of his visits was an important link to their shared past and an emblem of business loyalty. Marvin had known the original bosses of Lakeside Stables and every pair of them subsequently since the business began in the forties. He knew Earl's brother, Norman, who went on to be a successful lawyer, and Hank's brother, Burt, who died of cancer shortly after his stables tenure ended. When things got tough for the stables at times over the years due to high hay prices, insurance problems, or expensive accidents it was often Marvin who could suggest viable, if occasionally quasi-legal, solutions.

"Hey Marvin," Earl said climbing into the truck with a lead rope in his hand. "How are girls like poison ivy?"

"I'll bet you're itching to tell me," grinned Marvin.

"If you don't touch them, you won't get them."

One by one Wyatt and Earl led the horses down the ramp that descended from the back of the truck. Each horse first had to be captured by a lead rope around the neck inside and led out carefully and individually to prevent the herd from galloping down the ramp disastrously at once. The older peons exhibited skill in restraining the pace of the horses' controlled departure down the ramp, pulling back on the lead ropes deftly and looping a rope around each horse's nose to achieve even more control. Coolidge watched carefully.

When released each horse ran exuberantly into the spacious inner pasture bucking and even nipping other horses playfully as they explored their new home. One horse, a huge dark-leather-colored Belgium draft horse, Little Brother, seemed intent upon chasing each of the other horses one after the other, spinning at times to kick them as well. Only a tall bluish-colored thoroughbred, Cole, seemed willing to stand up to him and bite and kick back with equal vigor. How they managed to stay cramped up together in the truck and not kill each other was a mystery to Coolidge. *They are at war with each other out there.* The other horses, slightly less combative and more interested in grazing on the fresh grass than establishing relative dominance, looked like a who's who of horse types: a small dark Arabian named Straus who looked like he could fit in the back of Cal's Mustang, a pure white mare with a rotund belly named White Devil, a jittery golden quarter horse with fiery eyes named Annie, another lighter colored but still enormous Belgium named Big Brother, a small black and white horse with a weird face named Fred who looked like he stepped out of the Sunday comics, and a handful of others – a few quarter horses sleek and sophisticated, a pure bluish-black horse that moved like an old man named Velvet, and a huge but similarly old white gelding named Ross.

"It's going to be a noisy night. We'd better keep them in the inner pasture for a few days until they get used to things," said Cal leaning on the corral fence.

"All right, you assholes, they're yours now. Help me shovel out this bed into your spreader, and I'll leave you to it," said Marvin climbing back into his cab.

"Coolidge, grab a flat shovel from the barn and get in the back of the truck!" said Cal immediately. Coolidge looked scared and lost.

"Come on, Cool, I'll show you where the shovels are. You'll need a pitchfork too," said Wyatt heading toward the barn. Marvin pulled the truck forward, swung around, and angled the back to the side of the weird trailer by the barn. Earl dropped the gate of the truck next to the spreader and Wyatt and Coolidge climbed on.

It was like stepping into nothing Coolidge had ever seen or smelled before – soggy wet horse crap was stomped into giant compressed pancakes with random hunks of spilled hay sticking out between puddles of urine and blood. "Start here and work to the back," said Wyatt handing Coolidge a five-prong pitchfork and sliding his shovel under the muck closest to the back. He swung his first load past Coolidge and into the manure spreader, splattering drops everywhere. Coolidge held his breath and did the same. The heat of the stench was outrageous and a million small gnats pummeled his eyes each time he disturbed their apparent breeding grounds with his pitchfork.

"What's the blood?" Coolidge asked, carefully pitching another disgusting load into the spreader.

"One of the mares in heat. Probably Annie," said Wyatt. "She kicks, too. Gross, huh? Cole might get some action tonight. He's the tall one fighting with Big Brother out there. Neither of them have any nuts, but that doesn't stop them from fighting and getting a little from time to time."

"Oh," said Coolidge. He heard the screeching of Cole and Little Brother in the corral and the smack of a few well-landed kicks. *I have to work with these animals?* He remembered Earl a few minutes ago in that very truck he was cleaning out, squeezed between jittery horses trying to throw a rope over their heads before leading them dangerously down the ramp. He was glad Cal hadn't asked him to do that. *At least shoveling shit wasn't life threatening.* But maybe he wasn't too sure given the germs he was wallowing in right at that moment. He was glad he had on his new boots and gloves, at least.

"Thanks, boys," said Marvin after they were done cleaning the truck bed and the steaming manure was piled high in the spreader. They climbed out and shut the door.

"Don't let those bosses piss on you too much!"

"We won't. See you later, Marvin. Thanks for the horses," said Wyatt, and he and Earl gave Marvin a two fingered salute. Coolidge watched the truck make its slow way around the barn and out the entrance. After it turned, it seemed to go through a hundred gears before its sound faded into the background noise of the busy highway.

Bullshit and Fences

The action in the corral continued as the three peons joined their bosses leaning over the fence that separated the barnyard and wheel table from the corral. Horses were chasing each other around, biting, bucking, rearing up and screeching at the top of their lungs. Cal and Hank, both with one boot resting on the lower board and elbows out on the top of the fence, were missing only popcorn to make the entertainment complete.

"Wyatt, Earl, are you sure this fence is working?" said Cal. Hank started to smile.

Wyatt and Earl looked at each other and Earl said, "The fencer hummed like it should when I plugged it in. Looks like the light's on."

"Now, Earl, are you sure this fence is on?" insisted Cal.

"You know we can't afford to let these horses bust out tonight when they're chasing each other around like banshees, like they are," said Hank.

As if in answer, the closest white gelding, Ross, galloped after the small black and white gelding, Fred, and bit him fiercely on the ass. Fred skittered away with his ears back and Ross started calmly grazing where Fred had been a moment before.

"Well, now I suppose there is only one way to tell for sure, Hank, if the fence is on. There's only one tried and true method that I know of. Someone's going to have to touch it," replied Earl, knowing the inevitable was upon them.

"True. Someone reliable. Someone who won't bullshit and pretend it is on when it isn't like some worthless *unreliable* peon might do," said Cal.

"Are our peons going to be *worthless* this year, Cal?" asked Hank.

"I don't know, Hank. I sure hope not! Last year was pathetic!"

"Maybe we had better find out!" said Hank. Coolidge suddenly didn't like the way Hank and Cal were looking at him. *Touch the fence wire? Wasn't that electrified?* He looked at the bare wire running just along the inside of the top rail of the corral, insulators holding it out from the board. *They must be kidding.*

"Maybe it is time for Coolidge here to learn what a direct-order is," said Cal. "Wyatt, tell Coolidge here what a direct-order is, would you please?"

"So, a direct-order is when you have to obey or you lose your job. An emergency might come up and a boss will want you to do something right away that you might not want to do or you might have questions about, but there's no time to fuck around with an explanation so he gives you a direct-order," said Wyatt.

"Any peon above you can give a direct-order, but they damn well better be sure afterward that it was necessary," said Cal, looking at Wyatt and Earl. "You understand what we're saying to you Coolidge?"

Coolidge nodded but didn't have time to say anything because at that very moment Cole and Little Brother screeched a seeming death scream and backed into each other at the manger kicking with both legs at once and landing blows that sounded like rapid-fire shotgun blasts. The two one-ton geldings then turned around, reared up, and started biting and pawing at each other with their front hooves. Only the fence and twenty yards of pasture separated this display of raw animal fury from the hundred and ten-pound Coolidge and his fellow horse boys.

"Oh, man! We have got to get those two separated as soon as possible, Hank, before they kill each other! As soon as Parker gets here - where is that asshole? - we need to get the Hillcrest horses out of here."

Marvin kept his horses in a couple of different places. When they all get dumped off at once at the stables it takes a couple of nights for them to work out the pecking order. That's why all the fireworks. As much as they could, the bosses liked to keep the horses that are used to each other together at one or other of the two stables. Tonight, though, there was nothing they could do about it.

Hillcrest was the other location of the stables eight miles away, where Hank was the boss and Wyatt's brother, Parker, a fourth year peon, and a new first year peon, Lenny, rounded out the crew. It was a slightly less intense place to work considering that Wyatt and Parker's parents owned a cottage there on the lake and water skiing and spaghetti dinners were sometimes day off perks. Parker was probably at his parent's cabin tonight. He'd get the fence ready at Hillcrest in the morning most likely. Parker was a curly-headed pretty-boy ladies man, always ready with a smile and a killer imitation of Marvin and of Francis Kowalczyk, the bent-over octogenarian who delivered the hay. Wyatt was the more obviously serious and ambitious of the two brothers at the stables. A younger future peon, Justin, too early to start working yet was also in the family, and, to further complicate the nepotistic Moretti family connection to the stables, the stunning and sexually liberated older sister, Lynn, was an on again off again steady bed partner with Hank. Messing around with Lynn was the reason for Hank's late arrival at the stables – and his general excuse for most of his many screw-ups. Of the two bosses, Cal clearly carried the brunt of the worries and responsibilities.

It was a false hope that the reemerging distraction of the battling horses would make the bosses forget about the subject matter at hand. Cal looked right at Coolidge and said, "So, any questions about what a direct-order is, Coolidge?"

"No, sir."

"Good. 'Cause if Hank or I ever give you a direct-order you must obey right away, no questions asked. That's your duty as a horse boy. Just obey the order and ask questions later if you have to."

"Yes, sir." At that moment, Coolidge felt like he would never have any questions for either of his bosses. *I'm afraid of them.*

"Okay, Earl. The matter of this fence. How do we know this thing is working right here? I think these goddamn horses might break out tonight, don't you?"

Earl picked a long rounded blade of grass from beside the fence post next to Cal's knee and laid it tentatively across the wire. Earl was barely tall enough to peer over the top rail given his short frame. His arm shot back as the blade fell to the sand. "Yep, it's on," he exclaimed.

"Bullshit, how do I know you're not lying?" said Cal a flicker of a smile escaping his mustache. "That grass is a piss-poor conductor."

"Well, you probably can't," replied Earl. He picked up the blade again.

"Earl, you *bullshit* pretty well, don't you? Bullshit cops, girls, you probably bullshitted your way to straight A's last year in school too, didn't you?"

Earl just smiled. "I guess you could say that..."

"Frankly, I don't trust you. I need someone I can really trust to test this fence, and that's not you. Wyatt, are you a *bullshitter*?"

"I've been known to bullshit," said Wyatt, smiling.

"Damn right you are a bullshitter. You are so full of bullshit. Touch the fence, Wyatt!" Cal looked away at the horses.

Earl handed Wyatt the grass stem.

"Not with that bullshit piece of grass either," Cal said looking right back. "The only way to tell if the fence is on is to touch it. Now, touch it, Wyatt! I'm giving you a direct-order!"

Wyatt reached over the railing and pawed at the fence not unlike how Cole had pawed at Little Brother a moment ago, only more gingerly. Coolidge saw and heard an actual spark form at Wyatt's fingertip.

"Yeeow!" said Wyatt. "That's a live sucker!" He shook off his hand.

Cal and Hank gave themselves over to a brief and whooping belly laugh.

"Goddamn it, Wyatt, you're as big a bullshitter as Earl here," Cal said when he regained his voice. "Earl, now you touch the fence. With your finger this time, not that pussy piece of grass. I'm giving you a *direct-order*!"

The spark that popped on Earl's finger confirmed in Coolidge's mind what he was trying to not believe he saw. "Cheeyah!" exclaimed Earl hopping off the fence and shaking it off at his side, dancing a little in his boots.

"You are so full of *bullshit*, Earl," screamed Cal, a long necked beer mysteriously appearing in his hands. He and Hank both took long swigs from brown and sweaty bottles. Coolidge noticed an open cooler of ice and beer on the wheel table. "There's no way that fence is on! You are so totally faking it. Goddamn it, how are we going to know this fence is working, Hank?"

"I don't know Cal. Maybe we'd better find someone to test it who isn't such a *bullshitter*?"

"I wonder who that could be. Hmm. Hey Coolidge, are you a bullshitter?"

Coolidge didn't know how to answer this. *To be a bullshitter is to be a liar, right?* But if he said he wasn't a bullshitter he'd have to touch the fence because his bosses were looking for someone who was honest to see if the fence was on so the horses wouldn't get away. On the other hand, it was obvious that the damn thing was on and working just fine. *They were the liars, the bullshitters, not me. It's not fair the way they made Wyatt and Earl touch the fence.* He didn't have any desire to touch the wire at all. It looked like it hurt a lot to touch that wire. He was scared, and he wanted to walk away, but Wyatt, Earl, and everyone were standing right there by the fence smiling and laughing, and he didn't have any place else to go.

"Coolidge, did you hear me? ARE YOU A BULL-SHITTER?"

"I don't know..." said Coolidge glancing for help from Earl, but Earl was laughing with Wyatt and opening a couple of beers behind Hank.

"Yeah, I understand, Coolidge. There's *a lot* you don't know," continued Cal in a lower tone. "Just like there's a lot we don't know. Such as whether the fence is on or not, and that's important, don't you think, considering what we've got to keep locked up in the corral tonight?" He pointed at the horses.

The horses had migrated closer to where Coolidge was standing almost like an audience of gods to witness his torment. He couldn't help looking over at their massive bodies and jaws grinding whole thistle plants, the red heads of which were sticking out from their seemingly impervious lips.

"I suppose..."

"And I don't think you are a bullshitter, Coolidge, not yet anyways," continued Cal, "not like these asshole third year peons over there who no one can trust." He tipped his beer to Wyatt and Earl who tipped their beers back at him. "You want to be trustworthy don't you, Coolidge? You want to earn my trust, don't you?"

"Yes."

"Well then *touch* the fence, Coolidge."

"Yep," Hank chimed in, "Touch the fence, Coolidge. We really need to know if it is on or not."

"I don't want to..."

Cal's sideburns flinched. "Coolidge, goddamnit, these horses need you to be sure. Are you really going to let them down because you don't want to? Are you going to be trustworthy in your job or not? Now, son of bitch, I'm getting impatient with you! Touch that fence, you fucking worthless peon!!"

They were all looking at him with shit-eating grins, except Cal, whose stern-faced demeanor was too well rehearsed for him to break. *Is he going to hit me again?* Coolidge wasn't certain, but he sure didn't want to find out. He reached over the fence, but he couldn't make his fingers connect with the smooth but potent wire. His feet felt hot in his new boots. Tears came involuntarily to his face.

"Coolidge, I am giving you one last chance. This is a DIRECT-ORDER – touch the fence," said Cal.

Part of Coolidge's brain somehow disengaged and transferred Cal's direct-order to his right hand. He touched the wire and learned the reason they call it a "shock." No matter how much you anticipate it, there is no mitigating the surprise a strong jolt like that delivers to your system. Even though the voltage was low, the amperage was extreme, and the pain, and Coolidge's reaction to the pain, was simultaneous and intense. "Oh, shit!" he said. His arm shot back over the top board, wrist scrapping the rough edge at the top. "Oh, man, that hurts, that hurts, *that sucks*!" he groaned. The shocking pain finally subsided to a weird numbness in his fingertips. He had hit the wire with both his pointer and ring finger.

"Good one, Coolidge!" said Wyatt with a laugh.

"Yeah, nice technique," added Earl, his dark eyes smiling. A thin, astonished smile also crept onto Coolidge's face, even as his fingers still tingled and his heart was beating a million miles an hour. *I did it.*

"Well, looks like the fence is working just fine after all," said Hank. "I guess you guys aren't as a big a bunch of bull-shitters as we thought," he said over his shoulder to Wyatt and Earl. Then he reached over the fence and calmly touched the wire himself. "Whoa, potent this year," he exclaimed as his hand shot back involuntarily.

"Good job, peons!" added Cal as he too sparked the fence and draped his arm around his partner's shoulder. "And we're glad to know we have at least one first year peon who knows the meaning of a direct-order. "Grab a beer, Coolidge."

Getting the Business

The financial arrangement of the stables was basically one of indentured servitude. The "peons" worked for essentially nothing, hence their racist but financially accurate position title. The bosses split whatever profits were made during the course of a summer and the peons hoped that if they stuck around long enough they might themselves get the chance to be boss. For many years the stables existed as a partnership, and the peons cycled through to partnership, some making it, others dropping out, but in the mid-sixties Earl's older brother donated the attorney expertise to change the partnership structure to a corporation. This didn't really change much on the surface – the peons still worked their way up and took over from bosses who moved on from college to year-round careers. The unspoken rule still was that no one stayed a boss beyond college. The arrangement still gave loyal peons a chance to eventually cash in. It was the classic old boy network.

Of course, like all businesses at that time, Lakeside Stables, Inc. faced new and growing pressures. Horses, hay, and all the necessary saddles, bridles, and medicines were starting to get more expensive, and insurance became a real consideration. Camps were also beginning to figure out the bosses took home a wad of cash each summer and wanted a bigger cut of the action, so they started to charge a little bit for the food the horse boys scarfed down each day.

The decision to form a corporation was a clear reaction to the financial tightening experienced by the bosses prior to Cal and Hank. Now that lawsuits were more common, the dioceses of each camp required proof of liability insurance to cover their asses in case a camper fell off a horse and broke a neck on their property. Audits were also a new consideration, and while most, if not all, major expenses continued to be covered in skimmed cash from tourist rides and parents paying to register their campers for instruction rides and pack trips, better and more creative spread sheets were becoming necessary each year. Binding an insurance policy that named the camps as well as the stables, sending a copy of that reassuring policy to the camp directors, and then secretly cancelling the policy immediately before the first payment was due allowed the stables to operate at a modest profit as insurance prices skyrocketed, but that yearly little practice of fraud made the bosses nervous. Frankly, they knew they were always just one lawsuit or accident away from disaster, and the extra insulation of a corporation made it less likely to hurt them personally if the whole house of cards came tumbling down.

Thank God, then, for past bosses becoming lawyers! Thank God also for Marvin who officially "lent" his horses to the stables for the summer for free so "they could get some exercise" and then took his summer payment in cash. The horses were always returned to him in shape but exhausted from carrying riders every day all summer long for an average of twelve to fifteen hours.

Like any corporation, Lakeside Stables, Inc. played up its good citizenship angles: Youthful entrepreneurialism! Hard working young people dedicating their summers to providing superior horseback rides to Central Wisconsin riders! A business run exclusively by college students! Young horse-lovers teaching young campers the lost art of riding and how to care for animals! Healthy outdoor fun in Wisconsin's finest tourist destination! It was all bullshit – but good bullshit because the system worked fine for decades. Even though the organization could not have been more secretly illegal it was beloved by most everyone involved in it, not the least of which were the innocent young campers and tourists who filled the daily trail rides and truly did come to know, understand, and love the horses and the horse boys who entertained them on the trails. Cal's love for the stables was genuine, even if its structure was corrupt.

The stables didn't just rent horses from Marvin. It owned quite a few horses outright, and these were another reason for the organization to brag. It lent them out, "wintered them," for free to capable year-round residents who wanted to ride during the school year. It was a good deal for them and a great deal for the stables. The horses got loved and cared for over the off-season at no expense to the stables, and the people who adopted them got a chance to experience horse ownership without a long-term commitment. A few of the horses sometimes ended up in sketchy homes, but the bosses got Marvin to check up on them periodically in the winter to make sure everyone kept up their end of the bargain. The horses owned by the stables were by far the nicest ones in the herd – all capable of going out on the trail by themselves, and all very gentle with young riders.

Over the next few days the wintered horses began to arrive one after the other, pulled in small horse trailers by pickup trucks disgorging whole families to hug and say goodbye to their "pet" for the summer. Each horse reintroduced to the herd set off new fights to establish the pecking order. The need to move half the growing herd to the Hillcrest location became pressing - thirty horses in one pasture was just too crazy, and the two alpha horses, Big Brother and Cole needed their own undisputed "harem" immediately before they kicked each other to death. Campers would start arriving at the two camps soon on chartered buses or dumped off by secretly thrilled parents only temporarily feeling the impending loss of their children's company for the summer. It was time to get everything set for the first homesick riders from camp looking for fun to forget their homesickness, and even the tourists, already needing distraction from their lonely cabins in the woods around the lakes, were calling to ask when they could please go on a trail ride.

So the date was set. Cal would drive to Hillcrest in his Mustang and pick up Parker, Hank, and the new first year peon, Lenny, so that they could spend the night at Crane and ride the Hillcrest herd to Hillcrest early in the morning before tourist traffic on the winding country roads got too busy. There was a lot to do before the dawn departure – each horse had to be fitted with a saddle, bridle, and blanket, and their hooves needed to be cleaned and trimmed. Luckily the trails at both stables were all dirt and sand so shoes weren't required, but still four hooves per horse required a lot of picking and nipping. Cal and Hank did most of the trim work on the hooves – it required some skill to know just how deeply to cut the hooves back with the nippers and how to shape the hooves properly so that they held the horse's weight evenly and wouldn't split. If a trimmer cut too deeply the flap of skin on the very bottom of the horse's foot, the frog, the horse could come up lame or develop a serious infection. Each healthy horse out on the trail meant more money for the bosses, so great care was taken to trim their feet properly.

The best way to motivate a horse to stand still for the twenty minutes or so it took to trim all four hooves was to work in the relative coolness and isolation of the drive-through area of the barn. At Crane the old red barn was of a classic cow-barn design, with a small equipment room and two rows of stalls facing each other across a concrete walkway on one side of the drive-through, and a huge area for storing hay on the other side. When Francis Kowalczyk would deliver hay, he would back his 1940's era Chevy truck teetering with alfalfa or timothy into the drive-through and everyone would dump the incredibly dusty bales off the truck and stack them into the barn. The heavy burlap bags of oats he also brought were emptied into two gigantic wine barrels in the tack room.

The horses learned quickly each year that when the door to the barn from the corral was open delicious oats were waiting for them in the stalls. When Wyatt and Earl demonstrated for Coolidge how to capture, tame, and motivate a horse with a bucket of oats, it was a comforting revelation. Like otherwise wary cats that would let any human pet them as long as there was tuna fish in a bowl to eat, most of the horses in the herd were similarly passive when given a cup or two of oats in a bucket. On the rare occasions when a fence was down and a few horses escaped, the escapees would usually stay close to the rest of the horses left in the pasture because of the herding instinct, but without a bucket of oats or similar enticement, an equally strong instinct to shy away from an approaching human with a lead rope was oftentimes frustratingly insurmountable. Like humans, horses enjoy freedom, but they also like dependency. Learning to manipulate that paradox with give and take, push and pull, is how the horse boys convinced the money-makers to come in out of the pasture each morning, don a saddle and work their butts off all summer long for oats, hay, water, and an occasional foot trimming.

So, with one peon opening the barn door to the pasture and shaking a bucket of oats as a lure while the other peons walk behind the herd to corral them toward the door, it doesn't take long before all the horses are in the stall areas racing, jostling and biting each other to get to the oats. Into that straining sea of horseflesh wade the peons slipping on wet floorboards between the beasts, avoiding massive swinging heads, and clipping stall ropes around their necks. Earl was particularly effective at this morning gladiator game because his small size allowed him to slip between the horses and sneak ropes around their necks before most of them even realized he was there.

Earl was one of the fastest persons, in fact, Coolidge had ever seen. He could be anywhere he wanted to be in an instant on his short but active legs. Coolidge learned to imitate his calming vocalisms as well as his quickness. "Ho now, ho, ho...easy does it," Earl would coo as he darted about completing the herd's daily transition from wild animals to resigned, un-unionized laborers.

Coolidge also learned many things from Wyatt about personal survival in crowded stalls. Wyatt knew how to lean into the horses as he walked between them, his firm hand always announcing his presence on their haunches and backs. "Keep light on your feet, Coolidge, so you don't get stepped on." After a few days Coolidge also got good at using horse backs and necks as convenient platforms to lean on and hang on to in order to take weight off his legs. Sometimes, in fact, moving between the horses in the stalls felt a little like climbing around on a living animal jungle gym set up over a playground of manure. It was like a game but with mortally dangerous consequences if you made the wrong move.

The stench of the excrement in the close air of the barn was one thing, but getting stepped on by a horse was an experience Coolidge would never forget as long as he lived. It happened the first day the herd was in the barn, and the routine was as new for Coolidge as it was to the horses, lazy from their winter months of sloth. He was in the far stalls between Ross and Annie, both monstrously large beasts, trying to get the lead rope around Annie's neck. Her light mane hair covered her rapidly chewing jaws that were buried deep in the feed box. When Ross bullied his nose into her pile of oats she reacted by pushing back against him abruptly and strongly. (The best defense is a good offense sometimes in the equine world.) Of course, Coolidge was unfortunately caught between the two. Coolidge's booted foot shot back as his torso was crushed between the ribs of the two horses. His instep got caught under the front hoof of Ross who was redoubling his push back against Annie. The full weight of the front end of Ross – about five hundred pounds - pressed authoritatively down onto the top of Coolidge's boot with a frightening sensation of fatality, pain and pressure.

"Oh my God," yelled Coolidge. "Get off of me!" He put his shoulders into Ross's neck and pushed frantically, beating his fists into the horse's long white face until Ross finally gave up the quest for Annie's food and mercifully shifted his weight back to his other foot. The pressure and pain had been like nothing Coolidge had ever felt before, and he limped quickly from between the horses just as soon as he could pull his foot free.

"It's better to move Annie to the first stall and Ross farther to the front door," said Wyatt noticing Coolidge hopping around awkwardly holding his foot. "They don't like each other, but I guess you figured that out. You okay?"

"Ross stepped on me! Yeah, I guess, no...it hurts. Son of a bitch!" The pain radiated all the way from his foot to the back of his eyes. *Don't cry.*

"Yeah, try to avoid getting stepped on if you can. Walk it off. I'll get the rest of them on this side for you. You've got to push them apart if they're not giving you enough room in there." Wyatt went back to tying up the rest of the horses.

Coolidge's foot throbbed but wasn't broken. Over time he learned to shoulder his body between two tight horses in the stalls and then wedge his knee on one horse to push his back against the other horse to knock them both sideways to achieve some room for himself. He learned which horses to tie up first in the morning – the more selfish ones who cruised for the largest pile of oats. He learned which ones were the most jittery and dangerous, Annie among them. He quickly learned the tricks, but the survival dance in the horse stalls was not for the faint of heart.

Getting kicked was another serious danger. Annie was also famous for kicking often - and with uncanny accuracy. Coolidge learned never to surprise her coming up behind her, and certainly never to position her anywhere in a trail ride except carefully at the end of the line. Annie could never be on the same ride as White Devil, for instance, because both had a firmly established habit of kicking any horse behind them. Annie and White Devil tended to spend their summers at separate stables because of their mutual "caboose" status. The only time they were together was if there happened to be a third kicker in the herd, like the young appaloosa, Rim Tank, who would arrive mid-summer and was even worse. Still, in the course of any one summer Annie and White Devil each managed to catch a peon or two unawares with a firm shot to the thigh or knee, usually in a stall just prior to a ride going out when someone was busy and let their guard down. Leading a ride cheerfully after just getting kicked or stepped on by a horse in the barn was never any fun, but a peon always had to hide the on-going battle with the horses behind a smiling façade that presented the PR message that Lakeside Stables horses were the gentlest horses in the world and would never ever hurt a fly.

That it was a battle, rather than a whisper-fest, was clearly the primary cultural mindset of the horse boys toward horses, public relations notwithstanding. Horses that turned around in the stalls to nip a peon in back who was tightening a cinch too hard, or horses who tried to lie down and roll in the sand with a saddle on, were shouted at and immediately beaten about the neck and face as punishment. The peon would grab the lead rope, or if the horse had a bridle on, the reins, and then aim violent punches at the soft fleshy part of the nose. Invariably the horse would try to walk backwards to avoid the blows, fear flashing in its blinking eyes. An electric prod was kept in the tack room for the most severe of motivating or punishment circumstances. Shouts and warnings were also a prime way for peons to maintain dominance and control over the horses in the barn and on the trail.

Rarely, but occasionally, despite all precautions, a camper or tourist would get kicked or stepped on. Sometimes they even fell off a horse. A "fall" as the feared screw-up was called - and no matter the circumstance it was always considered a screw-up on a peon's part – was very bad PR and resulted in bosses punching them in a hidden part of the barn or in the cabin or granary later that night when the campers and tourists had all gone home.

When a customer did get the brunt end of a horse's mood, or if they were unlucky enough to get their foot caught under a hoof of a horse shifting its weight to swat a fly with its tail, the nearest peon would rush to rescue them, usually by shouting at the horse or delivering a motivating blow. Afterward he would ask if the rider was okay, then goofily invite the person to kick or step on the horse in return to "get even."

Amazingly, humor like that usually worked to diffuse the situation, to dry tears, and to prevent hard feelings. Coolidge noticed different variations. Earl and Wyatt had perfected a PR technique of rescuing the victim and then engaging in what amounted to an immediate wild and crazy post-trauma "counseling dialogue" between the offending horse and the victim, asking each to state their side of the story and offering mediation or judgment as in a trial. Parker's tried and true technique was grabbing the mouth of the guilty horse and manipulating its lips to make it look like it was delivering a sincere apology to the rider. If all else failed, the hurt and crying rider could usually be appeased by appealing to their stereotypical sense of the "dangers of the wild west" and how cowboys had to be tough, like the victim obviously was, to handle the challenges of riding horses, shooting bad guys, and rustling cattle.

No matter what the screw-up, the bosses, nervous about the survival of the stables, always demanded to be told as soon as possible about falls and other unfortunate, but inevitable, accidents because if they found out something bad happened on a ride from anyone other than the peons first, that would doubly piss them off and rob them of the opportunity to put a favorable spin on the situation. Every accidental fall, or other potential stables-ending screw-up, was "discussed" immediately with the culpable peon and also later one-on-one at the regular Tuesday night meetings that also doubled as beer night provided by the bosses. Whether punches were doled out or not at those meetings was always a topic of discussion by the peons waiting in the granary for their turn in the cabin to face the bosses. The older peons were usually called in first and then they worked their way down the ranks one peon at a time. That way by the time the bosses got to the first and second year peons the stories and circumstances of their screw-ups (and, to be fair, successes) were clear.

Saddle slips were the most common cause of someone falling off a horse on a ride. Horses like Annie, Big and Little Brother, and even the most ironically gentle horse around people, Cole, would purposefully hold their breath when getting saddled to keep the cinch comfortably looser afterward. It took a fierce kick to the ribs to get these particular horses to exhale enough in the stall to tighten the saddle safely. Forgetting to do so, or forgetting the standard safety practice of checking the cinches of these horses before each ride was a sure way to dump a rider, especially during a trot, or more fatally during a canter that was otherwise a ride's most satisfying highlight. The peon leading a ride was always responsible for checking each saddle of each horse on his ride. A fall caused by a saddle slip was always worth a punch or two.

Horses and Cliffs

B ut these were the everyday considerations of the stables in full swing with campers and tourists riding fourteen hours a day. Many things happened during those "routine" days (that were almost never routine), but it is best not to jump too far ahead lest this story omits some formative events in Coolidge's life at the stables. At this moment in his first year as a peon the camp was a week away and many things at the stables were not yet ready.

The bosses and horse boys worked hard in early June repairing and fitting saddles, blankets, and bridles to the horses, and trimming hooves. It seemed like they ate hotdogs and potato chips for every meal. The fence at the pasture at Hillcrest was repaired, and hay and oats were unloaded there in anticipation of the next morning's decision to finally split the herd. Cal and Hank, each wielding nippers and working with their own crew of peons, had put the final inspection to the freshly oiled saddles and were working on the last of the horses to trim. It had been a long few days. Coolidge, his boots fitting much better now that they had been treated with the same Neatsfoot oil he had been slopping onto the saddles and bridles all morning, was helping Cal and Earl with the trimming. Earl had shown him how to lift the front and back legs of a horse to expose the hoof. It was hard on the back. Hank, Parker, and the other new first year peon, a bulky kid with long blond hair named Lenny, formed another team working on the other side of the barn. He hadn't had much time yet to get to know Lenny, but he seemed like a nice guy albeit with a chipmunk sounding laugh. He smoked, though, which was technically not allowed, although he noticed the bosses didn't seem to enforce the rule too strictly, especially Hank.

"Hold it up higher, Coolidge. You're not getting tired are you?" said Cal, nippers in his gloved hand putting the finishing touches on the hooves of the bent front leg of the brown Arabian mare he was trimming. Sweat had soaked Cal's black work hat and was dripping off his mustache and sideburns onto the hoof that had a huge crescent piece hanging off of it ready for the last nip. "Almost done, Straus. Hold still. Just one more nip or two. Hang in there, girl," he said to the horse. Seemingly in response, Straus leaned even more into Coolidge holding up his front leg for Cal to work on. Some horses lifted their hooves and nicely shifted all their weight politely onto their other foot when getting trimmed, but many, like Straus, were smart enough to figure out that it was way more comfortable (not to mention satisfyingly passive aggressive) to lean into the peon and make him hold them up while the farrier did his work. It tended to shorten the overall process because humans tire quickly. It also was a big part of what often made that twenty-minute health maintenance routine so exhausting. It was possible to do the whole job alone, the farrier holding up the leg and trimming the hoof himself, but it was easier to have one person holding the reins, or nose twitch, another holding the foot, and the cutter working the nippers and pick. Earl was on duty at

Straus's head. He was only using a lead rope on Straus, but the twitch was nearby just in case. The nose twitch, a true torture device, was reserved for unbroken horses or the otherwise recalcitrant patients when the vet came by. It was basically a loop of rope or small chain on the end of a short broom handle that twisted onto the nose and lips of a horse so painfully as to render the horse completely passive. The local large animal vet, also a former boss at the stables, used it when having to plunge his prophylactic covered arms into rectums and birth canals of infected or pregnant horses. Straus didn't need a twitch. Annie, though, sometimes did.

"Okay, that's it," said Cal, putting the nippers and pick into his back pocket and pulling off his sweaty leather gloves. "Make sure all the saddles and bridles are labeled before you take them off and send the horses out, Earl, unless you want to do all the fitting over again. We'll bring just the Hillcrest horses in tomorrow early."

"Sounds good," said Earl leading Straus back to the barn. Straus pulled on the bridle to get to the water trough first, though, and Earl let him. It had been a hot twenty minutes.

Cal grabbed the hose and pulled the handle up on the faucet. He removed his hat, took a drink, and then let the stream of water wash over his head. Coolidge waited his turn, and took a long drink from the hose first before similarly wetting his hair and his already sweat-soaked t-shirt. "Don't forget to turn the hose off when you're done, Coolidge." He didn't have to say that twice. Lenny had gotten a peon punch from Hank for leaving the hose running in the water trough too long that morning. It flooded the yard badly. He received a backhanded smack to the triceps. Hank had given him the choice of his arm or his leg, and Lenny had chosen his arm. It was the ethic not to show pain, but Coolidge noticed he disappeared behind the barn for a cigarette afterward on the pretext of needing to piss.

Cal went to Hank now and watched his "Hillcrest" team finish up. Parker had done the trimming on White Devil, always a tricky horse to work on since she could kick you forward or backward with her back leg. This time she cooperated, probably because her feet must have felt so much better – it looked as if Marvin hadn't trimmed them all winter. Lenny led her back into the barn and put her newly labeled saddle and bridle into the tack room.

"Peons, get this barn clean so we can go swimming!" said Cal, heading for the granary with Hank for a beer.

"All right, this should go fast with all of us here," said Parker. "We'll do the far side, and you guys can do the near. See who finishes first!"

Parker and Lenny grabbed a hand broom and a big stiff industrial flat broom from the tack room and headed to the back stalls. The heavy doors from both the far and near stalls leading to the central drive-through area were rolled open, and Earl walked past the hay to open the barn gate to the corral.

"Unclip the horses from closest to the door to the farthest, Coolidge, one at a time," said Wyatt grabbing the rest of the brooms for him and Earl. "Don't leave the lead ropes on the floor – drape them over the boards."

The lead ropes were around each horse's neck and tied to holes in the feed stalls with barn knots. A barn knot was basically a simple over hand hitch, except that an end loop was pulled through the knot instead of the end of the rope. That way if a horse was panicking (which they did surprisingly often over seemingly ridiculous things like a fluttering piece of paper blown into the barn from outside, or a hat blown off of someone's head) all a peon had to do was pull on the end of the loop to untie the knot and prevent the animal from choking. Peons always carried jack knives, but pulling the release on a barn knot was quicker and simpler to think of in a crisis. It had taken Coolidge a few practice sessions to learn how to tie and release a barn knot, but he finally had it down, thanks to Wyatt's patience.

To let the horses out at the end of the day did not require pulling on lead rope barn knots, just unclipping them. The horses seemed to know immediately that freedom, and the cherished time to revert back to native wildness, was upon them. They whimpered and stomped their feet in anticipation as Coolidge unclipped his way down the line. The moment they were free, they eagerly clomped their way out of the barn. Ross and Little Brother decided to try to go through the door at the same time – taking turns was difficult for both of them, apparently. They got stuck and caused a horse jam behind them that threatened to spill into the tack room but resolved itself when Ross finally backed out reluctantly and let Little Brother's heavier frame prevail. Ross trotted after him immediately, his neck on Little Brother's rear end.

Coolidge, tired as he was, made a mental note never to compete with loose horses in doorways. He had a hard enough time learning to control them with a rope tied around their necks when they were calm. Getting in the way of loose horses headed for freedom was never a good idea. In fact, he'd learn later that cantering a trail ride toward the barn was extremely dangerous for the same reason – the junkie-like desire to go back to the comforts of the barn can sometimes overwhelm the decision-making center of even the most temperate horse. In the throes of cantering endorphins, a willful galloping horse given the chance to head for the barn is god-like in its purpose and fury, and the violent tugging of a frightened rider on the galloping beast is an infinitely ignorable minor irritation. If lucky, the stunned rider gets the ride of her life all the way back to the barn door – sometimes a mile or two of justified screaming and dodging of low-hanging pine boughs. If slightly unlucky, the rider gets tossed off early but unharmed onto the dusty trail and has to finish the rest of the ride behind the horse boy on the lead horse. If majorly unlucky it's a landing in a poison ivy patch with a broken bone and an emergency ride to the ER.

The manure spreader was located in front of the barn between the end doors of the two rows of stalls. After the horses exploded through the door to the corral bucking, galloping, huffing deeply, and chasing each other about, the horse boys swept and shoveled the day's collection of manure out the stall doors and into the spreader. Wyatt gave Coolidge the full-sized kitchen broom. "Get everything out of the corners of the stalls, and I will come behind you with the big broom to push it out the door," he said. Earl went to the hay pile and muscled a hay bale over the railing onto the drive-through's concrete floor. His job was to shake and fluff out the hay to get the dust out of it and put it in the feeding bins. He used a three-pronged hayfork to break the bale apart and shake it into a big pile. Then he walked with big forkfuls of hay down the center aisle between the two row of stalls.

Wyatt, in the meantime, was working the big push broom in a syncopated rhythm behind Coolidge. An initial pop of the stiff broom hitting the concrete preceded a long accelerating sweep that ended with a second and then third pop to knock the accumulated filth from the broom before the next pass. All of the "pops" were actually mini-sweeps forward, so the overall effect was to keep the sludge spraying inexorably toward the door. Coolidge tried hard but couldn't keep up with sweeping the manure and compressed hay from the stalls in time to feed Wyatt no matter how furiously he worked his smaller kitchen style broom. It kept getting gunked up in the wet and pasty manure.

"Here, I'll trade you," said Wyatt handing Coolidge the big broom. By the time Coolidge figured out the rhythm, Wyatt had all the stalls swept out. He used a mini-version of a cleaning pop on the smaller broom to clean it off between frenetic bouts of sweeping. Tricks of the trade. Wyatt ducked into the tack room and swapped out his small broom for two five-prong pitchforks, handing one to Coolidge. Parker and Lenny were also at the stage of shoveling the pushed out manure into the spreader. Earl was done with the hay, and was pouring oats on top of the soft beds of hay in each feeder. With five peons working, it only took ten minutes to clean out the barn.

"Well, it wasn't a record, but not bad," said Parker, shutting the barn door behind him and jogging for the granary. "Let's go!" Cal was already climbing into his convertible in his swimsuit and Hank was firing up the Harley. Lenny ran after Parker into the granary to put on his suit and grab a towel. He came tearing out a moment later, long blonde hair flying, laughing his way into Parker's classic Chevy pick-up truck. Coolidge hoped he could be friends with Lenny, but he seemed to be fitting in with the older guys better than with him so far. Coolidge rushed after Earl and Wyatt into the cabin to find his swimming trunks buried deep in his duffel. He was the last to climb into the back of the Mustang with Wyatt and, of course, a case of beer from the granary fridge. Untypically, Earl chose not to drive his Impala and was sitting up front with Cal. It felt good to Coolidge to leave his boots by his bed and put on a pair of flip-flops. At least he felt prepared for this activity from previous summers at the swimming club. How wrong that turned out to be.

It took about a half an hour to drive to the outskirts of Stonyred where five or six long abandoned quarries hid in the surrounding forests and fields. Many state and federal capital buildings had sourced their building materials from these quarries, but the easiest and best rock had all been extracted long ago and cold spring water now filled each of them to the ground water line. Of course locals soon discovered the delights of swimming there despite the no trespassing signs.

The quarries were majestically beautiful, full of sunny nooks and crannies in the steep walls to throw down a towel or lounge in a beach chair. The water was extremely deep in all places – often over 200 feet, in fact – and the tall cliffs overhanging were inviting to daredevil jumpers and divers. At this time the debate was about whether to make the quarries a city park or not. So many people had gotten drunk and killed themselves there over the decades that factions had arisen calling for a fence and guards to keep everyone out, but it would take decades before people on the city council would think that protecting themselves from law suits was possibly more important than keeping their secret swimming paradise from closing down.

The first thing Coolidge noticed hiking on the beaten trail from the dirt parking area to the most popular and well-known quarry – the "main quarry" as Wyatt referred to it – was the healthy patch of poison ivy growing on both sides of the path. As a youngster, Coolidge had once rubbed poison ivy plants growing in the ravine next to his suburban Coveside home all over his face and neck to prove to his best friend, Chad Van Bailey, that there was no need to worry about walking there in shorts because the three-leaved plants were "elm seedlings." He learned later, after a torturous week in bed with calamine lotion all over him, that there were other plant forms in this world with three leaves. Word soon spread among the middle school moms that Mikey's ailing mom let kids run wild in the woods, and after a while weekend visits and sleepovers dwindled away.

Back then, Michael wasn't too aware of the gradual social failings of his parents. When he had free time from the drama of Perry's anger and his mom's slow but inexorable decline into paralysis from MS, he loved swinging on a rope swing he rigged up that went high out behind the garage over the steep ravine walls. Even more mysteriously releasing for him were the long runs and hikes on deer trails in the ravine where he could pretend he was an indigenous hunter. Most of the time no one in his family even knew he was there, especially his dad who was fearful of him even going anywhere near the ravine. But Perry was usually off at work at the carwash on weekends, and to go out unsupervised to play and ride a bike around the neighborhood all day was just par for the course for Mikey. A couple of times his hiking adventures took him far downstream, through the long culvert beneath the railroad trestle, and far beyond to the mouth of the ravine opening onto the alewive-strewn Lake Michigan beaches of Doctor's Park. He had found a limping flicker there, a weird type of bird. He thought it was suffering and decided to put out of its misery with his penknife. It looked exhausted, couldn't fly, and had dirt and snails crawling around inside its beak. He didn't tell anyone about it, and it was a good thing because years later he learned that it was just an adolescent trying to feed itself before it could fly.

Guilt over misunderstandings about how nature worked is often a byproduct of a young person's unguided but sincere explorations. After his long and successful hike, Michael honestly felt he was helping the poor bird as a sort of king would in merciful control of his domain, and even the poison ivy fiasco mis-educating his friend about the flora of the ravine perhaps came from the same naively authoritative attitude over his chosen personal territory. Was this a subset of the "needing control" reaction he had away from home at school where only the best grades and achievements were acceptable to him? That the nature of school and Mother Nature in the ravine both pulled him like the pull of pasture freedom for the horses longing for the workday to end he had not yet conceptualized, but clearly the as yet un-self-aware strength of it was intense. Was the developing love for school and nature derived from needing attention and maybe even love-seeking behavior? Or merely from a need for some place in his life where there was a measure of ownership and security? Or perhaps it was the opposite, that school and nature provided mystery and adventure he could truly optimistically participate in at his level of development, whereas the adult problems and challenges at home provided no clear path for input other than cringing in his bedroom when fights erupted between his parents, or praying for his mother to once again be able to move her toes or transport herself from her wheelchair to the toilet.

Needless to say, Coolidge navigated his flip-flops carefully down the trail eyeing the dreaded and dangerous poison ivy plants along the beautiful wooded path to the glittering and majestic quarry ahead. The smell of the water and the heat emanating from the early afternoon June sun on the rocks was instantly relaxing.

"The water is going to be freezing," said Parker with relish. The hot days of summer were, after all, just beginning, and the ground water tenaciously held the long winter's cold in the deep darkness of the quarry waters. No one else had been parked at the quarry at this late hour, so Cal carried the case of beer on his shoulders and Wyatt and Earl grabbed the bags of cold cut sandwiches and potato chips.

Right away the path led to a flat set of low rocks with easy access to the water. This must have been the rubble side of the quarry when it was in operation, a pile of boulders where no doubt a road had meandered its way up from the bottom. It made for easy handholds and flat places to put your feet when climbing in or out. But Hank, Cal, and every-

one else kept going on the forest path around the edge of the
water toward the tall cliffs on the far side of the quarry. The
water was not much larger in area than maybe half a football
field.

"We don't drive old cars off the cliff anymore, but there
are a few stables cars at the bottom of this thing, for sure,"
said Earl.

"My old boss, Burt," said Cal with obvious admiration.
"We all watched it from down here. He drove it up there
through the trees, put a brick on the accelerator, dropped it
into gear, and jumped out. That piece of shit Ford did a full
180 before making the biggest splash I have ever seen. Locals
were pissed at all the oil it left in the water, but no one ever
figured out it was us."

"It's still down there if you dive deep enough." Cal continued. "Don't worry, Cool, it's way far down, you won't hit
it going in. Just make sure that you go straight out, though
– there's a boulder in the water on the left side you want to
miss for sure."

"All right!" said Lenny walking ahead of Coolidge. "Cliff
diving! Man, I can't wait!"

What the hell were these guys talking about? The cliff
was at least twenty feet high. He barely had mustered the
courage to jump off the club's twelve-foot high dive last summer. *Were they expecting him to dive off this thing?*

The path curved into the woods briefly and then
climbed back on a wider path to a clearing at the cliff's edge.
Coolidge could imagine a car accelerating from the woods
there and flying off. It scared him to think of it. *What if Burt
had not been able to jump out in time before the car hit the*

edge? He thought it wasn't too cool to pollute the water that way, either. *Hank's brother sure seemed like a wild person.* Wyatt had told him other stories about the bosses back then - stories told with a tone of wonderment and a kind of admiration, rough stories about drunken peon punching parties, wild driving adventures, and fist fights at distant bars where anonymity would protect the business while everyone let off testosterone-fueled steam.

"Earl, go first and show Lenny and Coolidge where to climb out," said Cal putting the case of beer under a tree and tossing his towel over it to hide it in case a local showed up unexpectedly. Most visitors didn't care if people drank and dove off the cliffs, and it was getting a little late for anyone else to settle in, but periodically the sheriff would swing by to make an occasional show of kicking people off the private property. Cal opened a beer for himself and Hank, and they each chugged it down in about two gulps.

Earl kicked off his loafers, pulled off his hat and t-shirt and stepped to the edge. It made Coolidge dizzy to get close enough to look at the glittering water far below. Indeed, he could see the outline of a boulder just below the water on the left side but only because it was in the shadow of the cliff they were standing on. *How do they know there aren't any other boulders down there?* Earl paused at the edge to look over at Wyatt. *Was he thinking the same thing?*

Coolidge watched Earl's left fist clench and unclench. Then Earl raised it to join the three fingers on his right hand, and with a grunt he thrust himself head first over the cliff. He arched like an Olympian through the air and knifed into the water with barely a splash. His arms made big splashes, though, a few moments later when he resurfaced and, whooping loudly, overhanded his way to the parking area side of the cliff and pulled himself out on a flat rock. Coolidge and Lenny watched carefully as Earl finally stopped hyperventilating and worked his way up the ladder of rocks to the path again. "That water is fucking cold!" said Earl, his voice echoing across the quarry.

"Just the way I like it," said Parker, who dove in next. His bigger frame and not quite as graceful style over-rotated him on the way down. He hit the water with a shotgun crack. Quite a bit of laughter and curly-haired head-rubbing accompanied his own whooping and desperate strokes to escape the freezing water. Nobody had a more exuberant or child-like baby-faced grin than Parker, even when the occasional lapse of judgment, physical or otherwise, led to less than perfect consequences. Hank and Cal laughed and handed Earl and Parker a beer when they got back to the top.

"Parker, you suck at diving. Maybe you should stick to jumping," said Hank.

"No way, man, too hard on the balls."

Wyatt was next. "I'm a jumper – I don't want to end up whacky in the head like my brother," he said over his shoulder to Lenny and Coolidge, but loud enough to rib Parker. "Jumping works, just cross your hands in front of your crotch and make sure you point your feet."

"Shouldn't be too hard to protect yours considering they're so small," said Parker.

Wyatt took a few steps back and ran off the edge with a quick yell followed by a big inhale. He landed in the water a few seconds later with a different sounding splash than the divers. He also seemed to take longer to resurface. Something about the physics of a jump makes a person descend farther into the water. Wyatt took a desperate breath when he finally came up and needed a moment to collect his bearings before he could splash his way to the escape rock. "Come on, Coolidge. You're next! Water is fine!" he managed to gasp. Even from so far away, Coolidge thought he could see the goose bumps forming on Wyatt's fair skin.

"I'll go," said Lenny, already stripped down to his trunks. He looked like he needed a cigarette, though, as he summoned his courage. "That's a long jump down," he repeated in a few different ways between spasms of nervous chipmunk laughs.

"Get your ass in the water, Lenny," said Hank. "Can't you see Coolidge is waiting for you?"

Coolidge felt like shaking his head vigorously in denial of that concept, but he had a feeling that that would not be such a good idea. Maybe Lenny would chicken out, and they could dip in the water down by the path where they first came into the quarry. He doubted it, though, remembering the electric fence testing. Reluctantly he shook off his flip-flops and stood up to watch Lenny.

Lenny, employing a brief delaying strategy, turned to Coolidge to see if he was indeed chomping at the bit. Seeing he wasn't, he laughed, but not meanly, and turned back to Hank and said, "Yeah, right. See you in the water, Coolidge!" and he too ran off the edge. His feet continued to run in the air the whole way down, and he landed on his side in a not quite reverse belly flop. Enough to score low on style points and high on impressive splashing. Coolidge could feel empathetic pain in his own side as he stared with concern at the white bubbles that had swallowed his fellow first-year peon. Lenny resurfaced, gasping and groaning. He made it to the flat rock, but the red marks on his thigh and ribs were severe.

"You okay, Lenny? Nice belly flop! You better get back up here and work on your technique!" laughed Hank. Lenny walked back to the top of the cliff. He was still a bit shaken but laughed and inspected his smarting skin as Hank handed him a beer.

"Your turn, Coolidge," said Cal.

"I think I'll jump, okay?"

"No one gives a shit how you do it. Get in that water before we lose our sunshine. Hank and I need to see if you are going to kill yourself before we go in.... I'm kidding you, goddammit. Just remember to take a deep breath on the way down!" Cal ran his fingers through his hair.

Coolidge couldn't look Cal in the face for fear of what else Cal might say, kidding or otherwise. Instead he looked at the spot at the edge of the grey cliff where each peon had departed the safety of land. He saw sand and pebbles resting precariously in a small crack in the granite leading to the edge. He kicked a few out of the way and watched them fly off and then disappear from sight before hitting the water with the tiniest of splashes. The waves from Lenny's jump were in the last stages of rebounding off the far cliffs and settling back to calm. He could smell the coolness of the water and the pine trees from the forest behind him. He tried to channel his knee-shaking fear into physical concentration. *Run a bit before jumping off, don't run in the air, land straight, hold your crotch.* He glanced back, trying not to show fear, but unable to smile or laugh as Lenny had done. Hank was pulling on a beer. Cal was wiping foam off his mustache on his muscular arm. Everyone else was watching him, no doubt wondering if he would chicken out. He certainly felt like it, but also not like it. He felt his mind disengage from places it had once felt safe, from the illusion of control over himself and his circumstances that had sustained him whenever he had previously been tested in his short life. He knew he would jump, *but would it hurt? Would I screw myself up forever? Drown?*

He looked out carefully over the water where he planned to aim his feet. He stepped back a few paces took a deep breath and accelerated toward the edge. His right foot pushed off last, and he felt an exhilarating acceleration. *Don't run in the air!* He put his body into a needle following his toes, but he was tipping too far forward! Instinctually he shot his hands back, regaining his trajectory. The speed was instantly blinding, the sensation of falling intense in his chest. He hit the water with pointed toes, arms up at the last moment but not all the way over his head.

The impact of the water was like an explosion forcing his arms upward with a smack and pressing on all sides of his body with a hammer-like force mixed with an incredible number of bubbles rushing by his chest and up his nose. The stinging pain in his forearms and triceps was immediate, and the pressure on his swimsuit was like a military grade wedgy. It hurt down there, but not like his arms. He didn't think much about pain, though, as the quarry water slowed his rocket descent and pressed harder and harder into his ears

– the cold was shockingly intense. He kicked frantically for the surface, lungs protesting for air. He broke through and every breath was a gasp. "Oh my god!" he managed to sputter. Freezing water was pouring out of his nose. *Where was that damn rock?* He saw the cliff and remembered to look right. There it was, so far away. He kept his head up gasping air and breaststroking like a maniac for the rock. When he finally reached it, it was hard to find handholds and footholds. *Out of this cold!* Finally, his foot found a little ledge in the side of the rock and he rolled himself out of the water onto its warmness.

"Yay, Coolidge! Way to go, Coolidge! Woohoo!" he heard everyone shouting from above. Seconds later he heard Hank land a cannon ball behind him followed by Cal's dive that was equally as graceful as Earl's. Coolidge made room for them to climb out onto the rock. It was interesting for him to see both his bosses shivering and gasping as he had been a moment before. As he followed them across the rocks and up the path to the beer and cold cut sandwiches, the pain in the skin of his arms gradually gave way to endorphins from the shock of the cold water. Back home in Milwaukee he had seen news coverage of crazy people in the Polar Bear Club dipping into Lake Michigan on January 1st. Considering how he felt now, maybe they weren't so crazy after all.

Splitting Up is Hard to Do

The roar of Hank's Harley coming to life before dawn the next morning woke the Hillcrest peons, Parker and Lenny, who spent the night in sleeping bags in the granary. They stumbled barefoot into the morning dew on the grass by the fence and peed between the boards into the corral.

"Get dressed, you peons," said Hank. "We've got to get to Hillcrest and back here by breakfast." He killed the engine and put the kickstand back down as if he had just remembered something. He cupped his hands and shouted at the cabin. "Cal, get your peons out here dressed and ready to work – we need the horses ready by the time we get back!"

Inside the cabin, Cal was the first one up. "You heard him, boys. Let's get those horses in!"

Coolidge climbed down from the bunk careful not to step on Earl who was pulling on his blue jeans and boots already.

"We'll eat when I get back from Hillcrest," Cal said to Earl and Wyatt. "Just bring the Hillcrest horses into the barn for now and saddle them up." He handed Wyatt a list of names on the back of an envelope resting on his nightstand.

Coolidge pulled on his jeans and a warm flannel shirt. He was careful not to bump into Earl next to him or into Cal putting on a chamois shirt beside the queen bed. The space between the beds was narrow and filled with duffel bags and boots. *Where were his boots?*

"Come on, Coolidge!" yelled Cal. "You're slow as shit. Wyatt and Earl are going to have those horses in before you are even dressed!"

"I can't find my boots," said Coolidge, an intense look on his face.

"What do you mean you can't find your boots?" said Cal to Hank who had just walked in slamming the screen door.

"You mean Coolidge can't find his boots either?" said Hank, amazed.

"What do mean either? Don't tell me your first year pe-on piece of shit can't find his boots too?" said Cal matching Hank's expression of amazement. These peons sure were a pain in the ass.

"That's right," replied Hank clicking his mouth and shaking his head.

"Get him in here!" said Cal.

"Lenny, get your worthless barefooted ass in here!" he yelled out the door. Coolidge noticed Earl giving Wyatt a wry smile. Something was up. *Were they in on it?*

"Wyatt, have you seen my boots?" Coolidge asked.

"Last I saw them they were under there," he said pointing to the floor by the bunk.

Coolidge got down on his knees and crammed his head under the lower bunk again just as Lenny tentatively stepped into the cabin next to Hank. From his angle on the floor Coolidge could look past the crowd at the door and see some red in the dawning sky. Cold air morning poured over him.

"Coolidge, get up!" said Cal. "Lenny, where the hell are your boots?"

"I don't know. I put them by the door of the granary last night, but they're gone."

"Are your boots broken in?" asked Cal. Hank started to laugh. Cal gave him a quick look and turned his frowning unibrow back to Lenny.

"I don't know. I got them before I came up."

"You didn't break them in?" asked Cal.

"I don't know. I guess. How do you break them in?" stuttered Lenny.

"Coolidge, your boots are missing, right? Did you break them in?"

"How do you break them in?" said Coolidge figuring at this point that pain of some sort was surely headed his way. Cal looked exasperated and pissed off.

"Look you peons, *my* boots are broken in," he said lifting his foot up for them to see. "Hank's boots are broken in. There they are. Earl and Wyatt, looks like your boots are reliable and broken in, right where they are supposed to be. Reliable boots, ready to serve, broken in! But your boots are missing! Why are they missing, Coolidge?"

Coolidge hesitated. "Because they aren't broken in...?"

"Exactly right, Coolidge! Boots are like pussy – you can't rely on them unless they are broken in! Do you know how to break in pussy, Coolidge?"

"Uh, no."

"Your damn right you don't. You can't even break in your boots properly. Fortunately, you're surrounded by experts, ain't that right, Hank?"

In reply, at first all Hank could do was try to suppress his laughter. He looked mildly in pain before succeeding and catching a breath. Then his mind caught up to the bullshit, and he retreated, like Cal, into a pissed off demeanor, only less scary because he couldn't fake it as convincingly. "You're damn right, Cal. We've been breaking in boots and pussy around here for a long time!" He smiled at Cal and glared at Coolidge and Lenny.

"That's right, Hank. You're lucky we were around to help you break in your boots, peons. Nothing's more worthless than a pair of unbroken-in boots, unless maybe it's first year peons trying to wear boots that aren't broken in when there's work to be done. Now you two go find your boots. They're someplace around the front of the barn, I think, and hurry up. Coolidge, you've got to help Earl and Wyatt get the horses in, and Lenny, you've got to go with Parker to get the fence ready at Hillcrest before breakfast. Hurry! Get going!"

Someplace in front of the barn he'd find his boots? Why? As Coolidge hurried out the door after Lenny, he glanced at Wyatt who gave him a smile and a fake shrug. Lenny had taken off his socks and stuffed them in his pocket. Good idea with all the sand and sticks in the yard, so Coolidge pulled off both socks quickly when he stepped outside and ran on tiptoe after Lenny toward the barn. The morning sky was light enough to see things now, and beautiful wisps of pinkish red clouds arched over the barn mimicking its color. His toes felt the moisture of the dew in the sand. Parker was looking over at him smiling from his truck where he had just tossed his rolled up sleeping bag. Wyatt, Earl, Cal, and Hank were laughing and walking after him toward the barn.

Lenny first went under the railing and looked around in the concrete drive-through area. Coolidge followed as far as the railing but didn't go under. *In front of the barn*, Cal had said. He walked to the left, passing the door to the near stalls and around the corner where they had cleaned the barn the night before. No boots anywhere.

"Hurry up, Coolidge!" Cal yelled. "Get your boots on!"

"Lenny, you, idiot," yelled Hank. "In front of the barn!"

Coolidge looked back at the group coming closer and shrugged his shoulders.

"Coolidge, figure this out," said Cal laughing. "Boots are like pussy. How do you break in pussy?"

"I have no idea," said Coolidge. Lenny walked up to stand with him at the corner of the barn.

"By fucking it?" answered Lenny, laughing at his own joke.

"Hmm, close, Lenny, you're getting warmer," answered Cal. "You break in pussy by spreading it!"

The spreader? Coolidge walked over to the manure spreader and looked inside. Sure enough, there were the four boots stuffed with horseshit and sitting primly on a mound of manure that was almost invisible behind the cloud of flies and gnats buzzing and breeding around it.

"Now what do you say, Coolidge?" asked Cal with a huge grin on his face. Hank was doubled over laughing. Earl and Wyatt were covering their mouths with their forearms.

Coolidge looked at Cal, unable to say what he was feeling or to answer his question. There was shit in his new boots, and he had to put them on. He reached in and lifted one of them by the strap. The weight of the boot was like an amputated limb. He turned it upside down. The smell was nauseating as the horse apples and smooched shit in straw tumbled out. He had to hit the boot on the edge of the spreader to get the filth out of the toes.

"I asked you a question. Maybe Lenny's got the answer. Lenny, what do you say to someone who has helped you out?"

"Thank you?" said Lenny reaching over the edge of the spreader for his own boots. Unlike Coolidge he could do it without leaning into the side of the spreader because he was taller.

"That's right, Lenny. Thank you, bosses, for breaking in my boots for me," said Cal. "I don't hear you!"

"Thank you, bosses, for breaking in my boots for me," mumbled Coolidge. Lenny chimed in with the same only louder.

Morning entertainment over, the bosses turned their grinning faces back to their cars. The first year peons rinsed their boots as best they could with the hose, rolled their socks over their damp and sandy feet, and pulled them on.

"Now, get those horses in," said Cal to Earl and Wyatt.

"Lenny, get your shit and go with Parker," said Hank.

"I'll meet you there," said Cal to Hank.

The morning air was losing its chill when Cal pulled away in his Mustang, top up, following Hank on the Harley, and Parker in his red truck. Earl and Wyatt were looking over the list by the barn. The problem was that all the horses were going to want to come into the barn for oats. It would be tricky to just let the Hillcrest horses in and not the others.

"As usual, Hillcrest gets all the good horses," complained Wyatt.

"Except for Annie," said Earl.

"Little Brother is so slow," said Wyatt.

"Better than Big Brother – he spooks."

"Yeah, I guess so. So, why don't we have Coolidge chase them in, and we can sort them at the barn door?" suggested Wyatt.

"Worth a try. Better than letting them all in and then chasing out the ones we don't want. Coolidge, looks like the herd is in the big pasture. Walk out there behind them and walk 'em in. Try not to rile them up too much. Go slow."

"Okay, Earl," said Coolidge, somewhat unenthusiastically. *Were his soggy boots completely ruined now?*

The sun was rising between the pine trees as Coolidge followed the fenced-in path from the corral to the ten-acre far pasture. Each step felt weird to him in his wet boots. The electric wire running along the top of the wooden fence looked ominous as he remembered the shock it delivered when he touched it. He imagined that the memory of its power would be enough to keep horses from escaping through the fence whether the juice was on or not, but they still managed to do so every once in a while, according to Wyatt. He hoped they wouldn't do that this morning while he was out there alone. He'd had a bad enough morning already. He saw a pile of horse shit on the path and stepped right in it deliberately. What difference did it make now?

He saw the herd hanging around on the near side of the pasture once he reached the end of the path. The dew on the grass had further soaked his boots and the tops of his jeans. There weren't many clouds in the sky, though, so the sun would dry him out soon. *By noon I'll be hot and sweaty.* The horses were grazing peacefully. A few were even lying down, so some equine diplomat had negotiated a cease-fire apparently. He noticed Cole and Little Brother were grazing on opposite sides of the herd.

As he circled around them, a few of the horses got the hint and headed for the path and the barn. Soon all the horses were up and trotting toward the path. "Whoa, whoa," he said, but there was nothing Coolidge could do to slow them down. In a moment he was alone in the pasture hoping the horses weren't mobbing Earl and Wyatt already at the door of the barn. Although it had been a relief to see Cal drive away that morning, Coolidge was still nervous about making any mistakes and getting punched. Wyatt had said not to rile the horses up. *Have I done something stupid?*

Indeed, as he entered the corral he saw Earl and Wyatt with their hats waving in their hands chasing some horses away from the barn door and letting others go through. All the horses wanted into the barn for the oats, or more likely they just didn't want to get left behind. It was a struggle. Straus managed to slip by Earl even though he was not on the list.

"Cool, go around to the front and get a bucket of oats and take it there to the outside manger. Hurry!" said Wyatt.

Coolidge hurried to the corral gate, let himself out, closed the gate, and ran across the yard to the barn. There were horses already in the stalls. *Tie them up? No, Wyatt said to get a bucket of oats.* He crossed in front of two horses trotting into the near stalls and grabbed a five-gallon bucket in the tack room. The heavy oak cover to the oat barrel wasn't too hard to slide off. In no time he filled a bucket of oats with his hands. He slipped his way past the loose horses again and out the stall door, the bucket slapping against his thigh. He ran back across the yard and into the corral spilling a few oats with each step.

"Spread the oats into the manger – it will distract the horses we want to stay out here," yelled Wyatt chasing White Devil away from the entrance to the barn.

The bucket of oats made Coolidge an instant attraction for the horses in the corral, especially when he started pouring them into the manger feeding stations. Fred put his entire head in the bucket while Coolidge was holding it just to be sure there weren't any more oats in it. Soon the pressure was off of Wyatt and Earl at the barn door. They went inside to tie the horses up and chase Straus back out. They then caught the rest of the horses on the list with an outstretched oat bucket in one hand and a lead rope in the other hidden behind their backs.

Standing in the corral watching them catch horses like that was a marvel for Coolidge. Earl was especially talented at pretending not to notice a horse approaching the bucket and then he would swirl and deftly clip a lead rope around its neck. Wyatt had a more aggressive approach, cornering a horse by the manger and then out-maneuvering it until the horse gave up and went for the oats.

There was an added nervousness to the atmosphere in the barn stalls that morning due to the fact that half the horses were left outside. There was lots of neighing back and forth, and it was clear the Crane horses in the pasture would never really stop trotting around and pawing the ground until the Hillcrest horses were finally gone.

Saddling was especially dangerous that morning with all the shifting, neighing, and stomping inside the barn. Before the carefully fitted and labeled saddles could be put on, each horse had to have the dirt and grime from the previous night removed from their coats. This involved using a currycomb and a big stiff horse brush. Wyatt showed Coolidge how to work the two tools in an overhand rhythm. The currycomb had rows of sharp metal teeth on a stiff round coil. It was very effective at loosening dirt and dust, and the brush on the next stroke swept it off the coat and into the air. Holding one's breath was advisable but not always possible when a lot of horses had to be saddled in a hurry. It was fastest to do an assembly-line approach with one peon brushing and the other two following with blankets and saddles. Earl took over the brushing and Wyatt showed Coolidge how to put the saddles on the horses.

"Pull the saddle off the rack like this," said Wyatt grabbing the horn of Velvet's saddle and pulling it toward him in the tack room. "Slide your other hand under the blankets and cradle them under the whole thing as you carry it. Grab the bridle off the nail with your other hand."

Wyatt carried the saddle, blanket and bridle out of the tack room and into the stall next to the big bluish thoroughbred. "Put the saddle down horn side down with the blanket draped over the back of the saddle like this. Hang up the bridle on the nail on the nearest post, there. Don't let the reins or the blankets touch the floor of the stall." He demonstrated. Velvet turned her head and looked at the saddle. "You have to put the blanket on folds to the front and slide them back from the neck like this to keep the mane hair straight and even under the blankets. Everything clean and smooth, that way you don't get saddle sores."

Coolidge watched how Wyatt pulled the blankets down Velvet's neck, stopping just when her back was covered. Wyatt lifted the saddle and swept the stirrup and rope cinch from the far side up onto the saddle's seat. He swung the saddle over Velvet's back letting the stirrups and cinch fall over the opposite side of her.

"Position the saddle high on the neck, just like you did with the blankets and pull it back over the blanket until the cinch is hanging just behind the front legs. See that?" He pointed to the hanging cinch under the horse on the other side.

"Okay," said Coolidge. "Got it."

Wyatt pulled the cinch under the front of the horse's barrel and held the round ring in his right hand. With his left he dropped an inch-long leather strap hanging on his side of the saddle through the ring. "This is the latigo. If you forget what it is called you can just lat it go. It goes through the ring on the cinch, back up to the latigo ring and around again. Pull it tight and feed it through the left side of the latigo ring, across its front and back around its right side, kind of like tying a tie." Coolidge watched carefully as Wyatt tied the simple leather knot across the ring.

"You know the tightness is about right if you can just fit two or three fingers inside the cinch," said Wyatt. "Velvet will fool you because sometimes she bloats. Watch out for bloaters. All the horses will do it sometimes, but this one is the worst. The only way to make sure they don't bloat is to kick them in the ribs as you tighten the cinch." Wyatt gave Velvet a firm knee to the barrel while pulling on the latigo at the same time.

"There that's about right. Check it out." Coolidge could only get two fingers into the cinch area. It seemed to be on nice and tight.

"Fortunately Velvet has tall withers. The ones you need to watch out for are horses with little or no withers to keep the saddle from sliding to the side. Those saddles have to be even tighter, and then the problem is saddle sores. Saddle sores come from dirty horses, uneven blankets, saddles that don't fit, and cinches that are too tight."

It was a lot to take in, but Wyatt had a sincere and patient way of teaching. Wyatt let him saddle Big Brother next. He was a monster to stand next to and a challenge to throw the saddle onto and have the cinch fall successfully on the other side. Big and round and a bloater, it took some hard kicking and pulling before the horse yielded and Wyatt was satisfied the saddle was on tight enough. As he worked his way down the stalls with Wyatt, Coolidge learned each horse had its own idiosyncrasies. He wondered if it was worth learning them since the horses were headed to Hillcrest.

"Horses go back and forth all the time. You've got to know everything about every horse in both stables," said Wyatt.

When Cal drove back in with everyone piled in the Mustang, the horses were ready, but the peons were not. You couldn't do a big cross-country ride on an empty stomach. Fortunately, Cal had done some more shopping. He set up a green Coleman stove on the table and put a Dutch oven and a big frying pan on the flames.

"Coolidge, wash your hands and crack all these eggs into this frying pan. Don't get any shells in there, whatever you do!"

Coolidge went behind the cabin to wash his hands. He was hungry enough to swallow the eggs raw, but when he saw the packages of bacon going into the Dutch oven he got even hungrier.

"The only way to cook bacon!" exclaimed Cal, stirring the mountain of unseparated raw bacon down into the recesses of the cast iron pot. He then unwrapped a whole stick of butter into the frying pan. "Crack all those eggs right in there," he said pointing to three-dozen eggs in the grocery bag. Coolidge complied putting the shells back into the cartons. The soupy eggs were an inch and a half thick in the pan as the bacon began to sizzle. The smell was amazing.

It took the scrambled eggs less time to cook than the bacon, so Cal kept stirring them over low heat to keep them warm. The bacon in the Dutch oven released its grease and bubbled in its boiling fat, eventually foaming up.

"See that foam, Coolidge? That's how you know your bacon is almost done." He stuck metal tongs into the oven and pulled out a mass of cooked bacon. "Perfect!" he said as he spread it out on a paper plate covered with a couple of paper towels. Coolidge had to admit that every piece of that bacon was evenly crispy, and it smelled incredible. He was pretty sure he could eat every slice himself with no problem.

Cal and Hank divvied out huge plates of eggs and bacon. There was a bag of Wonder Bread to sop up the grease and a gallon jug of orange juice with paper Dixie cups. Wyatt wrapped his eggs and bacon in a piece of bread and ate it like a burrito. Coolidge followed suit sitting to savor the meal in the now dry grass next to the fence.

"Great breakfast, Cal," said Wyatt. "You haven't lost your touch."

"Have Coleman will travel," replied Cal, pouring the hot bacon grease over the fence.

Parker folded his plate in half and shoveled the last bits of egg into his mouth. Belches followed, loud and demonstrative. There was already heat in the air even though the shadows were still long. The horses in the corral seemed to eye them suspiciously from over the fence as they continued their frenzied neighing with their saddled comrades in the barn. Coolidge licked the last bits of grease and bacon from his fingers and bent over to put his plate and white plastic fork into the black garbage bag. As he straightened up, the urgency to move his bowels hit him like a peon punch. It wasn't a diarrhea thing, just a natural peristaltic response to finally getting his stomach full. As he walked toward the outhouse, he thought again about how surprising it was when Cal and Hank had made a big deal yesterday about digging a new hole for the "Executive Palace." It seemed like work that would have been beneath them as partners and bosses. Not true. In fact, he discovered that the bosses did a lot of everyday work. They even put themselves into Sunday rotations, bringing in the horses and running the day's public trail rides, to give the peons a day off to do laundry or to go swimming. Coolidge learned to like Sundays because a busy tourist day usually meant a bonus, cash in the pocket he wouldn't normally earn, if, of course, the bosses had had a good week and were feeling generous that weekend. It was enough money to buy Band-Aids, baby powder, laundry soap, and a burger occasionally at the Burger Barn. How and when the bosses decided to do physical labor, though, was a mystery to him. All he knew was when they were around he was nervous, and when they weren't it was easier to follow Wyatt and Earl's lead on things.

In any case, he walked past the granary heading briefly down the dirt road leading to camp but turning almost right away onto a path among the pine trees leading to the Executive Palace, a double stalled, obviously homemade outhouse with a single piece of corrugated sheet metal for a roof. The roof shined in the sun. Coolidge was mighty glad it was there at that moment, considering the mood his body was in, although it was impossible to sit in that grand structure and not imagine spiders and other invasive creatures taking advantage of your butt's vulnerability. Dumping a cup of lime into the hole afterward was the equivalent of a flush. To forget the lime was to condemn the next user to intolerable atmospheric conditions.

The flimsy cardboard box of sanitary toilet seat covers was a weak nod to the comfort of unlucky tourists, who, God forbid, needed a restroom before or after a ride. Like many "PR" issues, this one too was dealt with verbally – with bullshit: "Oh, you need a bathroom? No, we don't have a bathroom! No siree Bob! We have an Executive Palace! Boy is it ever your lucky day! Just follow that golden path right there into the enchanted woods. You'll see it shining there. Woohoo! Sorry, you can only go once now, so enjoy it while you can! Don't forget to flush!" The showmanship play against a person's natural shyness about asking for a restroom was usually enough to intimidate a potential complainer from criticizing the inadequacies of the facility. Only occasionally did the terrible Lakeside Stables, Inc. outhouse experience motivate a tourist to suggest that an "upgrade of the bathroom facilities" might be a good thing to consider "for the comfort of your customers."

As he walked back from the Executive Palace, Coolidge saw Lenny behind the granary smoking a cigarette. "Want one?" asked Lenny.

"No."

Coolidge had spent a lifetime watching his dad smoke and could have snuck cigarettes anytime he wanted to but had no desire to pollute his lungs. He remembered asking his dad recently why he had never succeeded in quitting since they were so bad for you, and Perry had said he knew he should, "but they were *so* tasty." Coolidge thought Lenny exuded a different commitment to smoking. He wasn't after the taste, it seemed, but rather the posture of maturity it gave to his large frame. Coolidge noticed a grease stain on his white t-shirt from breakfast.

"Are you excited about heading to Hillcrest?" Coolidge asked.

"Yeah, I hear it's great. All kinds of chicks around the lake." He laughed at the thought, expelling chipmunk Marlboro smoke from his nostrils.

"Oh," Coolidge replied.

Coolidge understood the attraction of having girls around. He imagined Lenny to be really good at talking to them too. *What was that like? Wouldn't they be turned off by his cigarette breath? Maybe things like that don't matter...*

When Coolidge got back to the barnyard he could see things were moving into high gear. Parker and Hank were inspecting each horse's tack as Wyatt and Earl led them out of the barn one horse at a time. Coolidge, conscious of Cal's stern looks from the table, jogged in his boots across the yard to the barn.

Wyatt said, "Coolidge, water those horses at the trough. Let them drink all they want. You're going to ride Velvet, I think." Wyatt then led Big Brother across the yard.

There were five horses already tied up on a railing near the trailhead leading to the woods. They wouldn't head that way today, though, since Hillcrest was eight miles the opposite way across the highway. The trails at Crane meandered around the extensive acreage of the camp and eventually around a small lake cluttered with summer cabins. Today's ride would be in fields and on county roads.

Coolidge looked around at Cal. Hank was in the barn with Parker. "How do you do it?" he asked Wyatt softly.

"Oh," said Wyatt. "Here grab this horse, right here. The reins, under the chin. Holding the reins with the reins over the neck of the horse is better, gives you more control." Coolidge put his hands behind where Wyatt was holding the thin leather reins under Big Brother's massive neck. "Unless the reins are over a post, keep them on the neck, but don't ever wrap them around the saddle horn. Now walk him over to the trough. Stay ahead of him – you are leading the horse, not the other way around."

To lead that massive Belgian horse to the corrugated steel trough by the side of the barn felt a little like he was about to get run over by a large truck or by a charging elephant. Two flimsy lines of bridle leather attached to the sides of a tiny bar of metal in the horse's mouth seemed to be the only deterrent to becoming road kill. The high-stepping front hooves of Big Brother seemed to come down inches from the heels of Coolidge's boots, and as the horse got closer to the water Coolidge had to pull backward on the bit with ever increasing pressure to slow him down. At the end it was all Coolidge could do to step to the side and watch the massive head disappear into the trough and suck down the water with silent intensity. Coolidge held the reins and waited. Nearly a minute later the beast's head jerked upward spraying water all over Coolidge. Big Brother stared at the horses in the corral and let out a barrel shaking neigh and snort. He kicked the side of the trough with his front hoof and buried his head for a second round of sucking and swallowing.

"It's a long way to Hillcrest, and no water, so let him drink as much as he wants. When he's done, walk him back over to the railing and put the reins over the post. Don't let him step on the reins, though," said Wyatt. "Glad he's going to Hillcrest. Little Brother is slow and a pain in the ass, but at least he doesn't spook. That horse is an asshole."

Walking Big Brother back to the railing wasn't as hard as toward the water trough. Basic needs drive horses compellingly. Thirst moves flesh. So does hunger. Or freedom. Merely walking to a post was no big deal. Big Brother actually looked bored. He nuzzled around the post for grass to chew.

While Coolidge was practicing his leading skills with the other thirsty horses, Earl appeared by the barn door with baby powder. He unbuckled his blue jeans and shook a generous portion into the front and back of his underwear. He handed the powder to Wyatt who followed suit, then to Coolidge. "Prevents saddle sores," Wyatt said.

By far the trickiest part of the ride to Hillcrest was crossing Highway 50 in front of the stables. Although Coolidge was on the easiest horse to ride, he still had to lead another horse behind him on a lead rope. For someone who had never been on a horse before, this was a challenge. Compared to saddling a horse, though, actually riding a horse is a piece of cake. Pull the reins back to stop, kick the sides to go. It helped to be able to say "Whoa," when you are pulling back the reins, and to make clicking noises with your mouth when you want to go, but even those skills were a mere embellishment. Coolidge had good balance and was good at riding a bike. He took to riding with no problem at all. Western riding didn't require any fancy posting or rein work – just pull the neck of the horse where you wanted it to go and relax. A few turns around the barn yard, and he had it down.

But crossing the highway was a matter not to be taken lightly. Cal was there on foot to give the command, and everyone lined up on the driveway for the signal. Hank, Parker, Earl, Wyatt, Lenny, and Coolidge all were riding and leading a horse. The horses in the corral were going nuts, and the horses on the ride were nervous too, stomping their feet, neighing, and looking back toward the barn and the corral.

If the horses had their way, they would as a group head right back to the barn to join the rest of the herd left behind. Some of the horses in the corral felt the opposite pull and wanted to join their friends leaving. Fortunately, the electric fence is a powerful deterrent, but still the corralled horses were excitedly galloping about and hanging their heads over the fence on the highway side to see what was happening.

"All right, follow Hank when I give the signal. Get across the highway fast and up the ditch into Capp's field. Stick together. Coolidge, follow Earl and don't let go of that lead rope!" Although the lead rope in his hand was attached to Cole, the undisputed king of the pasture (when Little Brother wasn't around, that is), he was very cooperative. Cole was as gentle as a puppy around humans. He followed Velvet no problem down the dirt driveway behind the barn and was waiting patiently to go wherever Coolidge and Velvet were going.

Coolidge pulled his hat firmly over his forehead with the hand holding the lead rope. He wanted to hold onto the horn of the saddle, but Cal had yelled at him for doing so in the yard so he didn't. He watched a series of Army trucks and semis roll by in convoy on the highway. Earl pulled back on the reins and kicked the sides of his black and white horse, Guano, when he saw the army vehicles. Guano reared up on her hind legs in a stately pose for the passing soldiers. It was amazing to Coolidge that Earl could do that with control while holding the reins of another horse.

"Earl, stop fucking around!" yelled Cal from the end of the driveway. "After this last truck. Okay, go, Go, GO! Get across! Let's GO!" Cal stepped into the middle of the two lanes and waved everyone over. Hank led at a trot, followed by Parker, Lenny and Wyatt. Coolidge kicked Velvet and trotted out after Wyatt. The horses all crossed safely and surged their way up the steep ditch on the other side. Coolidge didn't care about style points at that moment – he hung onto the saddle horn with a vengeance. Earl followed gracefully on Guano, who at this point was a little worked up from the rearing. Foam and saliva were flying out the sides of her mouth. Earl got her settled down quickly, though, once they were on the flat landing field. Capp was a single-engine pilot who kept that field cut short for his Cessna. The horse boys quickly crossed the field and cut into a path in the woods to get out of sight of the barn and the dangers of the highway. They were trespassing on the field, but that was a small little rule they would violate several times on the ride in order to travel on a safer and more direct route.

Soon all the horses resigned themselves to the ride and settled down. The distant neighing of the horses left behind faded, and the gentle rhythm of the ride defined a decent but mellow pace. The soft leather feel of the reins felt good in Coolidge's gloved hand, and he understood now the advantage of tight boots – they stayed on whether he had his feet in the stirrups or not. The bright sun was hot, but the baby powder kept him from sweating too much down there where everything was getting moved interestingly by the saddle.

Soon the trail emerged from the woods by a small marshy area. Coolidge could see a country road on the other side of the marsh. They worked their way along the edge of the wet grass staying high on a bank. There were frogs croaking like mad and a few pairs of red winged blackbirds perched on last year's stubble of pussy willows. Their territorial cries were insistent and loud rising above the slightly decaying smell of the swamp.

When they reached the far side of the wetlands they came up against a barbed wire fence blocking their access to the road.

"Go a bit farther ahead," said Earl. "We cut through here last year. No need to make a new cut if we can help it." Hank had the eagle claw in his hand, but he nodded and stuck it back into his saddlebag. Sure enough, the fence ran along into a small patch of birch trees where the barbed wire had been spliced and wrapped around the trunks. Hank hopped off his horse and pulled the reins and lead rope over his arm. The eagle claw could nip barbed wire in half if it had to, or grab it and bend it like pliers. A few deft twists and Hank had the rusty barbed wire off the trees and safely pulled back from the fence posts. Single file the horse boys carefully crossed the fence line and waited for him by the shoulder of the road. No one drove by in the time it took Hank to reposition the wire. For all anybody knew, they had been riding on the road the whole time.

"Good practice for pack trips - cut fences only when you absolutely have no other choice," remarked Wyatt. "We did them a favor making sure that fence was secure," he added when he saw Coolidge's skeptical face.

After a mile or two following the meanderings of the two-lane country road, Cal's Mustang came up behind them. There had been a few cars and pickups that had passed them, most going at a safe and reasonable speed, and Cal was too, knowing as he did that the horses were somewhere on that road. Normally, though, the drive to Hillcrest was more or less an undeclared car race for the horse boys. No one could beat Hank's time on the Harley, but Earl came close. His skill as a driver was only matched by the level of terror he inflicted upon his passengers. That he would later become a commercial pilot who had to make an emergency landing on a main street in downtown Madison was not a surprise to anyone who knew him back then.

"You fucks are slow," remarked Cal pulling up beside the riders. "Party's at Hillcrest when you get there," he yelled waving as he accelerated away. From his vantage point on Velvet, Coolidge noticed a couple of cases of Old Milwaukee long necks in the back seat. *He must have made another run into Benny's.* Coolidge felt weird about alcohol. He hadn't actually consumed any beers since he had been at the stables, although he had been handed a few. They tasted weird to him, and after the electric wire testing and the quarry jumping, he learned to discretely put his beer down next to the case when no one was looking. He was only thirteen, after all. He had taken a few sips of kalua from his parents' liquor cabinet before, but the big black carpenter ants crawling on the bottle had turned him off. He was interested a bit in marijuana, though. The Jefferson Airplane and The Beatle's Magical Mystery Tour intrigued him. Was there something that could be learned by seeing things with a changed mind? John Lennon seemed to think so with the granny glasses and all. The album covers in his small collection next to his books spoke to him of many possible and mysterious parts of life. The sum total of what he actually knew about marijuana, though, was about the same as what he knew about girls.

That Lucy in the Sky with Diamonds was referring to LSD was completely beyond his awareness.

There certainly was mysterious life magic for him on Velvet that day, though. The conversation was sparse as they rode along the dirt shoulder of the road up and over small hills and past farmhouses and fields of cucumbers and alfalfa, but the countryside kept Coolidge company in a language he seemed to understand. Maybe it was all the time he spent alone at home exploring the ravine. He felt at ease among the Wisconsin trees and rolling hills.

He recognized tender shoots of asparagus growing in patches here and there among wild rose bushes and tiny wild strawberries plants in protected places. Velvet's hooves stirred up grasshoppers and butterflies in the grass, and he kept a gloved hand ready to slap away deer flies from her neck. When he was too late, the mean-looking flies left a bitten trail of blood on her neck and mane hairs. Big horseflies would also make their loud and clichéd appearance, usually landing on rumps despite swishing tails. Coolidge looked back occasionally to swat them off Velvet with his gloved hand before they could bite, and he got used to Velvet lurching forward a bit whenever he did that. He thought of commenting on them and on the asparagus with Earl and Wyatt, but turning back to look at them was hard. Lenny was ahead of him, but he really didn't know what to say to him either. Periodically, a car would pass them on the road and people would wave. Waving back felt interesting to Coolidge. It wasn't that often he had even seen anyone on a horse much less be the person riding one. *Is this really who I am?* He paused to let Velvet rip a convenient tuft of grass from the side of the road and then gave her a gentle kick.

"It's not really a concern as long as she is from around school," Earl was saying to Wyatt.

"Yeah, Lark Ridge chicks are clean, I don't worry about it either. I suppose there is always a chance, though..."

"You want a condom anyways," Earl said.

"Oh, yeah," laughed Wyatt. 'Unless you want to get married!"

"I would never pay to fuck a chick, but I could be talked into paying for a good blowjob," added Parker, smiling.

Lenny heard that and laughed. "You got that right!"

"So, Vanessa – you remember Vanessa?" Earl asked Wyatt.

"The one that was hanging around at the end of last summer?"

"Yeah, with her chubby friend, what was her name?"

"I don't remember, but it is always like that – you owe me for that one by the way," said Wyatt.

"First round of the summer is on me. Anyway, Vanessa shows up at my house around New Year's."

"You're kidding me. No shit! Did she bring her friend?"

"I wish she had so I could have had an excuse to blow her off..."

"Really? Yeah, that's scary. By herself, eh?"

"And loaded. I had to drive her car home for her and get a ride back."

"How was *that* ride?"

"She likes cocks."

"Sounds like she likes *you* – when's the wedding?"

"Not my type, but she's worth a roll in the hay if she's around this summer," laughed Earl.

"Maybe it's my turn this time. Mary – that's the porker friend. I remember now – with the bangs," said Wyatt.

"That's right!" Earl clicked his fingers.

"I'll go out with Mary," laughed Lenny. "I like fat chicks. More to hang on to."

Coolidge felt neither Wyatt nor Earl appreciated Lenny's addition to their conversation because Wyatt said, "Okay, Lenny. We'll keep that in mind," and that was the end of it.

"I can't wait for an Executive Shower!" said Parker about twenty minutes later. The sun was intense enough for saddle leather to feel hot to the touch now, and the sweat on Coolidge's pant legs was as much from Velvet's sides as it was from Coolidge. He had taken to tying his red handkerchief to his belt loop to dry out between wipes across his brow. *A shower? That sounds good.* The ride was late into its second hour, and he was getting tired and hungry. He stood up in the stirrups to give his butt a break. The riding experience on his genitals was weird - stimulating and numbing at the same time.

None too soon, Hank stopped and waited for the gaps between the horses to narrow.

"Cross here, and look out for cars coming around that bend," he yelled as he gave his horse a kick and crossed the road for a hidden trail on the other side. Everyone followed quickly at a trot. The trail they descended into was well worn, though some sumac branches that had grown up over the winter had to be pushed aside. A few hundred feet and the trail opened up to a small grassy yard in front of a large grey barn. Beyond it on the right was a long wooden structure, the front side of the stalls at Hillcrest, and tucked in the woods beyond that a small dark cabin, bigger than the one at Crane, but not by much. Down a little hill from the cabin Coolidge saw Cal's Mustang, and beyond it the continuation of the road they had crossed earlier heading past an old mill building and over a bridge.

The door to the cabin opened up. "About time you showed up. I thought I was going to have to drink all this beer myself!" said Cal. Coolidge noticed sandwiches of some sort next to the cabin on the top of the same huge oat barrel that was in the tack room at Crane. "Parker, make sure the saddles go where you want them to. There's new tape in there and a magic marker. The fence is on. Let's get these horses in the pasture so we can take a shower! How you doing Lenny?"

"Just fine, Cal! How are you?"

"Peachy. Just peachy. You ready to be a Hillcrest peon?"

"Yes sir!"

"Don't get lazy over here, you hear me?" said Cal.

"Just two of us here and three at Crane. Who are the lazy ones?" commented Parker, tying the lead rope of his extra horse to the hitching post and loosening the saddle from his mount. He carried the saddle through a small gate next to the cabin and into the corral.

Unlike the stables grounds at Crane which were flat, everything at Hillcrest was hilly. The corral, very small, arched over a bluff down to a small stream where the horses could water. The stalls were actually in the corral itself. It was just an open aired roofed structure with a small roped off tack room. The big barn was used for storage for the camp and wasn't available to hold hay bales. The hay had to be stacked under a big tarp on the stream side of the cabin. It was an easy chore to feed the horses there – just toss a bale over the fence and shake it into the stalls. At Crane one had to haul the bales out into the pasture as well as into the stalls in the barn. Everything seemed more intimate and compact at Hillcrest, simpler. The camp was also just across the street, so no need to drive in for meals or to recruit riders like at Crane. The whole place had a more family-like appeal rather than an institutional one, maybe because of the lake and the many vacation cabins right there by the bridge. The mellow country store and local bar set the atmospheric tone as opposed to the noisy and frenetic highway running by the stables at Crane. Coolidge wondered if Lenny would fit in here very well - *not too many nooks and crannies to hide out in and smoke.*

The horses were happy to shed their saddles and explore their small but adequate corral and cool bubbling stream after the long ride. There was little of the chasing each other around that Coolidge had expected when Velvet and Cole joined the crowd. After a long drink, the herd settled down to the hard work of chewing up all the virgin grass. Coolidge was amazed at the number of saddles and bridles Parker managed to organize and fit into the tack room. There wasn't much room but everything had its place: saddles on saddle racks three high on the wall, pitchforks and lead ropes hung neatly on nails, a fencer buzzing by the one outlet, flashlights, a small eight-track stereo cassette player, a mirror.

Where did people pee around here? Must be in the stalls. That was the only place relatively hidden from public view. At least Lenny won't have to clean out a whole barn every night. The stalls were dirt – a quick scrapping out with a five-prong fork was probably sufficient at the end of a day. *Maybe Hillcrest was an easier gig, after all.* Coolidge looked at his reflection in the mirror that was probably used for shaving. There was an enamel bowl for water resting on a shelf below it and a can of Noxzema. His eyes looked dark, and there was dust grime collected about his mouth.

"You ready for an executive shower, Coolidge?" said Parker.

"Where's the water?" asked Coolidge. Parker pointed out a hose coiled on the backside of the cabin.

"Fridge is inside if you want cold," he added laughing.

"Thanks," said Coolidge following Parker into the cabin. It was twice the size of the Crane cabin with a partition running lengthways down the middle dividing the space into two separate rooms, one side for Hank's big queen bed, a couch and some chairs, and the other for two smaller beds for Lenny and Parker. There were a couple of old wooden chest of drawers, a big electric fan, and screened in windows all around the entire cabin. A bunch of old towels and swimsuits hung on nails by the round-shouldered fridge humming by the door. Everyone was stripping down and putting on suits. Cal, already in baggy black swimming trunks, brought the sandwiches in and put them in the fridge. He deftly opened an Old Milwaukee on a short nail on the door beam.

"Grab a suit, you guys, and a towel. You'll need to put your boots back on to get to the shower," said Parker with a curly-haired smile – he was enjoying the surprise that was obviously in store for Lenny and Coolidge. Coolidge looked around. There was an old blue suit with a drawstring that looked like it would fit. He pulled off his shirt and blue jeans and put his clothes on top of one of the dressers. He couldn't get his bare feet back into his boots, so he had to put his filthy socks back on. It was a naked feeling to stand there in swim trunks and cowboy boots, but no one else seemed to think it was odd.

"Executive Shower! Yeehaw!" exclaimed Cal, polishing off his beer in two swallows. "Let's go!" he said leading the way out the door and through the gate by the stalls into the corral. Hank followed also carrying a beer in his hand along with his towel. *They were going for a shower in the corral?*

"No towel, Coolidge?" remarked Wyatt as he went out the door.

"These are okay?" Coolidge asked.

"They're community towels for swimming. They get left behind, mostly by chicks after midnight rides," said Wyatt. Coolidge grabbed a beach towel off the rack and followed him into the corral.

Parker, Hank, and Cal were halfway down the bluff and jogging for the stream. The horses trotted through the small trees to the back end of the corral when they saw them charging down the hill with their towels. Coolidge noticed an outhouse perched precariously on the hillside where the horses were now standing at attention watching them. He hoped he would never have to use that scary structure, especially at night. He saw Big Brother standing next to it like a defending Titan protecting some medieval monument to darkness and evil. *What could stop a horse like that from just running you over on the hillside if it wanted to?*

By the time Coolidge, Wyatt, Earl and Lenny reached the water's edge, Cal, Hank, and Parker were already wading out into the rippling water. Somehow they had gotten beyond the electric fence that hung on small metal posts in the streambed itself. They were headed upstream toward a huge dark space under an old concrete foundation that held up a massive two-story building perched over the stream. The water seemed to be coming from inside the building, or under it, rather. There was a lot of noise and spray going on in the dark space, like a monster was thrashing about or Charybdis had found a place to relocate on land.

"What is it?" asked Coolidge taking off his boots and putting his towel and socks carefully on top of them on the bank.

"The Old Mill," answered Wyatt. They were under the dam that held back Hillcrest Lake. The water crossed a spillway on the dam and ran under the road to the millworks where in the olden days it turned a big wooden paddle that in turn spun the giant millstones that ground the locally raised grains for a fee charged by the mill owner who lived above the dam. Long abandoned, the building was boarded up and quite hazardous to trespassers due to rotten floors and gears and equipment and such no longer securely attached to their moorings. That didn't stop the local teens from breaking in periodically to drink beer or get high. The real attraction though, was underneath the mill where spent water poured down a huge metal chute and pummeled the streambed below. The water fell several stories, and the force of its fall created a roar that was either completely deafening or nearly deafening depending upon the amount of water draining off of the lake. It had been a rainy spring, and today the monster was awake and roaring.

"Executive Shower! Everyone under!" shouted Cal walking carefully upstream over mud and small granite rocks toward the cellar-dark lair of the falling water.

Coolidge watched the others carefully duck under the hot wires of the fence and head for the mill. It wasn't easy to stand steadily in the stream, but he managed to follow them without electrocuting his back.

His head dipped into the flowing water briefly while ducking under the fence. The water was cool, not as cold as the quarry, and reddish in color like it had been filtered through a bed of rotting fall leaves. The smell was organic in that way, not cold and fresh like at the quarry. He wondered if there were leeches in the water. A few minnows swam near his toes, probably brown trout. At least he hadn't seen any poison ivy growing along the bank. Poison ivy liked a bit more sunshine. This was a dark, forested area.

The darkness increased as he tiptoed his way across the rocks and mud toward the mill. He could see the metal chute protruding from the bottom of the large building. The water was a torrent of violent white surrounding a smooth core of pure falling water until it disappeared into the mist and wild back-splash of the streambed. As he crossed over the threshold under the building his eyes adjusted, and he could see the Executive Shower more closely. Hank was hanging back, but Parker and Cal were already nearly to the waterfall.

Under the mill, Parker and Cal were waist deep in the swirling water. Coolidge could hear that they were yelling something to each other, and he could see Parker's laughing grin and wet curly hair shine through the mist. Cal moved forward and grabbed the end of the chute with both hands.

"Go, Cal!" he heard Wyatt shout out next to him. "Come on, Cool," he said moving closer to the waterfall. As he followed Wyatt closer to Cal and Parker, Coolidge saw Cal's head disappear under the water. The water careened off Cal's back and pounded him downward blow by powerful blow. Finally, forced to let go, Cal backed out quickly before getting swept under, and, staggering a bit to regain his balance, his yells competed successfully with the white roar of the water: "Oh, baby! That's what I'm talking about! What a slap in the face!" *Is he crazy?*

Parker was next, and he was actually able to stand the pummeling longer. He even managed to pretend he was scrubbing an armpit with his other hand before the water overcame him and he too had to stagger back out.

"Woohoo! Oh my frickin' God!" he said smiling broadly.

There is a hidden rhythm to falling water that most people are unaware of. That's because, of course, most humans don't get to swim under powerful waterfalls and live to analyze it. The roar of the mill's waterfall was caused by individual blobs of water hitting the rocks and stream, and since each blob of water was slightly different from its preceding brother, the sound inside the roar had a weird beat to it. Consistent, fast-paced, but moment to moment distinct in its uniqueness...and *terrifying*. The closer Coolidge got to the waterfall, and the more he witnessed each peon ducking a head under and submitting to that power, the faster his heart beat and the more he once again wished he had an out from this experience.

"Coolidge! Coolidge! Coolidge!" they were chanting when he was the last to go. Lenny had, of course, made a big show of enthusiastically embracing the shower. His chipmunk laugh echoed all around the watery chamber under the mill. It was clear to Coolidge, despite his laughter, that he was scared shitless too. *How could he not be? What if a rock came down with the water when your head was under there? What if that whole rusty chute fell off? It wasn't hanging on by much.* Indeed, everything about the mill was old and decrepit with damaged concrete walls and rotting boards hanging loose all over the place.

As Coolidge stepped forward to the shower, beside the all-encompassing noise, the first thing he noticed was backsplashing water traveling upward into his nose. Then, as his hands sought out the edge of the opening of the chute above him, the sheer friction of the water crossing his fingers felt like it might take the skin off his knuckles. He bent his head over to take a deep breath of whatever air was still around under there, and digging his feet firmly into the shifting stones below him, straightened up and walked forward under the falling water as he had seen Earl and the others do. *My ears are getting torn off!* The water hit the top of his head like a jackhammer. Instinctually he ducked his head forward, and like a school bully giving a ninety-pound weakling a swirly in the stall of the boy's room, the water shot him downward without asking permission. Coolidge immediately lost his grip on the chute and slid face first into the water. The crushing water rolled him over and spat him out before he even knew what was happening. Small rocks and violent bubbles flew about his head and shoulders. He pushed himself against the bottom of the streambed with his hands and finally got a knee under him. *I'm going to drown.* He felt a firm hand grip his arm, and Cal lifted him back up onto his feet. They were quite some ways downstream from the waterfall. He must have travelled ten feet in less than a second. His toes felt bruised but otherwise he was fine. Cal looked him fiercely in the eye but said nothing.

What was that look about? Is Cal angry at me for losing control? Or is he afraid that something bad might have happened to me and he would have been at fault because he was the boss?

Once again, Coolidge had been forced to do something scary that he didn't really want to do and that he knew many of his friends back at school would never have the courage to do. There was something positive and real in that, but he wondered if the enthusiasm emitted by Cal and the horse boys over this experience was ultimately bullshit. *Was he bullshitted into thinking he should enjoy this dangerous thing he just did? Or is anything one does in life only as exciting as the bullshit a person decides to believe in?*

Not that Coolidge had any real choice in the matter at that time. An executive shower was what was on the agenda set by others, whether he liked it or not, whether they were doing him a service toward his life, or a disservice.

The Meeting

I t was tricky to yank his boots back onto his wet feet and walk back up the bluff from the stream without getting dirty again. Several times the towel came in handy for wiping mud off his legs. Back at the cabin, even though he had to put on the same dirty clothes he wore that day, the swim felt good on Coolidge's skin. He could still hear the pounding of the executive shower in his ears as he gave his head one last toweling off and hung the towel back onto the nail next to the others. His legs were sore from the long ride that day, especially his butt when he sat down on the side of Lenny's bed to eat the ham and cheese sandwich Cal tossed him. Thumb-tacked above his head on the wall over the screened window there was a printed brown envelope, the type of envelope that came inside boxes with things that required assembly, and although he got the intended joke, to what product this envelope originally belonged to Coolidge couldn't imagine. "Erection Instructions" it said in big red letters.

The peons naturally gravitated to Parker and Lenny's side of the cabin, the one with the refrigerator and the view directly into the corral behind the cabin. Hank and Cal ate their sandwiches on the other side on a comfortable couch with the view of the parking lot below them. The Hillcrest road ran above the parking lot and over a bridge above the lake's spillway leading into the mill. Hank's Harley was parked just below the cabin on the hill above the dirt parking area, and Parker's red truck was below next to the Mustang. The early evening sun was filtering through the maple trees and catching the top of the big grey barn rising in front of the vehicles. A robin's matriarchal song was the only sound until an incoming car decelerated by the trail crossing above them where they had ridden in earlier that day, rounded the curve beyond the grey barn, and slowly made its way past the stables entrance, the mill, the town bar and sundries shop, and into the village.

"Parker, get that stereo of yours cranked up, will ya?" barked Cal. "It's time to get this meeting started!"

"Sure thing, Cal," replied Parker from his side of the room. The boxy wooden speakers to Parker's stereo were balanced on top of the partition and faced the peon's side. The turntable rested on a wooden box next to Parker's bed in the far corner. It had a bulky smoky-colored see-through plastic cover that rose on a hinge over the turntable. Parker lifted the cover up and tipped a Cream album out of its sleeve. Holding the album carefully by the sides he placed the album onto the turntable. Before dropping the needle, he removed a round record cleaner from its plastic tube, wetted it with some fluid from a small squeeze bottle, and ran the cleaner carefully around the spinning disc to remove dust and hair from its grooves. The needle dropped with a pop and crackle, and soon the bluesy sound of Eric Clapton's "Sunshine of Your Love" filled the cabin.

"Good choice, Parker. Get over here!" yelled Hank. Parker walked past the others on the bed, past the fridge and into the boss's side of the cabin. There was some exasperated shouting. He came back a moment later to get three frosty Old Milwaukees from the fridge and disappeared again. Coolidge and the others could hear that they were talking and sometimes laughing in there, but what they were saying was obscured by the music. After a bit Cal's head appeared at the passageway between the two sides of the cabin. He opened the fridge and pulled out three beers in each hand. Handing them to Wyatt and Earl. "For you peons," he said. "Bring three from the fridge when we call you."

"Thanks," said Wyatt.

"All right!" said Earl.

"Old Swill, my favorite," said Lenny feeling like he had to add his two cents. He had a cigarette cupped in his hand with a pack of matches but hadn't lit it. Coolidge didn't think he dared light it inside since he was clearly hiding his habit from Cal, but he noticed that Lenny often seemed to need to handle his cigarettes often, lit or unlit.

"It's so easy to get chicks over here, it's ridiculous," continued Wyatt to Earl picking up on the afternoon's conversation after opening his beer on the nail. Earl grunted assent and used a legitimate bottle opener hanging from a string by his head to carefully bend the cap off a bit at a time without distorting it. He put the beer on the floor, and laid the bottle cap between his thumb and middle finger on his good hand, bent his wrist backward, snapped his fingers and sent the cap spinning across the cabin. It careened off the far screen and landed on Parker's bed. Lenny laughed, and found his own discarded cap on the floor. He transferred the beer to the same hand as his cigarette and took a backhanded swig before trying to snap the bottle cap as he had seen Wyatt do. The cap fell limply to the floor. "Shit," he said and tried again.

"It doesn't hurt to have your parents' cabin nearby, either," added Earl.

"Yeah, but I think Lynn will be there most of the time Dad and Mom aren't," said Wyatt with a glance at the door to the boss side. Wyatt and Parker had a little brotherly possessive thing going on about their older sister. She spent a lot of time with Hank. Coolidge understood why when he finally met Lynn a few weeks later. She was kind, easy to talk to, voluptuously beautiful, and mostly braless. She had a natural athleticism that she tried unsuccessfully to hide behind smoking too many cigarettes and wearing flannel shirts. That anyone could even talk to someone so beautiful much less have sex with them was more than Coolidge could fathom. Instinctually he knew she was not another "chick to be gotten." She seemed to be in a category like Cal's steady, Sam, about whom the usual comments about bodies and "hustle-ability" were probably not appreciated.

"They get so bored. Walking over here for a midnight ride is the highlight of their summer," continued Wyatt.

They give rides at midnight? That's late. Earl handed Coolidge a beer.

"What's your favorite beer, Coolidge?" he asked.

"I don't know," said Coolidge, not wanting to sound stupid but truly not having any idea. His parents didn't keep beer in the house, although he had seen Old Milwaukee before, of course.

"Pabst is sweeter, but I like Schlitz, at least until you get toward the bottom of the bottle," said Earl.

"Yeah, like Point," said Wyatt.

"Brewed in Stevens Point and cheap, like People's Beer. They show you on the label just to what point it's tolerable to drink," said Earl, pointing to a spot fairly high up on his Old Milwaukee long neck. "Drink up, Cool."

Coolidge managed to get the cap off with the nail, but it spurted foam all over his hand. He held the beer out in front of him while it surged and spewed.

"Put your mouth over it!" said Lenny, laughing at him.

Coolidge looked at the mess he was making and immediately did what Lenny said. The foam filled the space between his lips and teeth and squirted out the sides of his mouth. A stream forced its way into his nose making his eyes water. It tasted like soda pop gone evil – yeasty and bitter.

"First chick I ever got to third base with was in that bed you're sitting on right there, Earl," said Wyatt.

"Surprised you can remember back that far," said Earl.

"She was three years older than me, off at college now," said Wyatt. "We rode White Devil out to the back forty and made out under the stars. When we got back here, there was no stopping her."

"Ha, like you tried!" said Earl. Coolidge tried to imagine what Wyatt's girlfriend had looked like. Probably like the girls in swimsuits he had seen in Fieldsburg. *Did he take her swimming at the executive shower? That would be dangerous at night, but maybe not if the moon was full.*

In a quiet space between songs, Coolidge heard the horses moving through the long grass in the corral just outside the window from where they were sitting on the bed. He heard them exhaling abruptly and tearing out clumps to chew as they grazed. He wondered what they thought of Eric Clapton. There was no doubt the music was reaching their big ears – it was loud.

Parker came back from the other side and gestured to Earl and Wyatt to go in next.

"Both of us?" asked Earl.

"Yep," said Parker.

"That's always a good sign," said Wyatt opening the fridge and pulling out four brews, handing two to Earl. He followed Earl into the front room.

Parker stepped past Coolidge and turned the album over, skipping the cleaning step this time. Ginger Baker's rhythms vibrated the walls, and Lenny started drumming his hands on the metal frame of the bed and on his knees. Coolidge noticed that Lenny's beer was gone already. Coolidge put his nearly full one up to his mouth and took a slightly bigger sip of the evil tasting stuff this time. He learned that the beer didn't foam up his nose as much if he tipped it slowly. A sudsy burp escaped his lips. The beer was starting to get warmer in his hands. It still tasted bad to him, though, like soda made from the contents of a manure spreader. *I wonder how much shit is still in my boots.*

"So, Parker, what are the campers like around here? Any hot ones?" said Lenny earnestly.

"Uh, uh," said Parker waving his finger. "Forget campers, off limits. Now CIT's, kitchen crew, counselors, they're all fair game. Hustle 'em all you want, but campers, no way. CIT's are even a little risky. Too stupid."

"Oh," said Lenny. "Okay, I'll remember that. No pussy under fourteen. How's that sound?" He laughed. Lenny could not himself have been much past thirteen or fourteen, but he had a large body for his age and looked older. His long blond hair gave him almost a college-aged look, especially when he was smoking.

Parker got up to get another beer. When he sat down on the edge of his bed again he ejected the album. The needle arm rose up and waved itself ritualistically over the turntable checking for another album before shutting itself off. He slid Cream back into its sleeve and cover and tipped out Blood, Sweat and Tears. In the interlude before the stereo kicked in again, Coolidge heard Cal and Hank talking in low serious tones with Earl and Wyatt on the other side of the wall. He heard Earl laugh and say something in that deep voice he had, one that was incongruous with his small frame but somehow fit his personality. Lenny got up to get another beer too. Sitting back down on the bed he managed after a few tries to get the cap to fly off his snapping fingers. He laughed and picked up the cap from near Coolidge's feet to try again. Coolidge looked from him to Parker reading the album cover, to the window overlooking the corral. He saw it was getting dark outside. Cold air was starting to pour in from the windows. *How long was this meeting going to last?* He was ready for a change of clothes and a long sleep back at the cabin. His eyes started to shut, and he lay back on the bed letting his beer rest on the floor by his feet.

Hours later, it seemed, Wyatt and Earl stumbled back from the other side. Earl opened the fridge and said, "Coolidge, Lenny, your turn. They want you together." Coolidge sat up suddenly fully awake and nervous. He took the two beers Earl handed him and accidentally kicked his own nearly full beer over with his foot. He had forgotten it was hiding there.

"Whoa, that's good beer, Coolidge. Don't waste it!" said Wyatt. Too late. It was all over the floor. *At least I didn't break the glass.*

Lenny stood up and took the other two beers from Earl. "You ready?" he asked Coolidge. Coolidge nodded weakly and followed him across to the other side.

"Sit down you two. First give me a beer," said Cal. He took one from Coolidge and when Hank gestured similarly, Lenny gave him the other extra beer as instructed. There were a lot of empties around, on the low table in front of the two tall wooden chairs where the bosses sat, and all around their feet. Lenny and Coolidge sat down on the edge of the couch, unsure if they should lean back or not.

"So, this is a meeting," started Hank. "It happens once a week, either here or, more often, at Crane. You tell us what's on your mind, and we tell you what's on ours. You have questions you don't want to ask in front of others, you ask in here. We have things we want to tell you in private, we tell you in here."

"Today, though, since this is your first meeting as horse boys we figured you'd probably have the same questions, or, more precisely, we have the same things to say to both of you, so we thought we'd save some time," said Cal. *Did we do something wrong?*

"So, what's the most important thing to remember around here?" Cal asks.

"Hands off the campers!" said Lenny, laughing.

"No, but you fool around with campers and we'll all get in trouble. It's way more important than that," said Cal.

"Always use a barn knot?" said Coolidge. Answering this question seriously and trusting that it was okay to be possibly wrong was not an easy thing for him to do given that since his arrival he had been forced to follow a direct-order and shock himself for no good reason, had been punched for making a harmless joke in a moment of weakness, had been talked into jumping off a very high cliff into freezing water, and had had his boots filled with manure in deference to some god of bullshit. Somehow, though, he felt a bullshit answer like Lenny's was not what the bosses were after at this moment. He remembered his drive into town with Cal in his mustang. *Cal cares about me.* "Because otherwise a horse could strangle to death if it pulls back in a panic?"

"Good answer, Coolidge," said Cal. "Safety. The rule about barn knots is about safety, yes, and we do nothing around here to jeopardize the safety of the horses, our riders, and each other. That is something we take very seriously, and I want you to listen to the older peons. They know, most of the time, what is safe and what is not with horses and riders. If they ever tell you something you don't think is right, you ask us about it, but 99% of the time you can count on doing what they ask is okay. You got that so far?"

"Safety first!" chimed Lenny looking at Coolidge. Coolidge just nodded.

"Don't water the horses right after oating them. They can bloat and die. It's called colic, and it's not pretty. I've seen Doc Chudzik have to puncture a horse's stomach to save it from bloating. Horse ended up dead anyway from an infection, so remember that," said Cal.

"Also, never trot or canter toward the barn. Know where the barn is at all times and make sure you are heading away from it before you lead a group in a trot or canter," said Hank. "You canter toward the stables across the highway here at Hillcrest, Lenny, and even if you have really good riders on your ride, that ride will be out of control and galloping across the highway - not a pretty sight!" said Hank. Cal nodded severely in agreement.

"Saddle slips and saddle sores are each worth punches to the responsible peon, I don't care what your rank. Brush the horses well, saddle them correctly with tight cinches, and watch out for hot spots. We have foam pads for anyone who gets a sore. Use them," said Cal.

"But remember a foam pad is going to mean you need a tighter cinch, so it's best just not get sores in the first place," added Hank.

"No hay gets fed without first shaking it and watering it. Heaving horses can get sick fast. Keep the dust out of their lungs!" said Cal.

"Now camp is going to start up soon, and we'll be eating meals with the campers and camp staff. None of them need to know anything about what goes on here. You understand that? Stables business stays with the stables. That includes gossip about the tourists, things that happen on rides, problems with horses, our social life, what goes on in meetings, all of that is off limits for discussion. This business is our business. You work for us. You are part of us and we protect each other. You protect us and keep your mouths shut. That includes letters to home," continued Cal. "When you are in camp you are the angels of all angels. Smile, even if you are sick or hung over. Everything is great whenever anyone asks you. The horses are great, the stables is great, you are great. PR is very important. Everything you say and do around the camp has to be good PR. You know what PR is, Coolidge?"

"Public relations." He knew that from his dad's failing carwash business. Getting robbed as often as his dad did was not good for PR, he remembered Perry saying one time after thieves had made off with cash and an office typewriter for the third time.

"That's right. Public relations," said Hank. "What you do in camp is all about public relations. Are we friendly to everyone? Yes, we are, more so than any other counselors in camp. You know why? So campers want to ride with us rather than do any of the other lame alternatives counselors offer like beading. That's how we make our money. Are we more responsible than anyone else? Yes, we are. We do what we say we will do. People can count on us because we can be counted on. You understand what we're saying about PR, you two?"

"Yes," said Coolidge.

"Good. You both did a good job on the ride over," said Cal, and Hank nodded his head. They took a quick swig from their beers. "Riding is not that hard. You just have to be aware at all times and know your horses. You'll get to know them soon enough, and then you'll be ready to lead your own rides. You better. Otherwise you're worthless. For now, you'll follow at the end. Pay attention, talk to the riders. Riding gets boring quick so it is up to you to entertain them. Do what Wyatt, Earl and Parker tell you, and smile. You're the life of the ride, don't forget that."

I hope I remember all this – I've got to. The room was darkening as the dusk faded outside, and only a single metal table lamp illuminated Hank and Cal's faces on the couch. Coolidge wished he could write some of this down as his bosses spoke, but he was afraid if he asked he would be too schoolish. This was not school. No, it seemed as if he was just supposed to get it, that if he missed it it would be because he was stupid, or incompetent, not because they didn't know what they were doing. Look at them. They were big, strong, sure of themselves. He was deathly afraid of failing, of getting punched for fucking up, of not being liked or understood, of having fear or insecurities, of saying the wrong thing, of not knowing if he belonged.

"Life of the party – I can do that! Partying is what I do best," said Lenny laughing and taking a sip of his beer. Coolidge repositioned the beer bottle between his legs where it wouldn't spill. He was done trying to put it on the floor. It felt vaguely insulting there, though, almost obscene sticking up awkwardly like it did, so he balanced it instead on the cardboard box that served as an end table next to the couch.

"Tell jokes, ask people where they are from, what they do. Make them laugh. Your job is to give them a fun ride. A safe ride, but also a fun ride," continued Cal.

"Check cinches!" said Hank.

"Right," said Cal. "Whose fault is it if a saddle slips on a ride?"

"The ride leader," said Lenny.

"Wrong," said Cal. "Every peon on the ride is responsible for checking cinches and making sure the stirrups are adjusted properly for each rider. There's only been one death at these stables, and it was due to a loose saddle. Now that's bad PR, for you. Fortunately, it was a long time ago when people were more understanding, so the stables survived. Not so now. People like to sue. So, save yourself and others some pain – tighten the cinches correctly for every horse before every ride. Check each horse at least twice before the ride goes out." He paused for a beer hit. "If someone asks you if anyone has ever died riding our horses, what do you say?"

"Uh," said Lenny. He looked at Coolidge.

"Probably... 'I don't know, never heard of anyone'?" said Coolidge.

"Not bad. You don't need to tell people the truth all the time. That's why there's bullshit. You can bullshit. No one has to know anything you might know, especially if it's bad PR. We're telling you about this because we don't want shit to happen again. It was ten years ago, and there hasn't been a death since, but the camps are real nervous about horses now. That's because we've had a few broken arms recently from horses that spooked – another reason to keep the saddles tight. Two fingers – three is too loose!"

"But if you try to bullshit *us*, we'll know," added Hank. "And you won't like the consequences."

Coolidge and Lenny both nodded their heads, but Coolidge felt somehow that Lenny would catch on to the bullshit thing easier than he would. His cigarette breaks already managed to work themselves around quasi-legitimate reasons to disappear like forgetting his gloves somewhere, or looking for a pitchfork.

"So, any questions for us?" asked Cal. "Now is your chance." They drank and waited.

"I don't have any," said Lenny. "Do you, Coolidge?" Coolidge shook his head no, although he wondered who had led the rides when the broken arms happened. If it weren't for the adrenaline running through his arteries keeping him awake, he might have asked Cal about that and if they were going back to Crane soon. He resisted his sudden need to yawn and rub his eyes.

"Well, then, this meeting has come to an end! Peons get in here!" yelled Cal over the partition.

Wyatt, Earl and Parker rolled in from the other side.

"What do you think this is, the first year peon couch?" asked Cal suddenly pissed again. "Go get peon chairs from the other side!"

Lenny laughed, but Coolidge, glad to finally move, was the first to hurry past the grinning older peons. When he returned with a couple of folding chairs, Earl and Wyatt were on the couch feet draped over the worn out arms. Parker was opening a new round of beers.

"That's a lot of beer you assholes haven't drunk yet!" exclaimed Hank. "I don't know, Cal, doesn't seem like our peons appreciate the brews we generously bought them. What's the matter, you guys don't like Old Milwaukee?"

"Finest beer in the country. No one has ever topped Old Swill!" grinned Earl taking a slug. Earl had a way of holding his beer in his crippled hand that hid his missing fingers somehow. The mouth of the beer bottle was so deeply hidden he seemed to drink from the middle of his palm. Like a magician, he instinctually knew how to keep your attention away from his hand by distracting you with gestures with his other hand, and his general cleverness and warm smile usually had folks looking him in the face and laughing rather than noticing his deformity.

"Earl, you are full of shit. Wyatt do you agree with him?" asked Cal.

"Well, Pabst is all right, but I like Old Swill just fine," said Wyatt.

"Oh, you'd prefer Pabst? Well maybe next time we'll have to pony up for the good stuff, eh, Cal?" said Hank.

"I guess we will have to," said Cal, "seeing as how they can't seem to drink this beer fast enough!"

"You said it – slow. Earl, are you a slower beer drinker than Wyatt? I can't remember..."

"Wyatt is a pussy when it comes to drinking beer. He's from Chicago, remember?" smiled Earl.

"Hey, I resent that," said Parker sticking up for his brother. He waved the four open beers in his fingers menacingly with a big grin on his baby face.

"All right, enough talk. Let's see if Wyatt is still the slowest drinker around here. Parker, give Wyatt and Earl a fresh beer. Are you boys ready? I'm timing," said Hank.

Coolidge grabbed his bottle just in time from the box before Parker snatched it and placed it in the center of the open space in front of the couch. "Step up, boys!" he said giving them each a brew. Cal and Hank leaned back in their chairs. Earl and Wyatt took the beers and stood by the box.

Coolidge noticed their eyes were slightly blood shot and a bit droopy.

"Beers on the table. First one to finish and return the bottle to the table is the winner," said Cal, pulling a stopwatch out of his chamois shirt pocket. "You ready? On your marks, get set, Go!"

The eyes were what impressed Coolidge the most about the next eight and half seconds. Earl's in particular bugged out the most, although Wyatt's watered in a frightening way too. There was earnestness in both their expressions as they eyed each other and worked their Adams apples up and down. Stress too, and pain. By the end both of them were leaking tears with similar velocity into the foam escaping the sides of their mouths. Wyatt had to pause halfway through to let the fizz drain from his nostrils onto the floor. Earl's empty-ish bottle hit the box top first. Foam obscured the sides of the bottle in his shaking hand. He turned the red-labeled longneck upside down to show it was drained adequately. Wyatt slammed his bottle down next, and both commenced a truly impressive series of belches. They bent over and held their hips as if they had just finished a 100-yard dash. Wyatt's nose continued to drain beer onto the cabin floor.

"Don't know how you do it, Earl. Must be your upbringing!" laughed Hank. "Parker, you'd better defend your honor!"

"Oh it wouldn't be fair to chug him now," replied Parker. "He's used up. I'd kick his ass."

Earl smiled and wiped off his mouth with a red handkerchief. "I'll go again," he said.

"Tell you what, Parker. If you can chug two beers in the time it takes Earl to chug one right now, you would be the undisputed champ," chuckled Cal.

"I'm game for that!" said Parker. "Let's go, Earl, you pussy! Two for one," he said with a joyful gleam in his eye. He grabbed two beers, one in each hand.

"On your marks, get set, go!" said Cal, forgetting about his stopwatch this time.

For all intents and purposes it was a tie. Parker alternated between bottles, shaking both enough to spill half of each on the floor, and Earl had to pause twice, like Wyatt did earlier, to de-foam his nasal passages and belch out enough room to keep going. Both of them staggered a bit when they finally fell back against the couch.

"The only way I get drunk faster than chugging is by shooting," Parker said. Shooting, Coolidge learned later, is done with a can of beer. You open a hole in the bottom with a can opener, put your mouth under it and pull the pull-tab. The beer flows down your throat and into your brain like water down the mill pipe.

"Next up, Coolidge and Lenny. Set 'em up. Let's see who wins this contest!" said Cal.

"Just open up your throat and pour it down," said Earl handing Coolidge a freshly opened beer. Coolidge glanced at his almost full previous bottle now hidden behind the couch. Wyatt gave Lenny a beer.

"Thanks, Earl. Ready to chug, Coolidge?" Lenny's chipmunk laugh had a distinct slur to it.

Cal yelled "go" and when the beer hit Coolidge's mouth, it felt that he had stretched his face around the wake of a speedboat at full throttle. The cold, foul tasting beer rushed immediately down his throat and out his nose with what could only be described as a jet of misery. *Oh my God!* Coolidge's eyes felt so much pressure that when he sneezed and coughed at the same time, he was genuinely worried they had popped out of his head.

"Chug, Coolidge!" Cal yelled.

"Go, Lenny," yelled Hank.

Coolidge felt like the voices were coming from behind a muffled screen, maybe from a different dimension. He lowered his bottle. His whole being and consciousness was concentrated in his nasal passages and burning throat.

"No giving up! Come on Coolidge!"

He put the bottle to his lips again but this time took a smaller chug. He settled into a drink, swallow, burp race that seemed interminable. Yes and also with a bit of breathing thrown in there for good measure, gasping breaths taken among genuine fears of dying. He noticed in a watery blur Lenny's arm crashing down on the box, slopping beer everywhere.

"I won," yelled Lenny. He belched and wiped his eyes.

"Finish, Coolidge. You can do it!" yelled Parker, laughing.

And Coolidge did, falling afterwards to his knees to keep from tipping over. Finally, the burp came, huge and explosively painful in his throat. *Did that come out my eyes?*

"I don't know, Hank, looks like Lenny spilled half his beer instead of chugging it," said Cal.

"Did not! No way!" said Lenny.

Coolidge raised his hand conceding the victory to Lenny. *No rematch!* The pain in his throat was still there, and his nose was dribbling beer, but he felt pleasantly elated somehow, like this thing he just did was actually funny. He started laughing to himself at first and then out loud. "Yeow!" he yelled out loud happily, surprising himself.

Then he realized he had to pee. He put his hand out on the box and got up slowly off his knees. *Why is everything spinning counter clockwise?*

"I've got to piss," he said, his detached head following his suddenly wobbly legs toward the door. He was vaguely aware of laughing faces looking at him as he headed past the couch. He heard the Beatles playing music with horns. *Sergeant Pepper, not unlike Blood, Sweat and Tears.*

"I need a piss too," said Lenny following him, patting his shirt pocket.

At the door, Coolidge watched his hand somehow navigate the soft air between his eyes and the doorknob. It felt weird to feel his hand turn the knob and the cold air hit his face as he stumbled outside. *Where was he? That's right, Hillcrest. Go left into the corral to piss. Don't forget to close the gate. Oh, Lenny's behind me. He'll close it. Horses in here. They piss here too. My piss and their piss on the ground!*

"Man, did that get me drunk!" said Lenny behind him peeing down the bluff toward the outhouse. There was a cigarette in his hand.

Drunk, yes! This is drunk. My dad... His body still lurched awkwardly behind his head as he willed himself to move through space into the corral. He unzipped and peed. *Ow, that hurts! Burns! Must be the riding...saddle sore? That long ride on Velvet! Did that really happen today? There are horses right there - which one is Velvet?* "Hey, Velvet!" he said. "How ya doin'?"

"Come on, Coolidge, the beer's inside, man," said Lenny.

Yes, go back inside. Good idea. More beer. He zipped up his jeans and followed Lenny back toward the cabin remembering to latch the gate behind him. *Let the horses out would be bad...don't touch that wire.* The smell of beer that washed over him in the social atmosphere of the cabin contrasted starkly to the cold pine air and animal smells outside. This may have registered in his reptilian brain, but his conscious mind at this point was all about not running into anything. The music drowned out the lively conversations that the others seemed to be having. He moved farther into the spinning cloud of the cabin's interior and leaned unsteadily against the arm of the couch, blinking his eyes against the light. Hank and Cal were chugging beers in their chairs, laughing. He looked at Wyatt and Earl having some kind of argument with Parker about his truck. Lenny hovered near Parker shaking his long hair to the music. Coolidge tried a little dance step himself and asked Lenny who was playing. "Chicago," he shouted. *Wasn't that where Wyatt and Parker were from? Chicago?*

For a moment he felt at a loss. *What was next?* Then his hand remembered, found the now warm beer he had hidden behind the couch. *Clever of me to stash it here for later!*

Effort and Betrayal

There was not much he could remember about the rest of that night, but the pain and nausea in the top bunk at Crane the next morning was unforgettable. *Did I get hit by something?* He vaguely recalled a cold and windy ride in the back of the Mustang. He didn't remember getting into bed, but somehow he had kicked off his boots. His formerly white socks felt hot now on his feet even though the air in the cabin was cool. *Maybe they were generating their own heat like compost?* There was mud on his calves. *Did I walk down to the stream for another swim last night at Hillcrest?* He remembered his dad had once told him a story about a guy on his baseball team at Yale that they teased by calling him sweat sock. "Can you imagine a more disgusting nickname?" Perry had said.

"How you feeling, Cool?" he heard Earl ask from the bunk below. He heard a short laugh from Wyatt. Apparently nobody was up yet. He looked over at Cal's bed. He was asleep with a pillow over his head.

"Uh, not so great. My head hurts." Coolidge sat up, not that he wanted to. *I have to pee. Can I climb down off this thing without my head exploding?* He wasn't sure. *Might be good to get outside, though, in case I throw up.* The waves of nausea had increased with verticality.

"Did you chug water last night, Earl?" asked Wyatt.

"No, just the aspirin," said Earl moving to the inside of the bed to avoid getting stepped on by Coolidge. "Aspirin works every time, if I remember to take it."

"Did you chug water last night, Coolidge?" asked Wyatt, grinning at him. Coolidge was standing now between the beds eyeing the door unsteadily.

"Beer," said Coolidge. "I chugged beer, unfortunately."

"You sure did," said Earl. "The floor of the Hillcrest cabin will never be the same!"

Coolidge didn't know if Earl meant he had spilled a lot of beer on the floor when he was chugging or if he had thrown up - or worse - on it. He didn't ask. He headed outside for the fence and the sink. The horses were standing nearby just over the fence in the morning mist, but Coolidge didn't notice anything but burning again as his dehydrated pee arched a flaming yellow stream against the corral post. The pain spread all the way from his urethra up to the back of his neck where it merged with his monstrous headache. *Better remember the water and aspirin trick for the next meeting, or never drink again...*

Now that the extra horses were gone, the routine of the days at Lakeside Stables quickly settled upon them, hangovers notwithstanding. Every day while Cal slept in, the peons got up early, brought the horses in and saddled them before breakfast so that everything would be prepared for the first camp riders in the morning. Sometimes those riders walked the long dirt road from camp to the red barn early enough to go for a ride before breakfast and eat a peon-cooked meal in the woods – usually bacon in a Dutch oven and scrambled eggs. Sometimes the first riders came after breakfast for instruction rides – half-hour lessons around the barnyard followed by a half hour of riding. Horseback riding was a very popular camp activity and every ride was usually more or less full in spite of the fact that an extra fee was charged. On the rare occasions when a ride wasn't full, a lucky peon could sometimes catch a quick nap. Naps were welcomed because there were usually dinner rides at night and a tourist ride at dusk before the workday ended and the horses were let loose into the pasture. Days were long and hard, as most days are for indentured servants, or in this case, apprentices of the fine horse craft of business exploitation.

That and apprentices of comedic entertainment, because being funny was quickly what Coolidge learned the whole enterprise was about. Horse boys were entertaining, the favorite "counselors" at the camp, and the ones who delivered the most excitement. Setting was part of it, the barn and all that. There were also old abandoned train cars hidden in the woods that the horse boys ambushed like Indians. They whooped stereotypically hitting their mouths with their open hands as the kids trotted behind them learning to do the same. Finally, there was the small lake to ride around with a public access beach that allowed for the horses to splash about in the sandy water while getting a drink.

Gross outs, and bullshit: Those were the two basic flavors to the entertainment. Well, actually three because bullshit had two subcategories: believable bullshit, and crazy bullshit. Coolidge, by virtue of being a bad liar, could not pull off the believable bullshit like Earl or Wyatt could, so he ultimately gravitated to crazy bullshit, but only after desperation set in because he got punched when some campers reported to Cal that his rides were "boring," and "not as fun as Wyatt's or Earl's rides."

Every peon participated in the gross outs. The most basic of all entertaining gross outs, of course, involves horseshit, which, at the stables was readily available. For city kids, the simple natural experience of seeing a horse pooping is enough to make any ride memorable and worth the price of admission. This is true for children, but also for self-conscious teenagers and sensation-seeking adults hoping to capture a slice of "real country life" for their seven-dollar fifty-cent riding fee.

So, of course, no horse poop went unacknowledged by the horse boys. When Wyatt noticed a horse raising its tail and getting ready to let loose, he liked to immediately stand by the horse's saddle and lean over and squeeze the horse's rear end on both sides and earnestly say, "Come on Ross, you can do it! You can do it!" Sometimes, if the horse was a gentle one, he would pump the horse's tail up and down as if it were a well or a lever on a slot machine. Earl relied more often on clever toss-off lines like addressing the poop directly with a "Nice of you to drop by, but you need a shower." If the audience was just a bunch of campers, the easiest way to deliver satisfying gross out giggles was simply to pick up a horse apple and say, "My, my, what a lovely and delicious apple!" When Earl then opens his mouth and pretends to eat one, it burns the memory indelibly into the minds of the campers who go back to their tents and tell all their friends about it.

Scatological humor gave young riders a way to cope with the supreme grossness of things like a horse having to stop in the middle of a ride to "pee," or more accurately explode, gush, and flood the immediately surrounding world with deeply foul smelling urine. For the mares peeing was a shower that often invited a close inspection from a gelding's nose riding behind. For the geldings, peeing involved a dipping down of the back legs prior to release, an abrupt, scary and mystifying experience for the rider until she hears the torrent splashing beneath her. When this happens on breakfast rides the peon's line was often, "Oh good, Orange juice! Quick, grab a cup - save it for breakfast!" Or simply, "What's wrong with Sam? He's sprung a leak! Anyone have a cork?" The idea was that through the joking commentary the uniqueness of the sensory experience was forever wedded with the crazy thing the crazy horse boys said instead of with just the pure gross-out nature of the disgusting experience. The camper's fun of later saying "Horse boys think horse pee is orange juice! Wyatt and Earl are so weird!" keeps them, and their friends, coming back for more.

Sometimes, though, skating the edges of appropriateness in the interest of commercially valuable humor resulted in inadvertent bad PR. Like the time a few young camp riders threw up from getting grossed out by the peons on a dinner ride.

Dinner rides were usually hugely popular and big money makers for the bosses, so they would drive out and help with the dinner preparations while the peons rode the horses to the fire pit and picnic table deep in the woods. There was lots of enthusiastic bullshitting about the world famous high quality of the burger patties (cheap) and specially imported Boston Baked Beans (from cans) being served, and lots of jokes about the fine silverware (plastic), china (Dixie cups), and fine silk napkins (paper), with which the royal guests were honored. Peons chugged "bug juice," and ate burgers in buns turned the wrong way out with ketchup, lettuce and pickles on the outside insisting all the time that that was the proper way to eat them and the campers were crazy to say otherwise. Cal had a famous shtick where he put on an apron and pretended he was a doctor examining a patient who was gravely ill, a watermelon. Of course the patent ultimately required surgery, and after much hoopla and exploration (intended in part to waste time and give the horses more time to rest) Cal would cut into the watermelon and pull out a handful of red flesh. "Ooooh, yuck!" the campers inevitably exclaimed in pure grossed-out delight before being served the patent's hand, or foot, or eyeball.

So, one day when Cal wasn't around, Earl was cooking the burgers and beans, and Coolidge and Wyatt led the ride to the cookout area. After helping the riders dismount, they tied up the horses carefully to small trees, small enough to break instead of the reins if the horses pulled back in a panic, but big enough generally to keep them in place. The meal went as usual with Earl straight-facing the campers about how these were the very woods where Wisconsin flying skunks (non-existent) were first discovered. Only a few mosquitoes were out, but the Off and the smoke from the campfire kept them at bay. Also, mosquitoes prefer biting horses, so the campers were at least safe from that threat.

The set up for the gag came early when Coolidge mentioned off-handedly at the burger course that he felt "a little off." Wyatt laughed and said, "You mean you feel like a little can?" pointing to the bug spray. Coolidge laughed and filled a fresh Dixie cup halfway with red bug juice. He stood up and went over to the food by the campfire, leaving the group at the picnic table. There he discretely tore up bits of burger, lettuce, tomatoes, and carrots on the serving tray and slid them into the cup. They sunk in the bug juice and almost filled the cup full. Hiding the cup behind his back, he sat back down at the table.

"No, it's absolutely true. Flying skunks do exist in Wisconsin. In fact, there was a big debate in Madison whether to make them the state mammal instead of badgers, but then they decided that since the flying skunks were only found in this woods and the badgers were found everywhere else that the badgers were a better choice. But I like the flying skunks better than badgers, although they can make the rain around here a little stinky," said Earl in earnest seriousness taking his hat off and rubbing his hands through his long black hair. Coolidge brings the cup out from behind his back hiding it under the table. Slowly he raises it to his chin and nods at Wyatt. Coolidge stands up and abruptly spills the contents of the cup forward from his chin all over the table in front of him while simultaneously making the loudest puking sounds he could summon from the depths of his chest.

"Oh, Coolidge! Are you sick?" asked Wyatt also standing up from the table. The campers, serious and concerned, all scoot away from the spreading puddle of chunky fake puke. "Oh boy! Puke! All right!" says Wyatt, happily reaching over to pick up chunks from the "puke" pile and put them in his mouth, chewing exaggeratedly. "Yummy! Don't you want some? Help yourself, everyone. Gee, thanks, Cool! Tastes great!"

One might suppose it was the three campers who added genuine puke of their own to the table that purged that bit of entertainment from the repertoire of the peons forever. Cal had to endure a firm request from the good Father Able via the kitchen staff, who always had their finger on the happenings around camp, to "make sure no food was ever again wasted on the dinner and breakfast rides." Wyatt as well as Coolidge and Earl got firm punches in the upper arms from Cal at the next meeting. They had told Cal right away, of course, that some campers had gotten sick on the ride, but they neglected to say specifically why. They would have gotten more than one punch each, except that even Cal was laughing when he was trying to be pissed. "You fucking peons are disgusting!" he said. Coolidge had a better PR filter after that, but he never regretted the gag because he had finally done a bullshit gag with Wyatt on an equal basis.

It was a wonder the campers came to the stables at all considering the terrible flies that thrived there. To walk anywhere in the barn felt a little like Moses parting the Red Sea except the waters were layers of houseflies. There was no avoiding them. Sometimes the swarms were so thick on the beams of the barn that the wood disappeared beneath them and the surface undulated from the dance of their reflective wings. To make things worse, the green-headed ones actually bit especially when supercharged by the sun. It was a constant losing battle to keep the flies out of the cabin and the granary, although everyone tried to go in and out the screen door as fast as possible. The flies even sought the moisture on the sides of everyone's mouth when they were asleep.

Bullshitting was necessary to deflect customer attention from the germ-laden flies everywhere. Earl pretended they didn't even exist. "What flies? You see flies around here? What are you, nuts?" Wyatt pretended they were pets and had names. "Oh look, there's Mary and Patsy, and there's Timothy and his brother, Leary. Who do you see?" and a game of naming the flies would ensue. "That's not Joey. You're mistaken. That's Susan. Don't you know boys from girls? Hi Susan! What? She's mad at you for calling her Joey..." Coolidge learned from Earl how to catch flies with his hands, stun them by throwing them onto the concrete, and then tie a hair onto their heads or legs. The best nooses were from a long hair plucked from the head of a surprised camper. When the flies regained consciousness they would soar in entertaining loops like pets.

There were attempts to control the flies, all futile. The long rolls of sticky fly paper that came with their own thumbtacks, provided amusement, but only for an hour or so before they were so full they had to be thrown away. The yellow sticky strips were more effective in the cabin where the flies were fewer than in the barn, but Coolidge got his hair caught in one hanging by the bunk bed one time and it took a scissors to rid his hair of the fly-encrusted gunk. That was not amusing. In the stalls of course, the horses murdered dozens of flies at a time with each swish of their tails creating little piles of corpses behind them that had to be swept out with the manure at the end of the day. During the aerobic workout of cleaning the barn each night, it was common for a peon to swallow a fly or two by accident. They were just too thick to avoid.

Since this was farm country and farmers had their own 200-hundred-gallon gasoline refill tanks, the bosses signed a summer lease for one to avoid having to drive into town so often. The Shell gasoline delivery guy, Jimmy, wore a bright yellow uniform and peddled the company's pesticide products on the side: No-Pest Strips, baits, etc. One day he came with his truck to fill the tank and Cal offhandedly asked him if the Shell No-Pest Strips were safe for cabins. "Of course," Jimmy said, unwrapping one of the yellow cartons sitting next to him on the seat. To everyone's amazement he removed the cheesy looking strip completely out of its hanger, held it up to his mouth and took a decent-sized bite out of it. "Safe as hell," he said chewing. "I've been selling them for years. Never had any problems with them!" Cal passed on the strips, but in honor of Jimmy's unique sales pitch and willingness to sacrifice life and limb to uphold his company's bullshit, he did take some sugar-based bait samples for the barn. Turns out the flies preferred good old manure better than processed sugar, but the ones that landed by accident on the poison died a weird death on the barnyard floor, buzzing around in circles for several minutes before finally lying on their backs with their feet twitching. Nothing, of course, even the sugar deaths, put a dent in their plague-like population. Flies were just part of the stables landscape, inevitable as tourist girls hanging around the barn, or a horse walking through poison ivy.

To lead a ride meant that the peon had to watch where he was steering his horse but always to look back at the ride to make sure there were no problems like saddles slipping or hotdog riders trying to peel away for an unauthorized canter. Unbeknownst to most customers, only a handful of the horses were actually capable of leading off on their own. Most lacked initiative, and like all herd animals, they were content to follow another's tail anywhere it might lead, especially back to the barn. Trail horses always walk more quickly toward the barn, and that is when peons had to be most in control of a ride, keeping it tight, and staying in tune with each horse and rider. Even a horse that wouldn't lead could be talked into a dangerous gallop toward the barn by a rider more invested in thrills than personal survival. Putting people on the right horses for them and building trusting rapport with them early in the ride was essential to keeping things safe.

Fortunately, the ability to sniff out a hotdog the moment they step out of their vehicle was an easy one to acquire. Hotdogs are usually males between the ages of eighteen and forty, and they almost always whooped or yeehah-ed when they get out of the car. They "want to go fast," but they are nervous and clearly have never even stood close to a horse before. They "don't want a nag," but they can't remember any breed of horse they may have ridden before, even if they are "expert riders." They are usually dressed in shorts and tennis shoes or sandals and a baseball cap or some variation if they aren't in just swim trunks and a t-shirt. Aviator sunglasses were another sign. Hotdogs usually got Little Brother with the following lines of standard peon bullshit: "Well, we are giving you the biggest and strongest horse because you look like you might be able to handle Little Brother here. He's the king of the herd and not for a meek rider. You've got to be willing to kick this animal to show him who's boss! Are you up for the challenge?" In actuality, although Little Brother was indeed the strongest and fastest horse in the herd, that was true only in the pasture where, like Cole, he chased the other geldings around all night to show them who was in charge. He chased his share of mares around too, most likely "due to an undescended testicle," according to Marvin. On a trail ride, though, Little Brother was smart enough to know there was nothing at all to be gained by keeping up with a ride. He was always put at or near the end because huge gaps inevitably opened in front of him as he lazily lagged behind. It was all a rider could do to kick him hard enough for the entire ride to keep him caught up. Thus he was the perfect choice of horse for hot dogs. Usually about halfway through a ride on Little Brother a hotdog is handed a stick to use because his legs are worn out from kicking. A stick was still only mildly effective at motivating Little Brother. He needed to preserve his energy for after work.

"Marvin, you've got to take back this Little Brother," Earl had pleaded with the horse dealer one time, knowing full well he never would. "He's impossible. Won't keep up on rides and then runs all the horses ragged at night."

"You assholes don't know how to ride him. One of the best pieces of horseflesh in the county this horse is. Do you know he can pull a plow?"

"He goes about as fast as a plow horse, that's for sure," replied Earl.

"Just tire him out!" said Marvin.

So for a week at the beginning of the day before breakfast and at the end of the day when all the horses were let out, one of the peons, usually Earl, grabbed a huge club of a stick and cantered Little Brother around the lake – a full half hour ride at full speed. Little Brother would come back from his workout completely lathered up and angry. No horse could keep up with that routine for a week and not be exhausted at night. Not so with Little Brother. It just got him in shape and the pasture antics increased in vigor and fury.

"What a horse!" smiled Marvin when he heard.

Well, at least he was useful for cooling hotdogs.

He was also good for scaring the holy shit out of Coolidge one night. It had been a meeting night at Crane, and although Lenny had demonstrated his prowess at shooting cans of beer, Coolidge knew his limits a bit better since the first meeting at Hillcrest. He still had to get up in the wee hours to take a wiz, though, probably from the aspirin he took and all the water he chugged at the outdoor sink to avoid another hangover. Nighttime was a good time to pee at places along the barnyard fence that were too exposed during the day. The prime daytime peeing places, in the shadows of the cabin and behind the granary, got stinky fast, so the ethic was to spread your pee around a bit if you were out at night.

Anyway, the ghostly images of the horses were just on the other side of the barnyard fence when Coolidge stumbled out to pay his rent on one Schlitz and gallon of water. He didn't pay much attention to the fact that the horses were not out in the big pasture – it was normal for them at night to roam freely all over the place including the inner corral – and besides, the moon was compellingly near full and amazing to look at in the chilly night sky. As Coolidge yawned and stared at the moon a blood-curdling horse screech blasted his right ear. Little Brother was right there across the fence looming over him. His mane was shaking wildly in the moonlight. Coolidge, startled, lurched away from the fence to instinctually escape being crushed by the towering mass of horseflesh grunting and quivering above him. That's when he saw the mare underneath Little Brother.

Of course, it was the illusion of proximity, of sudden loud noises seeming closer than they really were, that scared him. The copulating horses did not crash through the fence onto him as Coolidge had feared, but it took seeing the wet glitter of the massive brown and pink three-foot penis withdrawing sloppily from the mare for him to finally realize what he had accidentally witnessed up close and personal. When Little Brother's front hooves slid off the staggering mare's back – was it White Devil? - and landed on the ground with a deep thud it vibrated Coolidge's already shaking knees as he looked up between the fence boards at the so-called gelding baring his teeth to the moon and shaking his head back and forth. As his fear subsided and the horses slowly disappeared into the moon shadows of the pine trees surrounding the pasture side of the corral, Coolidge wondered if he should wake somebody up about this. Then, as he regained his feet and finished the business that had brought him there, he was afraid no one would believe him. As he shuffled back to the safety of the cabin, he thought about what luck it had been to witness that primordial storm of raw sexual power from seemingly gentle trail animals. He felt blessed somehow as he quietly slipped through the screen door of the cabin and back to his sleeping bag.

Coolidge's feelings about horse sexuality, or, in particular, horse penises, however, became even more complex the very next day. Whether it was because of the previous evening's amorous activities or not, Little Brother seemed to grow an erection like clockwork every fifteen minutes or so. Didn't matter whether he was in the barn, getting water at the trough, or being mounted for a ride, there it was his horse penis for all to marvel at, angling stiffly downward like some ancient organic plow Egyptian farmers once used to plant papyrus. The flies appreciated the moisture it offered, and their grotesque accompaniment somehow lent it even greater spectacle.

It was the brief lull between lunch and the one o'clock tourist ride. Cal had eaten earlier in town at Garcia's and was talking on the phone with Marvin about an untamed appaloosa the horse dealer wanted the stables to break. Cal and Hank loved a free horse, even if it wasn't broken because if they broke it successfully they could use it free all summer and Marvin would get a trained horse back. Good deal all around, provided the horse wasn't completely crazy. Often these horses ended up sufficiently broken but at best marginal trail horses, and often the bosses gave them names that were suspiciously similar to those of authority figures in the camps. Apparently the bosses felt the PR risk of possibly deeply offending someone was well worth the sophomoric humor of, for instance, naming a somewhat dim gelding Unable in honor of the good Father Able.

"Sure, Marvin. Bring it by anytime. We'll give it a shot. You know we love a rodeo," said Cal hanging up. He belched from the enchiladas he had eaten at Garcia's and headed for the cable table to sit in the shade and digest.

Earl, at the wheel of the Impala with the top down, was driving Wyatt and Coolidge back from a camp lunch of cheese sandwiches and tomato soup served on indestructible light green plastic plates and bowls. Emerging from the pines by the granary, he saw that no one was in the parking area so, as expected, he cranked his steering wheel and spun his patented donut and a half before parking abruptly but perfectly next to the granary. It was the least frightening car move in Earl's repertoire. Coolidge liked the thrill of it, but even more the calm and cool way Earl kept a straight face behind the wheel and while stepping out of the car afterwards. "Didn't everyone park this way?' he seemed to be saying with his body language. It cracked Coolidge up every time. Earl's trick of sometimes turning the lights off at night on wild drives to Hillcrest was frightening, though. That one and taking blind curves so fast that at any moment the car seemed ready to fly sideways off the road and into the trees. "Radials are incredible," or "G's" was all that Earl would calmly say stepping even harder on the gas pedal. Earl loved his cars.

The peons pile out of the Impala and head to the barn to bring the horses out for the upcoming tourist ride, and the first horse out of the barn is Little Brother sporting his member. "Jesus, Wyatt, what did you do to that horse?" laughed Cal jumping down from the cable table and walking toward the railing by the parking lot where Wyatt was looping Little Brother's reins over a post.

"I don't know, Cal, I think Little Brother is happy to see you!" replied Wyatt.

"You, you mean," said Cal. "You were the one in the barn with him just now." Earl laughed and tied Fred next to Little

Brother, followed by Coolidge with White Devil. Coolidge hurried to follow Earl and Wyatt back toward the barn to get another round of horses. He usually tried to avoid being alone anywhere with Cal, and doing the work at hand that the others were engaged in was usually the best and safest strategy.

"Wait a minute," said Cal stopping them. "I'm not sure Little Brother is really okay. Do you think he's okay, Wyatt?"

"Oh, I think he's doing just fine!" said Wyatt.

"No, no, I'm not so sure," said Cal his most serious look of angry and assertive concern on his face. If what was coming was truth or bullshit, Coolidge had no way of knowing.

"It looks like his cock is not connected solidly."

"You're kidding," said Wyatt catching on. "Hmm...looks pretty solid to me..."

"No, Wyatt, you know you can't tell by just looking," said Cal squatting on his knees to get a better view under Little Brother. "You better grab that cock to see."

Somehow Wyatt had managed to slip on his pair of work gloves. "No gloves, Wyatt. You can't do a proper test of firmness and skin connectivity with gloves on. You know that."

"Right, I forgot, Cal. What do you think, Earl? Do you think Little Brother's cock is connected okay?"

"Seems to be connected fine to me. What do you think, Cool?" said Earl, his face deadpan.

Is he serious? Looking again at the enormous penis close range and remembering Little Brother's violent but obviously physically healthy mounting of White Devil in the corral the night before, Coolidge was tempted to tell them the story, but he suspected Cal wouldn't be interested. Where this conversation was really leading, though, he wasn't sure. "It looks okay to me, I think," he said.

"You peons can't think!" yelled Cal. "You've got to be sure. This horse is going out on a ride in a few minutes. What if his cock falls off?"

"That would be bad PR," commented Earl.

"Very bad PR. Not to mention sucking for Little Brother," said Wyatt.

"Right," said Cal. "So, Wyatt, take that stupid glove off and grab that cock. Move it around and make sure it's connected okay."

Wyatt glanced across the front of the barn hoping tourists would pull in early for their ride and rescue him, but no such luck. He yanked the gloves off his hands and stuffed them in his back pocket.

"Coolidge, hold the reins while Wyatt grabs that cock," said Cal. Coolidge grabbed the reins below Little Brother's enormous mouth. The disheveled mane was over his glazed eyes a bit. Coolidge remembered what that hair looked like recently swinging wildly in the moonlight. Wyatt squatted down next the saddle. "Grab that cock, Wyatt," repeated Cal.

Coolidge saw Wyatt's left hand disappear underneath Little Brother. A flash of awareness electrified Little Brother's eye in front of Coolidge's face. Little Brother, shifted his back feet a bit and Wyatt stood up quickly.

"So, what do you think, Wyatt?" asked Cal.

"I don't know, Cal. Seems pretty well connected to me," said Wyatt. *Had he really touched that thing? Why didn't Little Brother kill him?*

"Earl, get over here and grab this cock! Wyatt doesn't know anything about horse cocks he's so used to grabbing his own!"

Earl traded places with Wyatt. He saw Wyatt stand next to Cal to view the scene. Again, Little Brother shifted when Earl stuck his hand underneath his back side. "Oh God, that is totally gross," he said, wiping his hand on his blue jeans. "But very well connected. Yes, indeed. Little Brother's got good connections."

"Good," said Cal, and he turned and walked back toward the cabin, his freshly shined boots reflecting the sun directly overhead. *Is it over?* Coolidge put the reins back over the post and went to fetch another horse from the barn.

"Hey, Coolidge," said Wyatt standing with Earl still near Little Brother. "Where're you going?"

"Getting more horses out for the one o'clock," said Coolidge.

"But you haven't had a chance to grab this cock yet!" said Wyatt. "Don't you want to see what it feels like?"

"Yeah, Cool. You need to tell us what you think of this cock here," said Earl. *Was this revenge somehow, for Cal forcing them to touch it?* He walked back to where they were standing by the horse, cock still hanging down with stiff inertia. The hard thing jerked forward briefly. Coolidge felt his own groin suddenly, and a knot formed in his stomach. His chest tightened.

"Grab that cock, Coolidge!" said Earl pointing under Little Brother. "The riders will be here soon."

"Yeah, grab the cock. That's a direct-order!" said Wyatt, holding onto Little Brother's reins.

They're serious about this. Coolidge put his left hand on Little Brother's saddle seat and crouched down as he had seen the others do moments before. Little Brother's enormous bulk put off waves of heat he could smell even in the already hot air of the yard, and the size of his underbelly and back legs was truly phenomenal. *One quick kick or step forward could crush me. This is stupid. I would kick me if I were this horse.*

"Come on, Coolidge. Hurry up. The ride's going to get here. Grab that cock. Move it up and down!" He heard them both laugh a little under their breath.

Reaching into the shadowy space below the groin of Little Brother felt like reaching for the trigger of a bomb, only the trigger was composed not of a wire or a switch but of some alien worm of protoplasm designed to automatically set off an explosion. As the fingers of his left hand touched and closed on the patchwork of dark colors that covered the thin skin around the baseball bat-sized organ, similar fingers seemed to close inside his throat and reach deep within his gut searching for and priming the juices of revulsion and nausea.

Little Brother's organ was not easy to hold and move once Coolidge realized the horse had not yet killed him for touching its genitals, and he could actually do what the third year peons were telling him to do. Still, he hesitated, revolted. *Can this hurt him? Wouldn't moving this thing bother the horse even more than grabbing it?* Holding his breath, he planted his foot and jerked his hand forward swinging the stiff cock like a cadaver's rigor mortis arm toward himself and the front legs. The mass of flesh felt firm and warm beneath the loose skin of the penis, and that was the last sensation Coolidge's guts could handle. As Earl and Wyatt laughed, he rolled out of his crouch, avoided Little Brother's now shifting front feet, and crawled out of harm's way toward the barn. His eyes were watered and his throat retched. Coolidge gagged back the tomato soup rising into his mouth from lunch. Getting to his feet he saw though blurry eyes a Volkswagen bus pull into the parking space followed by a couple of other sedans.

"Well, I guess we better get this ride ready to go. I'll lead this one, Earl. Coolidge, you follow on Little Brother. I think he likes you now!" said Wyatt with a laugh.

"He'll remember you in his dreams, Coolidge," remarked Earl passing him on the way to the barn. Coolidge couldn't wave to the tourists as Wyatt and Earl had done. When he got up, all he could see were flies swirling around his boots as they dragged through the sand on his slow walk to the barn.

Getting Chicks and Other Objects

Michael is eight years old in his yard at Coveside. He has picked the asparagus in the garden for his mother, and is back outside to play alone. The garden occupied a small patch of the front part of the two-acre property, while the back consisted of a tiny one-story artist studio-inspired residence. The modest house was perched back on a peninsula of land looking over two ravines that converged below them and meandered its way several miles to Lake Michigan. It was a surprisingly wild place to live in the middle of what was otherwise a boring, flat, middle to upper class suburban neighborhood. The workers who labored at Perry's carwash would come periodically on the weekends to mow the front lawn and tend the garden that produced string beans, bush beans, tomatoes, strawberries, and rhubarb. Raspberry bushes and grape vines formed the barrier to the neighbors to the west, and a thick forest of oaks and maples defined the property line to the east.

It was autumn, and the thick and multicolored leaves were covering the ground. The yellow birch leaves, small and difficult to rake up, were interspersed lightly among the dominant wider leaves of the majestic black oaks and sugar maples. The elms, smooth of limb and equally as impressive as the oaks and maples, had succumbed to Dutch elm disease only just recently, and Michael marveled at how their sudden absence left behind mounds of sawdust and sunshine in the canopy.

Michael picked up a fallen oak branch, unusually long and straight. There had been a storm the night before, one of those scary Wisconsin thunderstorms with booming thunder and severe lightning lasting more than an hour with winds tossing the branches of the big trees to and fro. "One of these big maples is coming down on the house someday," said Perry the night before. "Can't afford to cut them down, though. Too expensive, and they sure are beautiful." The massive tree trunks grew only inches from the side of the house.

Michael remembered his father's words and stabbed the end of the branch into a big maple leaf. The palm shaped leaf stuck to the end delivering a certain feeling of satisfaction. He poked another leaf, one of thousands littering the lawn and garden. It also stuck, pushing the first leaf up the stick. Soon he had a full column of leaves on the shaft of the oak branch. He worked his way around the lawn like a human sewing machine, up and down, stabbing leaves. There was a partially filled black garbage bag up left by a worker against the trunk of a maple by his parents' bedroom window. He opened the bag and rested it across his knees. With his other hand he slid the stuck leaves off satisfyingly into the bag.

Look at the space I cleared already in the lawn. Dad will be happy. He became obsessed, stabbing leaves in a widening circle around the house jogging back to the bag to empty the stick when it became too full. He resented the time it took to pull the leaves off the stick because the stabbing was what he liked – each poke resulted in immediate and measurable progress on the lawn. He took to dragging the heavy bag to the areas he was working to save time. Eventually he found another bag on the workbench in the garage. He left the old one by the garbage-burning barrel near the lawn mower. He kept going, filling the new bag and smelling the moisture from underneath each leaf he stabbed. He worked obsessively with no concept of time passing.

Clearing a whole yard with just a stick – that's something! He imagined headlines in the Milwaukee Journal: "Boy Cleans All the Leaves in His Yard with Just a Stick." *I can do this.* He felt amazed that he could have such an impact on the land with something as simple as tenacious physical effort.

There would be no headlines in the Journal, though. Had he stopped to think about it more carefully, he would have enjoyed recognition from the Sentinel more – The Milwaukee Sentinel, after all, had better comics.

Coolidge remembered this one afternoon while tediously putting hay in the pasture at Crane. He reviewed all he had learned about feeding horses as he stood beside the manger:

A bale of hay is a deceptively powerful and dynamic entity. Take a section of a more or less wild grass field, water it with fresh rain, bake it in intense sunshine for a few weeks, cut the stems off at ground level, dry everything in the sun some more, and crush the resulting plant matter into forty to eighty pound packages tied tightly with two strong pieces of twine, and there you have it – an amazingly compact package of calories and nutrition, clean and fresh smelling like a walk in the country.

Until, of course, it gets wet, or eaten. Either event results in the same thing – immense energy release, and manure. A couple of armfuls of hay can keep one of the largest animals on land living, breathing, and running for an entire day and produce an impressive pile of shit. Bale up a bunch of hay before it is dry enough, or just let a moderate rain soak into the bales before you can get them under cover, and the hay will ferment and heat up enough in a barn to burst into flames.

Every late afternoon the evening hay for the horses needed to be put into the mangers, about a half a bale per working horse. Whoever is not on the evening ride is usually the one to pull hay duty. Today Coolidge was the one hauling the bales from the barn out the door to the corral. It had been a rainy few days, stormy, in fact. Rides were cancelled the previous afternoon and the peons, hanging around in the barn, watched dark storm clouds spin menacingly above them before the skies let loose with fierce lightning and hail, prompting Earl to run and park his Impala in the barn. It was the storm, probably, that reminded Coolidge of his home back in Milwaukee and all the leaves.

Weather was always a consideration at a riding stables because lightning loves a moist body high above the ground. In fact, even without riders on them, lightning kills scores of Wisconsin horses - and other livestock - each year because in a flat pasture animals are often the tallest targets around. Still, even with the horses getting a bit of a rest and extra hay-eating time lately in the barn, they were out now and would still need overnight feed, so Coolidge was sinking his boots extra deep in the muddy corral carrying the evening's bales from the barn to the mangers. The first step was to clean out any old hay that was rotten from the mangers, and as Coolidge dug the pitchfork into the hot compost at the bottom of the wooden manger his nose made him think that one of the horses must have turned around and pooped into it. Essentially, a horse might as well have done that. Biologically it didn't make much difference. Wet hay is as efficiently digested by the bacteria in the manger as it would have been by the bacteria in the intestines of a horse. Hay bales had to be shaken and watered to protect horse's lungs from dust, especially lungs of horses that are ridden ten or more hours a day. Not enough water, the horses sneeze. Too much water, and they eat manure along with their hay. It's a balance that has to be achieved – a balance accompanied by a lot of manger cleaning.

In the dry barn, though, a huge pile of stacked hay is steadfast as a cash investment. It is like having many acres of available pastureland controlled and condensed in the barn, and climbing on the slippery bales in cowboy boots is like experiencing all that nature and sunshine without having to go outside.

The smell of hay in the barn, whether fresh or not, is pervasive, rich, and almost strong enough to drive out the manure smell wafting from the stalls on the other side of the barn. Stacking the bales when Francis brought new loads and hefting the bales about during the day to fill the mangers and the feeding troughs in the stalls is the main way the peons built muscles in peon arms and chests. There was no way to escape getting in shape if you are moving hay around for fifteen horses. Riding endless hours built up core muscles, and hauling hay around finished the job with the rest of their bodies.

The huge stack of hay bales dominating the corral side of the barn was also soft and inviting for naps and other activities. When the thrill of cliff jumping wasn't in the cards, a huge hemp rope tied to the barn's long beam high above the stack provided ample thrills. Parker was particularly daring, holding the rope over his shoulder as he climbed high up the support beams framing the tall parabolic wall of the barn over the hay. Pushing himself away from the wall with his feet, he would swing on the rope in a high arch out and back to the wall on the other side where he would push off again and spin and pendulum around back to his original launch position ten yards or so above the bales. Sometimes he could manage three full rotations on a single leap. Sometimes his timing was off and he would hit the wall with his back instead of with his feet. In that case the rope would drag his back painfully along the boards. Eventually, no matter what the style points earned, Parker's arms would tire and he would drop skillfully into the hay with his patented smile and laugh. Unlike cliff diving, there were degrees of beams one could jump from, lower ones that were simple to master on up to the highest beams that propelled you off the wall with enough momentum to launch you onto the concrete of the drive-through if your grip wasn't tight enough.

Coolidge actually mastered the rope in the barn quickly and liked the swinging sessions the peons engaged in after-hours. He had secretly rigged a rope swing behind the garage over the ravine at his house one summer that had provided similar thrills. He cringed, though, when he heard that

Hank's older brother, Burt, had gotten drunk and while swinging spectacularly (apparently Burt never did anything less than spectacularly) had put his boot through the wall boards of the barn causing him to let go of the rope and get caught there. The impact immediately broke his leg. Luckily the hay prevented him from also breaking his neck when he was finally able to twist free and fall to the bales below.

Rope swinging was also a handy method of showing off when girls were hanging around the barn. If the term "chick magnet" didn't originate around a stables full of horses, it probably should have. There were guys who liked horses and riding, of course (often because they figured out that girls liked guys who rode) but no doubt from the youngest female riders to the oldest no one loved horses with more unashamed flirtatious passion than the girls. They were always the first to show up for scheduled rides – sometimes hours ahead of time – and they were always the last to leave, leaning on the barn's removable railing across the drive-through with the sun shining on their t-shirts or halter tops, or peaking over the tall and sturdy barn doors at the horses in the stalls.

Managing the groups of interested and worshipful females was broken down according to an unspoken code, as Coolidge ascertained by watching his mentors negotiate the daily flow. They goofed around with regular campers and listened to their gossip about life at camp, mostly about how boring it was (except for riding) or about how much they prefer being at camp than at home (which was even more boring). PR with campers was important because if the regular camp riders liked the peons, the rest of their cabin mates usually fell in line, which made for safer and better rides. What horses they got to ride was always a big deal for them. They all had favorites, and as much as possible, Wyatt and Earl would accommodate them, usually by telling them before the horses came out of the barn that they were going to get the very horse they hated the most, and then bringing out the ones they wanted all along.

"Earl, can I ride Fred today? Please! Fred is my favorite horse! Fred, Fred, Fred, I want Fred! Please!" whined Tammy, an eleven-year old full-summer camper wearing blue jeans and boots she insisted her parents send her after she discovered the stables.

"You rode Fred yesterday, Tammy Bananny. I think White Devil is the better horse for you today. Fred is tired. He wants to stay in the barn and watch television," replied Earl from the stall door of the barn.

"No! Not White Devil. I hate that horse! She is so slow! Can't I have Fred? Please, please, please!...Horses don't watch television!"

"Well, Fred does, and his favorite show is on now – Mr. Ed," said Earl looking over his shoulder back at the horses in the stall.

"No! You're lying. Fred doesn't watch Mr. Ed."

"I'm not lying. Wyatt, doesn't Fred like Mr. Ed?"

"It's his favorite show," said Wyatt from inside the barn. "He's watching it right now in his Lazy Boy."

"He is not! Please don't make me ride White Devil. I'll *die* if I have to ride White Devil!"

"Someone has to ride White Devil or she'll get depressed and think nobody likes her. You don't want that do you?

White Devil wants you to ride her. She asked us especially this morning. Why don't you like White Devil? Is it her breath? Or the wedding dress she wears every day?"

"She doesn't wear a wedding dress!"

"She sure does. She has it on right now and she's getting married on this very next ride. Don't you want to be on the bride when she says 'I do' to Little Brother?"

"White Devil's not marrying Little Brother! You're crazy! Horses don't get married!"

"She sure is. Winder is the minister and Bessie is the flower girl. White Devil gets married every day. Yesterday she married Ross."

"But I want to ride Fred!"

"Sorry, Tammy. There is absolutely no way I would ever deprive you of the once in a lifetime opportunity to ride White Devil on this historic ride. Horse Bride Magazine is going to be there taking pictures. She's getting married, and you're invited. I hope you brought her a wedding present," said Earl disappearing into the stalls to grab her horse.

And then Earl would bring out Fred for Tammy to ride.

With older girls from camp who hung around, such as counselors in training, the content of Wyatt and Earl's bullshit became slightly more sophisticated and self-acknowledging while achieving similar goals of situational manipulation and conversational control.

"So, what's your mode?" Earl would ask a group of newly arrived railing leaners looking to kill some time before a ride, or to walk back a group of younger riders coming back from the trail.

"Hi Earl! What...?" a cute, but ineligible, CIT would respond for the group.

"Your mode. What's your mode today?" Earl would say in a serious tone to the whole group, as if "mode" was a vital thing to have one's handle on.

"We're here to take the 10:00 instruction riders to swimming."

"Backstroke or breaststroke?"

"Kickboards for this group. They suck." Titters from the group, nodding their heads.

"Whatever it takes. You can't get wet unless you're in the water. How do you guys like to swim? Strokes or boards?"

"Oh, we're strokers all the way! You better watch out for us, Earl!" More titters. "How come we never see you swimming in the lake, by the way?"

"Oh, I swim there. You just can't see me 'cause I am too fast. I'm in and out in a flash. Want to help me pick up some apples?"

"Ooo, no! Yuck!"

"Suit yourself. I'm in work mode," and he'd grab the wheel barrow and a five prong fork for a tour of the morning piles in the yard, his muscular arms bulging, and his periodic smile rewarding the admiring eyes of the group hanging around and following his every move. Wyatt's approach was very similar – engage them with charm and enough subtle innuendo to keep them guessing and interested, but never crossing any lines that could get the stables in trouble with the camp. Get them to try to hustle you all you want, but hustling them back was forbidden.

Counselors and tourists, however, were an entirely different situation altogether. Counselors were considered adults and fair game, even if some of them were under eighteen, but Wyatt and Earl tended to avoid the full-on hustle with them because of the hang-around factor. If something didn't go well for some reason, if unspoken expectations were crushed and feelings were hurt for instance, one still had to eat meals with them every day, so the vetting process for hustle-able counselors was intense, and only a chosen few ever ended up in the hay for a bottle of wine and an overnight tussle. Those who did had to previously verbally demonstrate a thorough understanding that any midnight dalliances were meaningless beyond just a wild party night, and that the social separation between the stables world and the camp counselor's world was not to ever be bridged either in their minds or in reality. This was usually accomplished through goofing around and meaningless bullshit conversations that slowly grew in suggestion and innuendo until expectations and conditions of trust and non-commitment for any upcoming partying were reliably established.

The Earl/Wyatt verbal contract approach to hustling tourist "chicks" was similar but significantly accelerated. The PR minefields were virtually non-existent for tourist chicks, whereas counselors and kitchen crew workers could cause all kinds of rumors and political headaches around the camp. Any rumors started by flirting tourists who drove themselves to the stables late at night for dates with the peons would reflect more on them than on the stables, it was figured. They could be toyed with for a night and then discarded without consequence beyond the momentary challenge of moving on from them after they had been "gotten." For this reason, tourists were without question the preferred pool of available after-hours entertainment.

Although it took a while for Coolidge to develop an ability to be entertaining as a ride leader – he eventually tapped into his love of reading to go off on free-association rants that were crazy and weird enough to make riders laugh – he learned to lead safe rides almost immediately, and so he was put into the rotation, spelling Earl and Wyatt at the front every third ride or so. He would have been asked to lead more rides, since leading was a very exhausting and demanding task, and he was lowest on the totem pole, but there was an ethic to split the rides more or less evenly for safety reasons. The only motivation for a peon to offer to take an extra ride, or two rides in a row, was if something was happening at the stables that hour that was even more exhausting, like unloading hay, or something that required specialized skill such as breaking a horse. Coolidge noticed early on, though, that the leader schedule goes out the window if a group of hustle-able chicks show up for a ride.

"So, Coolidge," whispered Wyatt in the stall as they were getting the horses bridled for a one o'clock tourist ride, "Earl and I are going to take this ride. Put the blonde on Fred up front behind Earl and the other cute one on Ross in front of me. We'll help them up, just be sure they go out in that order, okay?"

"I gotcha, Wyatt!"

Coolidge had heard enough discussions between Earl and Wyatt to catch on that there were certain visual opportunities on rides, particularly during trots, that went along with the rule of always keeping your eye on the riders and the horses. He was not at all immune to the erotic stimulation of riding, nor to the beauty of many of the young women bouncing along with their shorts rubbing against the saddles. He imagined the physical sensation of touching them, thought about it a lot, especially during unnecessary trips to the outhouse, but the whole process of talking to them, getting them to like him in that way, and then inviting them back for a date was flummoxing.

Not so for Wyatt and Earl, who, of course, were several years older and already in high school where, Coolidge imagined, all mysteries of life were probably revealed. In any case, he was happy to let Earl and Wyatt take his scheduled ride that day. He knew what they wanted – to hustle the chicks – but beyond the stables talk about "getting them," and "who was hot and who wasn't," and "who had to take the turn with the ugly one so the other guy could get the good one because, darn it, they always come paired like that," he had no clue what line of bullshit and what specific moves were required. That bullshit was the key, he had no doubt, however. He lived among hustling masters, and Earl and Wyatt were clearly not looking for steady, meaningful girlfriends. They were looking for sex, pure and simple, and they were up front with each other about it. It was a singular and simple goal, discussed openly and considered a higher mission of the summer.

Only it wasn't simple, of course, not at all. The process itself of succeeding at the goal of getting sex wasn't easy, and the process of then living with the complexity of the bullshit required to "get a chick" wasn't simple either. But in the rarified atmosphere of the stables where more or less anything goes, the peons, supervised by those who were cut from the same cloth and barely older or more mature than they were, were encouraged to hone their hustling skills. By the middle of July that first summer, Coolidge came to recognize that no one succeeded in achieving the simple goal of the sexual conquest of chicks better than Earl and Wyatt.

Of course, Coolidge, being too young and awkward to be trusted on a double date with the older peons, could only hear snatches of the conversations his mentors used to make the girls laugh and decide to sneak out and return to the stables late at night for a midnight ride and a roll in the hay.

It would happen more or less like this: girls would go on a trail ride in a normal seeming fashion, happy but just girls going for a ride, and then return excited and focused. They would lean on Wyatt and Earl as they helped them dismount from their horses, and stick around laughing and smiling long after everyone else had paid and departed. Coolidge, leading the next ride by himself, would imagine Wyatt and Earl joking around more with them in the barn while he was gone, or maybe even necking with them in the hay. Sometimes he would hear that they had let the girls help shake some hay into the manger, or that they all swung on the rope in the barn.

Cal always approved of hustling and allowed for truncated barn cleanings if Earl and Wyatt needed to get showered early for a trip to the drive-in movie or whatever date excitement they had up their sleeves for a night with "chicks." Often free beer would appear in the fridge, courtesy of Cal's latest run to Benny's. Alcohol, and the opportunity to drink it unimpeded at the stables, was a big draw for bored girls stuck for the summer in their family cabins around the lakes nearby. A few times, specially invited girls would even come back on a Sunday to go drinking and swimming with the handsome and virile horse boys at the quarry. When this happened it disappointed Coolidge to be left behind and miss the swimming, even though he understood the priorities. He depended upon Wyatt and Earl's good will for transportation to places, like to camp for meals, and to the laundry mat in town once a week or so. A trip to the quarry now and again left him feeling refreshed even if jumping off the cliffs was terrifying. *Do the girls lose their tops in the water?*

Coolidge was always on the outside looking in, but the view never lost its fascination for him. At night in the cabin, Coolidge would hear Wyatt and Earl laughing and walking with girls out to the pasture with twine in their hands to make makeshift bridles to catch and ride horses around bareback in the moonlight. He would hear the laughter continue in the barn afterward, and notice that Wyatt and Earl were not in their beds late at night when he got up to take a whiz. A glance at the parking lot would confirm the girls were still around someplace, probably losing their clothes in the relative privacy of the granary or on a blanket spread out in a makeshift room of hay bales in the barn. There was a certain loneliness mixed with awe in Coolidge when he witnessed these events. *What am I missing out on? What does it feel like to sleep with a chick? Would I dare touch one? Kiss one even? Would a chick ever even want to sleep with me? What's the bullshit that works to do this?*

On one occasion, two girls from town showed up in separate cars. Later in the evening, Wyatt's girl in the barn got tired and took off, but Earl had his girl in the Impala for hours with the windows rolled up and draped with towels for privacy. How he managed to talk to her and keep her there doing whatever they were doing, obviously sexual, was an eye-opening puzzle to Coolidge, and Earl's casual ability the next day to go on and plan the next conquest and act as if nothing unusual happened to him the night before was equally awe-inspiring and mysterious. *What's his secret? How can I actually accomplish something so amazing and still act cool about it? Why doesn't he stick with one chick? All that work to get her to have sex - why not just keep having sex with her again?* Coolidge saw the advantages of the constantly changing parade of flirtatious girls who came to lean on the open barn doors and corral fences of the stables, but he was afraid that if any one of them actually showed a sexual interest in him he might very well want to live with that person for life. Naturally, he was too embarrassed to share this thought with anybody.

There were frequent stories of Hillcrest conquests as well. Parker had a truck and a fake ID, so it was easy for him to pick up girls in bars, and the cabin was big enough that his bed in the corner was relatively cozy and private. Hank spent most nights with Parker's sister, Lynn, and Lenny's conquests were hit or miss, but to go by his bragging, mostly hits.

"You just invite them to go for a midnight ride, Coolidge," Lenny bragged one Tuesday meeting night. "They hop up behind you and hug you with their boobs in your back, and the horse does the rest of the work. Warms 'em right up. By the time the ride is over chicks are ready for anything you want to do to them." Lenny laughed and tipped a Pabst. *Is he lying?* Coolidge wasn't sure, but the thought of being held like that by a girl, whether on a horse or not, made him cross his legs.

Rodeo

The Fourth of July was a big tourist day at both stables. Camps pretty much ran their own program for the kids with special attendance-required holiday activities and trips to local lakes to watch fireworks. That left the stables free to book rides for the hordes of vacationers up from Milwaukee and Chicago looking for some wholesome country fun.

The bosses knew this meant for a couple of long riding days for the peons, and so they offered rare but appreciated bonus incentives – an afternoon of rides where the peons could keep and split the collected fees. Cal and Hank even led a few rides themselves in the morning to give peons a chance to grab a missed meal, catch up on hydration, dump more baby powder onto their sore butts, brush their teeth, and maybe even take a nap. The horses, also feeling the constant grind, were given extra oats at lunch and plenty of water between rides. Still, horse bickering broke out sometimes with combatants squaring off and kicking the shit out of each other while their petrified riders hung onto the saddle horns for dear life. "Oh, Ross is just giving Straus a few love taps to remind her he's her boyfriend and to stop looking at Little Brother. Nothing to worry about! They're fine now. Let's just put you in a different place in line, okay?" It was a successful day.

"Okay, peons, that's it. We're going to the rodeo tomorrow!" said Cal to the Crane crew that Thursday night. The horses were all rolling in the corral scratching their sweaty backs, and Wyatt, Earl and Coolidge were trying their best to clean the barn and get into camp for a shower before they fell asleep on their feet. Coolidge's feet felt melted into his boots from riding all day in the sun, and the boil on his butt felt like it was about to burst. He had asked Earl to look at it in the shower the night before because it hurt like a bullet wound and he was afraid his whole leg was going to get infected. "Look up your own butt," was Earl's reply. Coolidge dumped some rubbing alcohol he found in the tack room on it and hoped for the best. All day he rode standing on one stirrup to take the pressure off the infected cheek.

"You mean everyone?" asked Earl.

"Yep, we're cancelling everything tomorrow after the instruction rides."

"All right!" said Wyatt and Earl at the same time.

There was no breakfast ride on Friday. The first ride was an instruction ride - campers cantering on the trail and learning how to feed horses and clean stalls in the barn. By the time the last instruction ride was over at 11:00, the barn was clean and the horses had extra weekend hay in the mangers. Work was finally over for the week. Cal returned from his run to Benny's with three cases of Schlitz, and the whooping Hillcrest peons arrived in Parker's truck led by Hank on his Harley.

The bosses allowed the horse boys to attend a number of summertime big events - the car races at Elkhart Lake, the

County Fair in Fieldsburg, the rodeo in Manawa – but there was no money provided for entrance fees.

At Elkhart that summer, the bosses paid to drive a vehicle through the entrance, but the peons were on their own to sneak in under the fence. They would drink beer, catch up with friends from Milwaukee or Chicago, and watch the racecars and model Corvettes go around the track. Coolidge spent most of the time sleeping under a tree on the grass.

Another event they attended one evening was the county fair. There the peons walked around the back of the Fieldsburg fairgrounds where an extended horse barn with a long slanted roof backed up to the fence. Under the cover of darkness, they snuck up a tree trunk next to the fence, climbed out over a convenient branch, and dropped onto the metal roof making enough noise with their boots to spook the horses and piss off the show participants underneath who were meticulously grooming their livestock. Coolidge, following Earl's every move, stomped to the front of the roof, hung off the edge and quickly dropped into the shadows of the gathering commotion. "What the hell is going on? Who's doing that?" the men in the crowd below were saying. Earl blended right in: "What the hell is going on? Who the hell did that?" he echoed, standing up and joining the gathering and angry crowd. Coolidge, doing the same, imitated his angry tones: "Who's making all that noise? Idiots! God dammit. Don't these people know we have horses to get ready in here? Where are those jackasses who were on the roof! Probably people trying to sneak in. Jesus!" And of course, obeying a deep-seated herding instinct, even the legitimate 4-H contestants and their parents who might have noticed that the peons hadn't been around the stalls before, looked at the boots and hats and chose to believe the bullshit. Still acting like they were looking for the perpetrators, the peons strutted away angrily into the crowd by the rides, slipped into porta-potties and changed safely into different shirts they had wisely tied about their waists.

Getting into the professional rodeo free on a Saturday morning, however, was a trickier bullshitting challenge. How do you sneak seven people into the completely fenced-in and patrolled arena, a place full of buff, testosterone-ridden men (and women) who were ready and willing to pound the crap out of anyone they caught cheating or otherwise simply didn't like? A place where alcohol-enhanced frustrations were encouraged to be taken out on animals but just as often were taken out on humans? Cal didn't seem too worried about it. He just said, "Grab a few of the newer saddles, peons, and get in the back of the truck. Parker, you drive. Hank, ride in the cab with me; this isn't a biker crowd."

All the way to the fairgrounds in Manawa, the peons in the back of the truck drank beers to celebrate their day off and help them to forget about the wind in their eyes and the bumps from the stiff suspension of the '55 Chevy pickup. Coolidge rested his uninfected butt cheek on a saddle blanket and closed his eyes against the dust. When they passed through small towns, Parker would shout back at them, "Beer's down," and Wyatt, Earl, and Lenny would hide the bottles in their shirts or under the sides of the truck bed. Pissing out the back was forbidden when the truck was going over thirty, or if anyone was following closely. Coolidge solved that problem by only pretending to drink beer the whole way so he wouldn't have to go.

At the rodeo grounds driveway, Parker pulled over, and Cal took his place at the wheel. "Remember, we just went into town for supplies," said Cal to Parker and Hank in the cab. He then leaned out the window, "Beers away, boys. Look serious like you're about to ride. You laugh, I'll kick your ass, got it?"

The truck pulled into the line of cars and pick-ups approaching the entrance. A young cowboy with a yellow rodeo badge in the shape of a bucking horse pinned to his pearl-buttoned cowboy shirt tipped his hat at Cal and approached the truck, eyeing the saddles and the young but rough looking horse boys in the back.

"Where to? Parking or participants?" he asked.

"Participants. Traffic sucks around here! Are we late?" asked Cal.

"A little bit, but you should be able to make it if you hurry. That gate over there." He pointed at the open gate leading to the driveway behind the stands to the holding pens and chutes. Two bouncer cowboys, also with badges, were standing in front of the gate with gloved arms crossed in front of their chests. They looked about six feet tall and two hundred fifty pounds apiece, not including their mustaches and sideburns that rivaled Cal's.

"Thank you," grunted Cal, and gunned it for the gate. He stopped with a little skid in the dust when it was clear that the gatekeeper apes weren't going to get out of his way. One stayed put in front of the gate, arms now on his hips, and the other walked to Cal's window side.

"Pass, please," said the cowboy, pointing to his yellow badge.

Cal put on his most serious, hassled, and business-like face. "We had to go get some supplies!" he said in a pissed off tone.

"Do you have a pass?" asked the cowboy, wavering a bit when he saw the saddles and anxious cowboys in the back. The peons had slipped on their leather gloves and were flexing their fingers at Wyatt's suggestion.

"What do you mean, pass!" exclaimed Cal doubling his exasperated anger. "I've been in and out of here four times already!"

"Oh, okay sir. Sorry. Go right on in," the cowboy said waving off his buddy and stepping back.

Cal drove ahead shaking his head. The peons tipped their hats as the truck entered the gate and Cal quickly weaved his way and disappeared into the labyrinth of horse trailers and pick-ups already parked there.

Of course once they were inside the sanctuary and parked, they were just like any of the other circuit rodeo cowboys and their entourages milling about with gloves and beers and serious expressions on their faces. The peons knew well how to play this acting game. They climbed onto the fence railings with the real cowboys and cheered on the contestants who dropped onto the backs of broncos and bulls in the chutes below them. Parker produced a bag of Red Man chewing tobacco, and the challenge of not falling off the eight-foot oak fencing was compounded by a new type of dizziness from nicotine as well as from Schlitz. Coolidge, hanging onto the railings as hard as the cowboys were hang-

ing onto the bronco straps couldn't believe that he was looking out from the dark passageways of a true rodeo sanctuary
at the cheering crowd in the outdoor arena. *Lucky I have
these real boots.* Why no one had questioned his possession of
a beer when he clearly looked way under eighteen made him
feel older all of a sudden, not like he belonged there exactly,
but perhaps a cousin of like he belonged. Whenever he felt
self-conscious he just buried his feeling in a cowboy holler.
No one will bother me if I look like I am really into this.

After the bronco-riding event was over, Cal and Hank
climbed down from the railing to go back to the truck for
more beer before the bull riding climaxed the evening. On
the way they passed a huge black bull in the tight passageway
getting prepped for the next event. Cowboys were shocking
it with an electric poker to rile it up and positioning a cinch-
strap around its groin.

"Hey Coolidge, get down here!" he heard Cal yelling
back at him. "Get over here, Coolidge!" Even in a rowdy
crowd, Cal's pissed off voice was distinctive.

Coolidge jumped down and dodged his way between
cowboys lining up to ride the bulls to see what Cal wanted.
There he was, Hank next to him, and through the fence not
a foot away was the massive rear end of the biggest animal
Coolidge had ever seen. The bull was very agitated, and not
just by the amazing number of flies it had all over its rear
end. It had a stubby little tail with a tuft of manure-caked
hair hanging down from it. The tuft twitched nervously back
and forth, and the powerful back legs stomped ready to kick
down the corral at any moment. The animal was the next one
up for riding. It knew what was coming and didn't like it one

bit. The handlers tightened the cinches about his chest and groin, and Coolidge could see the young cowboy, not much older than Cal, getting ready to drape his legs around that impossible frenzy of bucking and twisting.

"Coolidge, what is that?" yelled Cal at him pointing through the fence boards at the butt of the writhing bull.

"I don't know..." yelled Coolidge back.

The bull raised its tail and released a soft and massive river of manure down its butt and legs.

"That, Coolidge! What's that?" A couple of cowboys standing nearby caught on and laughed a little at their drunken colleague.

"Bullshit?" said Coolidge.

"What is it?" said Cal cupping his ear like he couldn't hear, an angry expression on his face.

"That's bullshit!" yelled Coolidge. Hank was doubled over laughing. A dozen other cowboy spectators were laughing too.

"What did you say that is right there?" Cal asked once more, even more fiercely, reaching into the fence and pointing right at the pile at the bull's back feet.

"That's bullshit," screamed Coolidge this time as loud as he could.

"That's right, Coolidge. That's bullshit! And don't you ever forget it, either!" said Cal walking away. The cowboys pulled the gate open and the bull disappeared into the arena.

"Hey, Hank," asked Earl through the back window of the truck after the rodeo was over and Parker was navigating the line of trucks and horse trailers out of the parking lot, "we're out of the county, right?"

"Yep, but you didn't tell us you were holding!" whispered Hank angrily over his shoulder. Coolidge imagined he was drunk, but he couldn't tell. Hank seemed to be able to drink at will and never get loaded.

"We're not, but I thought maybe you were. Could make the ride back more interesting," said Earl.

"I see," said Hank. "Probably true." He turned to face forward again.

Parker said something to Cal, and the truck pulled over next to some horse trailers. Cal switched places with Parker, taking over the driving again. Cal was another person Coolidge had never seen falling down drunk, although most of the Schlitz was gone, so Cal had probably downed at least ten of them. That put him in close company with just about everyone else around them revving their V-8 engines and squealing out of the parking lot. It would have been easy pickings for the State Patrol sobriety units had they really cared to do their jobs. Although Cal did take note of a few cop cars ahead waiting on the road, rural Wisconsin was known for being more friendly to bars than to sobriety, so most DUI's, if they were issued at all, were only tacked onto actual accidents and then more as an afterthought than an incentive not to drink and drive.

The State's attitude toward hippies and pot was another matter, however.

The long line of departing rodeo fans and cowboys poured out onto the highway and gradually splintered off onto various winding rural roads leading back to isolated small towns and farms. Eventually, Cal left the traffic behind and was careening along a back road that turned quickly to dirt and washboards. The vibrations were bouncing the peons around in the back pretty badly.

"Hey, we're losing our teeth back here," yelled Earl. Cal slowed down and pulled over near a dark cornfield, killing the lights. Hank opened a metal flip lighter and lit a fat, home-rolled joint. He took a deep swooshing drag that pulled air into his lungs along with the smoke and passed it to Parker. Parker did the same, but he passed it back to Earl instead of Cal. Earl took a hit and so did Wyatt. Wyatt offered the joint to Coolidge who took it in his fingers but passed it on to Lenny. "No thanks," he said. *I need to think about this.* He was fascinated by marijuana, but it had been a long night, and the beers he had drunk were making him really tired in the cold and windy truck bed.

"Oh man, I'm game," said Lenny taking a big hit. Coolidge imagined Lenny's lungs were used to smoke, so he was surprised when Lenny started coughing uncontrollably. "Wow, strong shit," he said, the sweet-smelling smoke escaping from his lips. He passed the joint back up front where it made three more full rounds, the last one on a tiny alligator clip. Lenny coughed hard each time, and Hank ate the roach before Cal started the truck again and pulled back onto the road.

The washboards went on for a few more miles, then Cal thankfully turned onto a smooth highway again. "You guys reek," he said. He lit up a Swisher cigar, and its own legal version of sweet smoke infused the swirling winds on the long ride home.

Midnight Construction

"You don't smoke, Cool?" asked Wyatt a few days later when Earl was out on a ride and they were alone in the barn shaking hay.

"No, my dad smokes. I wish he didn't," said Coolidge.

"I mean, you know, Mary Joe Wanna," said Wyatt.

"Oh, never had any," said Coolidge.

"It would probably take you a few times to get high," said Wyatt leaning on the railing and looking out on the yard.

"Oh," said Coolidge. "Do you have some?" He put down his three-pronged pitchfork.

"Maybe, but it's hidden. Can't do any around here. Got to plan for it with Cal and Hank and go out of the county."

"Why? I mean, I get it not around here, but what do you mean, county?"

"It's a felony, so if someone gets caught, Cal doesn't want the trial to be in Barret County. Bad PR," said Wyatt. *So that's why Cal didn't take any hits...?*

"Has anyone ever been caught?" *That would suck.* He had heard of people going to jail for possession of pot, and even though he had read that it wasn't nearly as bad to smoke as people said it was, he wasn't sure. Even if smoking it could expand your mind, he wasn't sure he would ever take the risk of getting caught.

"Nope," said Wyatt. "We're real careful," and he walked under the railing to greet a tourist car pulling into the yard to sign up for a ride.

Another thing Coolidge soon learned the horse boys were real careful about was stealing stuff, again an activity that primarily happened out of the county.

"Cal says we're doing some midnight construction tonight," said Earl to Wyatt in the barn a few weeks later after a ride. Coolidge looked over and saw Cal chatting on the phone outside the granary with the long black cord of the receiver stretching from the screen door.

"Is that right?" said Wyatt. "What's up?"

"You know those logs we told him about when we went out of the county?" said Earl.

"Those big mothers?"

"Yep. Parker's coming with the truck. It's going to take all of us."

"Those things are heavy," said Wyatt.

"The plan is to pull them onto the truck with the Mustang's hitch."

"No way."

"Yep."

"That's going to be tricky."

"And noisy."

"But we'll get a breaking corral out of it."

"Yeah, those logs are oak. The corral will be there forever."

"Wow."

"Yep. You ready for a little midnight construction, Coolidge? You're going to need your gloves," said Earl. "And a few muscles..."

That evening Coolidge took the seven o'clock tourist ride and came back happy to see that Wyatt and Earl had already cleaned the barn. "Just let these horses out right into the corral," Earl said to him, meeting the ride. It was a young family celebrating a birthday with their nine-year old daughter and invited friends. Coolidge had spent the ride blithering on about TV characters who were related to other TV characters they couldn't possibly have been related to and about how all TV characters are required to have super powers whether they admit to having them or not.

"Well, I'm really glad you girls came on a ride with me tonight. Otherwise you would never have learned the truth about Porky Pig and his mother, Phyllis Diller. Jackie Gleason is his daddy. He can swallow watermelons whole."

"You're crazy, Coolidge!"

"I may be crazy, but I'd trade it for the ability to read minds and fly on vacuum cleaners like Mr. Rogers can."

"Mr. Rogers can't fly!"

"Oh yes he can. I've seen him, and so can alphabet soup! Ever see a chimpanzee eat Campbell's? Letters fly all over the place!"

"Ha, ha. You're nuts!"

Coolidge collected a five-dollar tip from the dad after all the kids hugged their horses goodbye. It was a good haul for him – laundry money, maybe even a cheeseburger at the Burger Barn. It was great to have all the horses out early too. He was exhausted.

"Shower time, maybe a nap, peons," said Cal when they walked into the cabin. He had his enormous black checkbook register spread out on his bed. "We head out at midnight. Full moon, but bring your flashlights and gloves." He closed the ledger and grabbed his towel and a change of clothes.

The Crane camp shower house was across the circular driveway from the dining hall, a mile drive from the barn. It had a boys and a girls side, but in the evening it was reserved for counselors and other adults at the camp. Usually, it was abandoned at that hour, but tonight there were a few women on the girls side.

Cal recognized a voice. "Hey Sarah, I need someone to scrub my back over here. You game?" She was an eighteen-year old counselor who had been there for many previous summers. Coolidge saw Cal smiling under the stream of hot water.

"You wish! Jackass," she yelled back, making everyone over there laugh. She surprised the horse boys a moment later by appearing on their side dressed only in a skimpy towel and holding a soapy washcloth in her hand. She walked up to Cal and slapped it on his back so hard she lost her towel. *Whoa!*

"Aah," said Cal. "Just what I needed! You really know how to keep a guy clean."

"It'll take more than soap," she said, picking up her towel. She threw the washcloth at him and marched back out the door scowling. Cheers greeted her return on the girls side.

She's gorgeous. Coolidge put his own towel in his lap even though he had yet to have his turn under the water. Cal got dressed and left.

Earl and Wyatt laughed about it afterward as Earl drove his Impala back to the stables in record time, raising dust the whole way and culminating with an especially creative and prolonged display of barnyard donuts. *They want me to nap after that?*

It seemed like only minutes after hitting the pillow in the top bunk that the sound of Parker's truck pulling in from Hillcrest woke him up several hours later.

"Get up, Coolidge. Time to get going. Gloves, jacket, flashlight," said Cal standing in the doorway.

Coolidge saw that Earl and Wyatt were already gone from the cabin. *When did they get up?* He rubbed his eyes. He jumped down from the bunk and pulled on his jeans and boots. *What are we doing, anyway?*

Outside he saw Hank toss a big hemp rope from the tack room into the back of Parker's pickup. Lenny nodded to him under the yard light that seemed too bright to Coolidge as he headed for the fence to take a leak. Maybe it was the head-lights from the running vehicles reflecting off the white corral fence that made him squint. Every light source was attracting moths and all sorts of other flying and crawling insects. He remembered Wyatt the other evening capturing a deer fly, a honeybee, a bumblebee, a centipede, a yellow jacket, and a potter's wasp all in the same jar to see who could duke it out to the end. Coolidge had bet on the yellow jacket because one had recently stung him on the tongue while he was eating a drumstick on a supper ride. He couldn't seem to kill it no matter how many times he tried to slap it away. But he was wrong - the centipede kicked everyone's ass, even the bumblebee by far the largest and most active combatant. Wyatt had bet on the bumblebee, and it came close, but the centipede's venom eventually stopped it cold. "Just shows you to be careful who you bump into," remarked Earl, collecting his winnings.

"Okay, Parker, follow me. We're headed toward Princeton. Hank knows where we're going," said Cal gesturing for the Crane crew to pile into his Mustang. "When we get there, it's a dirt driveway, narrow. Back in toward the logs so we can leave fast. We're going to need to work hard and smart." Coolidge noticed a thick piece of plywood in the back of Parker's truck as he climbed into the Mustang.

The highway was deserted as they pulled out of the stables and headed East away from Fieldsburg, but Cal didn't stay on it long. Soon they were headed south, out of the county, on a paved but obscure country road similar to the one that meandered from Crane to Hillcrest. In the back seat with Wyatt, Coolidge could see the shadows of trees on the edges of the fields they were passing in the moonlight. It was light enough to go for a walk, or even ride a horse. He imagined himself riding at that moment as if in a dream. Little wafts of cold night air pushed in around the edges of the window between the canvas roof of the convertible and the frame of the back window. It was almost too noisy to hear the conversation in the front seat. *I've got to stay awake.*

"Parker's truck can handle this many logs?" he heard Earl ask Cal.

"It'll ride on the axle, but we'll go back slow. Getting it loaded will be the trick," said Cal.

"With all of us we definitely can lift each end onto the back," said Earl.

"That's the idea, then the rope will pull them on. Wrap 'em twice, then use a barn knot."

"It's going to be noisy," continued Earl seriously.

"The house is a mile away. We should be fine, if we work fast. Shit!"

The panic-braking sent Coolidge's dozing head into the seat in front of him before Cal released the pedal and sped up again right away to prevent Parker's truck from back-ending him. Coolidge saw a flash of white and golden brown go by the window on the side of the road. *Huh?*

"Fuckin' A, deer," said Cal, pissed.

"Close one," replied Wyatt. "Nice maneuver."

"I wonder if Parker even saw them?" said Cal. He looked into his rearview mirror.

"He's okay," said Wyatt looking back over his shoulder.

Cal kept driving, a little slower now, but not much. Coolidge, adrenaline receding, somehow incorporated the near miss into his dream and drifted off again. He woke up when Cal finally stopped in front of what looked like a dirt driveway with a thin rope tied across it between two trees. Cal backed away from the driveway, put the car in park and jumped out. He cut the rope with his buck knife and gestured to Parker to swing by him. Parker waved and pulled ahead of the entrance and backed into the driveway. His headlights swept the forest around him revealing nettles and poison ivy in the far ditch. *Better wash with brown soap when*

I get back. It's hard to see what you are stepping on in the dark, even if the moon is out. Coolidge flexed his hands in his gloves and forced himself to wake up.

Cal quickly backed in following Parker's truck. The narrow, dirt logging road climbed a small hill and down the other side to a clearing. The logs were piled neatly here and there between huge brush piles of cut branches and leaves. As Coolidge followed everyone out of the vehicles, the smell of urine - the signature sour smell of oak - hit his nostrils. It reminded him of the ravine back home. Cal and Hank trained their flashlights onto the largest pile behind the truck. The logs were as wide as basketballs and cut in ten-foot lengths.

"Okay," Cal whispered. "Parker, back up a little more. Hank, hand me that rope and stretch it over the bed to the hitch. Earl, help me wrap this log right here. Let's go!"

Hank jumped into the cab and uncoiled the rope, relying on the ample moonlight to see what he was doing. Parker started the truck and eased the clutch out to position the back of the truck near the pile.

"All right, Coolidge, Wyatt, Earl, everybody, get a hold of this sucker and lift!" whispered Cal a little louder now. Coolidge found his way onto the pile and straddled the log behind the others.

"One, two, three, lift!" said Hank, and the end of the log came up enough for Cal to wrap the pale yellow rope around twice and tie it off on itself with a barn knot. Coolidge's leg slipped on the top of one of the logs below him, but he caught himself before he lost his footing.

Cal sprinted to the Mustang and wrapped the other end of the rope around the hitch on the back bumper. The red brake lights on the truck were shining on Coolidge's face behind Wyatt's torso in front of him. He heard the Mustang start and felt the jerk of the rope on the log. It moved forward between his legs. "Don't drop it," said Wyatt stumbling forward with the log in his arms.

"Lift! Lift!" said Hank, yelling now, in spite of himself. The edge of the log went up and forward onto the plywood on the truck bed, and the peons let go and scurried off the pile. From the side Hank and Earl guided the log as the rope pulled it farther onto the truck. When the balance point was reached it teetered into the bed, depressing the springs.

"Stop, Cal!" Hank yelled, and Cal did so and backed up the Mustang to create slack. Hank pulled the barn knot and released the rope. "Okay, peons, push this mother the rest of the way in," he said. Wyatt got behind the back of the log and leaned into it, and everyone else lifted and pushed from the side. The log slid the rest of the way to the front of the bed. It still stuck out a good four feet. They were committed now. One in. A bunch more to go.

"All right, next one. Hurry," said Hank. Despite the cold night air, sweat glistened on his forehead in the moonlight. Coolidge was a fully awake and breathing hard.

The second log was both easier and more difficult to get onto the truck. The first log interfered a bit with the path of entry and provided places for hands and feet to get disastrously trapped, but the communication was good, and the routine, although dangerous, wasn't rocket science: Lift the log, wrap the rope, pull the log with the car, untie the rope, push the log into place. The second log maxed out the springs on the truck, but the goal was at least eight posts for the breaking corral. They kept going. The logs in the truck pressed against the upright stakes in the sides of the bed.

They worked fast. Soon there was just enough room for one final log. "Let's get this last one, boys," said Hank. *It can't hold another one, can it?* The final log would require extreme lifting to land the edge of it on top of the others already on the truck. They managed it, but as Hank was wrapping the rope, the leaves in the trees above them brightened like a lampshade, and the sound of an engine suddenly coming up the hill startled everybody.

"Fuck," said Earl. "Someone's coming."

"Act cool," said Hank. "We're just workers doing a job. Hey Cal!"

But Cal had already seen the lights through his windshield. He got out of the Mustang and walked back to the truck, shoulders tight, to talk to Hank. *Is it the police? We're definitely caught - why else would somebody be driving here in the middle of the night? Run away! But where would I go? How would I even know where I am much less find my way back? And back where? The stables? Milwaukee?* He felt a liquid sensation of fear grow around his eyes and flow around his ears and down into his chest. *These logs do not belong to us. We're stealing.*

"Coolidge, don't look at the lights. Just keep working," whispered Wyatt. Coolidge obeyed and joined Wyatt as he lifted the log so Hank could finish wrapping the rope.

A truck door opened. "I thought you said guys weren't coming back until Monday?" a strange voice yelled. Coolidge snuck a look at the man standing now in the headlights of his pickup truck, door left open behind him.

"Yeah, sucks - we got double booked," said Cal looking him straight in the eye.

"Well, it's a little late to be logging, ain't it?" said the man suspiciously. He came closer and looked at the peons and the rope wrapped around the last log.

"Yeah, it's a bitch," replied Cal, "but we need to get these logs out of here before the rain, and this training crew wants the overtime. You didn't get the message? Hope we're not disturbing you..." He turned back to the logs as if he was anxious to get back to work.

"Oh, no," the man said. He raised his hand to his forehead and scratched. "Just wondering what was going on, that's all..."

"Yeah, well, nice cool night to work, so we're not complaining," said Cal turning back and tipping his hat. "Come on, boys. The sooner we get this load on the sooner we can finish this job!"

The peons lifted the last log once again and Parker repositioned the rope. The man watched them work a moment longer then walked back to his vehicle shaking his head. He put the truck in gear. His headlights brushed the treetops again as he backed down the hill. *I can't believe he let us go.*

"Come on, let's get this one loaded before that guy figures it out and calls the sheriff," grunted Cal attaching the rope one last time to his hitch. The final log, a monster, fell into place. Earl and Wyatt pushed it forward and unwrapped the rope from the log. They then tied it across the load to each side panel of the truck and jumped down. "Let's get the hell out of Dodge," said Earl, laughing as he fell into the Mustang's front passenger seat. "No shit, Sherlock," said Wyatt piling in next to Coolidge and Lenny in the back. Cal said nothing, but he pulled a tab on a can of Pabst Blue Ribbon and started slowly down the driveway.

Coolidge looked back at Parker's truck behind them with Parker smiling at the wheel and Hank laughing in the dash lights next to him. As Cal led the way, Coolidge kept himself turned backward toward the crime scene transfixed by Parker's truck straining and lurching down the rutted road, a mechanical red tortoise carrying a world of too much wrong on its back.

The Corral

Despite fatigue from the long slow drive back to Crane on untraveled back roads, pushing the logs out of the truck behind the granary was way easier than getting them in, and the Hillcrest crew was able to successfully drive back to their cabin before the sun came up. Mission accomplished.

The giant logs looked like fallen Roman columns to Coolidge when he passed by them on his morning trudge to the outhouse, even more trudge-like this morning after so little sleep. They smelled like the forest the night before, only fainter. *Did that really all happen?* An empty Pabst can was in the sand between two of the logs. He picked it up, crushed it in his hands, and stuck it in his back pocket. *Bad PR to leave beer cans around, especially here near the road to camp.* There was no breakfast ride that morning, *thank God*, but they brought the horses in before breakfast anyway. "We've got to make those logs look like they've been here a long time," said Cal to them in the barn. "Earl, lay out that breaking corral the way you need it, and I'll pick up the rails."

So, it was full day of leading rides for Coolidge, one after the other, but each time he circled back to the barn to mount the next ride he saw progress on the corral. After the nine o'clock instruction ride, Wyatt and Earl had dug eight post holes in a circle the diameter of Cal's Mustang.

Piles of dirt and rock were next to each hole. A posthole digger rested nearby, and Earl and Wyatt both were completely sweaty when they took a break and helped riders on and off the horses. Coolidge was actually happy that day to lead each ride. Despite his festering saddle sores, making jokes in the cool morning sunshine and pulling on dew-covered pine branches to drop water on the camp riders behind him for laughs seemed way better than digging for hours with a post hole digger.

After the ten o'clock ride, he saw Cal was back from town with boards hanging out of the back of his car. The giant oak posts were all standing up in their holes now. *How did they lift those logs like that?* He saw tire tracks, some smaller logs scattered about, and big metal bars they must have used for leverage somehow. When the eleven o'clock ride returned at noon, the posts were all tamped in, the railings were nailed up around the circle and a strong gate was hanging between the front two posts. The structure was basically a giant cage, Stonehenge-like, and Earl looked almost too tired to drive his Impala to lunch. Cal and Wyatt were spent as well. With the ground raked clean around the structure, though, it was true that the whole thing looked like it had been there a long time. Cal had gotten his wish. If possession is nine tenths of the law, these posts clearly belonged to the stables now. It would take a crane to lift them back out of those holes.

And no one did come to question the stables about the logs. The man in the pick-up truck, presumably the owner of the land, clearly hadn't thought of writing down license plate numbers, and that's understandable. It's hard to think straight in those situations, late as it was. A theft report was undoubtedly filed in the other county, but no one noticed who might have put two and two together.

There were other midnight construction projects: a utility truck left over-night in a field had some locks cut and tools purloined. A pile of lumber slated for county use as a picnic structure for a park mysteriously disappeared. Coolidge strongly disliked these adventures – they made him anxious as hell and screwed up his needed sleep, actually - but there was not much he could say about them. He was a horse boy now too, after all.

It wasn't long before they could put Wyatt's breaking corral design to the test on an untrained horse. Marvin called to say he finally had time to put the thing on his truck and swing by. "This is a young gelding, a real asshole," he said to Cal on the phone. "He's a fast motherfucker in the pasture, but unbreakable, according to the owner. Bucks everyone off. Sent the guy to the hospital with a broken leg. I know it's late in the summer for you, but if you feel like giving this appaloosa a shot, there's no charge. I'm sending him to Canada if you don't want him." Canadians loved horse meat, according to Marvin, and although Marvin didn't tell too many people about it for PR reasons, that's where he liked to ship his old or impossibly recalcitrant horses. "Those bastards will eat anything up there," he said when Cal pushed him on the politics of the subject.

"Sure, I told you we'd take him," said Cal. "You didn't think Tequila could ever be broken, and now he's a great lead horse," he added. Coolidge, getting water from the refrigerator and overhearing the conversation, had really not had a chance to see if Tequila was great as a lead horse. Tequila was impossible for him to even catch much less get on. When Earl and Wyatt rode him, they needed to constantly pull back hard on the reins to keep him from galloping. He was a high-strung prancer with jumpy eyes and saliva that flung from his mouth with every shake of his head. Riding Tequila looked scary, but interestingly challenging in a way, like cliff diving. He was Earl's favorite horse, probably because the horse's acceleration and hoof marks in the sand reminded him of his Impala, and the thrill of successfully riding him required finesse and skill not unlike completing a perfect thirty-foot dive off the highest cliff at the quarry.

But this new appaloosa put Tequila to shame. The first thing the horse did after arriving in Marvin's truck early the next morning was to kick or crush anyone foolish enough to get near him. Wyatt got the closest, but the kicking was just too wild for him to untie the lead rope from the front of the truck.

"Marvin, how the hell did you get this horse in the truck?" Wyatt asked.

"I drugged the bastard," he said.

Finally, Cal climbed up over the side panels and reached down from above to untie the lead rope. The horse turned around immediately and jumped off the ramp, and it was all Cal could do to jump off the truck with him and keep a grip on the lead rope while the frightened horse snorted and pranced around the yard. "Son of a bitch!" said Cal.

"You'd think he still had his nuts on him the way he's acting," said Marvin once Cal finally succeeded in twisting a rope onto the horse's nose. Appaloosas are famous for having spooky eyes, and this horse was no exception. The look was pure terror, even though the horse was choosing to stand at the moment because of the invasive pain Cal was inflicting on his compressed nostrils. Coolidge couldn't imagine the nightmare this horse must have been for its previous owner. It was clearly one that had grown up without any handling in a big wild pasture someplace. *A wild horse from hell.*

"Okay, Marvin. Leave it to you to always find the winners," said Cal. "Earl, go clear out a stall. Let's tie this beast in the barn for now."

"Good luck, assholes!" said Marvin climbing back into his truck.

It was Wyatt who discovered the horse's phenomenal aim with his back feet. After Cal tied it up to the front of the stall it unleashed a furious forward kick with its back hoof, clipping him in the shin. "You fucking piece of shit!' Cal yelled. "Rim Tank! I'm calling you Rim Tank after Tim Reinke! Sneaky, backstabbing, worthless, maintenance crew asshole of a horse. We're breaking you today, you fucking two-faced piece of dog crap!" he said. He punched the horse as hard as he could in the front thigh. Rim Tank didn't seem to even notice but just gave Cal the evil eye. Cal gave its hind end a wide berth when he left the stall rubbing his leg.

Wyatt had a broom in his hand in the next stall over. "Let's see something," he said, after Cal was out of the way. He extended the broom head behind Rim Tank. Crack! The back hoof snapped the broom and sent the head flying into the wall of the barn. It landed in a fresh pile of manure.

"Whoa, now that's accuracy!" said Wyatt. Wyatt repeated the test with a board, a yard stick, a bucket on a broom handle - it didn't matter; Rim Tank hit them all dead on. "Fuckin' A amazing," said Wyatt. "I suggest we not go behind this one for a while."

"I've got a better idea," said Earl. He picked up the broken board and grabbed a long thin rope from the tack room. Carefully, he rigged what looked like a child's swing over the rear end of Rim Tank. He held the board far behind the horse and safely out of range until it was set up. Then, when everything was measured the way he wanted it, he released it. It swung down from the rafters and hit Rim Tank squarely on the hocks prompting the expected reaction of a deadly and accurate kick to the board. This time, though, instead of splintering and falling away, the board simply swung up and came back to hit the horse again in the same place. Again Rim Tank kicked the board, and again the swing flew up wildly only to return as before, over and over.

Two things happened as the horse boys enjoyed the show – the first was that Rim Tank became even more accurate in his kicks. He anticipated the return of the swing and hit the board with another kick sometimes before it even reached his hocks. The second was that, after a good fifteen minutes or so, he eventually gave up kicking the board. It came to rest on his quivering and sweaty back legs.

"This horse is either extremely smart, or extremely dumb. I can't figure out which," said Earl.

In any case, the first instruction riders of the morning had arrived, and soon Coolidge and Wyatt were busy teaching them the parts of the horse and taking them out to learn to trot. When they came back from the lesson, Coolidge saw that Cal and Earl had somehow moved Rim Tank to the new breaking corral. Amazingly, they had also managed to get a bridle on its head and a blanket onto its back. Cal was holding the reins and Earl was cooing and patting it on the neck. He slowly laid the blanket on its back and removed it over and over again. Rim Tank tolerated it but with jittery and menacing eyes. Wyatt let the campers watch for a little bit before sending them back down the road. "Rim Tank's so beautiful! He has spots! I want to ride him!" they said as they raced each other back to their cabins.

It was a light morning, and no one from in town had come by or even called for a ride yet, so Wyatt and Coolidge watered the horses and put them back in the barn stalls to rest. By the time they finished and came back to the corral to watch the action, Earl had a small saddle on Rim Tank. They watched as he took it off and put it on over and over again, each time Rim Tank tolerating it a bit better. Cal loosened his grip on the bridle. He seemed to be losing some patience watching Earl work so slowly. Earl, for his part, was happy to proceed one baby step at a time. He had his eye on Rim Tank's karate-like back feet.

"All right, Earl, enough pussy-footing around. Let's test this fancy corral of yours and break this horse!" said Cal.

"Okay," said Earl. He tightened the cinch on the saddle, grabbed the saddle horn, and gingerly leaned his torso onto the seat. Rim Tank reacted and skittered sideways into the boards. Earl stayed with him and continued to apply increasing weight to the saddle while Cal hung on tightly to the reins. Earl persisted adding more weight. He cooed, "There now, whoa, whoa, Rim Tank, shhh, shhh..." Rim Tank turned his spotted head abruptly back toward Earl. *Was he going to bite him?* Cal jerked his head forward again.

"Come on, Earl. Goddammit, get on this horse! How do they get anything done down under screwing around like this all day?" Cal spit on the sandy ground.

Coolidge wondered if Earl would take offense to this. He knew Earl was proud of the time he spent last year in Australia on a ranch that raised Santa Gertrudis cattle and where they always broke their horses in this type of corral. Earl was always talking about the ranchers down there, and Coolidge figured he had probably learned the rope swing trick from them that had worked so well. Earl seemed to know what he was doing around wild horses, but Cal was the boss, so Earl went ahead and put his foot in the stirrup and applied pressure.

Whereas Rim Tank up to this point had only exhibited nervous and dubious curiosity about the breaking corral proceedings, his reaction when Earl finally straddled him with his full weight was immediate and violent. Rim Tank lunged forward, jerking Cal's arm and shoulder, and leaped immediately into a bucking frenzy. He seemed to rise straight up and down without paying any heed to the supposed inhibiting effects of the closeness of the railings and posts. Earl, holding tight to the saddle horn, managed to stay on for a while, but then the saddle slipped sideways and tipped him toward the fence. He dropped the horn and lunged for the top board. He clawed at it like a desperate cat and pulled himself off the horse. Rim Tank skittered sideways and tried to kick off the saddle dangling upside down under its belly. He eventually succeeded, despite Cal hitting him on the nose with his fist and yelling, "Whoa, you piece of shit!" Rim Tank backed up against the railing, the saddle beneath his hooves. It was a standoff.

"Earl, get that saddle back on this horse!" Cal said once Rim Tank calmed down a bit. Earl lifted the blanket and saddle carefully from the ground and kicked them with his heel to knock the sand off. He let Rim Tank smell the blanket before he began the same slow process of placing it on his back and then the saddle on and off, over and over.

"Yank on that cinch as much as you can this time, Earl," said Cal. You could tell Rim Tank didn't like that idea, but he just stood with his legs spread and snorted a few times when Earl tugged on the latigo. Cal handed Earl the reins, and they switched places.

"All right, Rim Tank, let's see what you're really made of," said Cal and in a flash he was on his back. Again, Rim Tank exploded, bucking back and forth across the cramped corral. Cal, whooping, held onto the horn with one hand and his hat with the other. Between the tightness of the space and Earl pulling down on Rim Tank's head with all his might, it was true that the corral partially curtailed the power of his bucking. Still, Cal only lasted ten seconds or so before he was eating dust and scrambling for the railings to avoid Rim Tank's deadly feet. "Jesus Christ, that horse has spirit!" he said. "We're either going to break this fucker, or he's going to break us!" A moment later he was back on for a repeat ride. In a flash Rim Tank bucked him off again. "Son of a two-bit whore," said Cal, rubbing his legs where they had smashed into the railing. "We need some fresh riders."

"Wyatt, Coolidge, get in here. Earl and I need a break, and this horse needs to be ridden."

"Are you ready, Cool?" asked Wyatt. "It's our turn at the rodeo. Just hold on as long as you can and get away from his feet fast when you fall off." He pulled his hat down firmly on his head and ducked under the bottom railing into the corral.

Reluctantly, Coolidge bent down to follow. He remembered the beer can he had found in the sand there that morning and wished he could drink a full one for courage. His peripheral vision was suddenly blurring. *I'm shaking with fear. Corral or portal to the underworld?* His gloved hands gripped the bottom rail tightly as he rolled in after Wyatt.

"Grab the reins from Earl, Coolidge," said Cal from the top railing. *I'm trapped – like the insects in the jar.* Coolidge's mouth was as dry as the sand beneath his boots.

"Hold the reins down as much as you can when Wyatt gets on," said Earl from between the railings, "and stay in front of him no matter what happens."

"Whoa, Rim Tank. That's a boy. Whoa," said Wyatt stepping next to Coolidge and gently lifting his armpit over Rim Tank's nose. "Put his nose in your armpit - it helps if they know your scent," he said to Coolidge moving away to give him room, but Coolidge couldn't do that because Rim Tank's eye, an optical Cerberus to everything fearsome, was focused right on him. *Put his nose in my pit? No way.*

"Hold the reins tight, now, Coolidge. Stay nimble and strong. Easy, boy. Whoa now. Here we go!" said Wyatt as he put his boot in the stirrup and hauled himself up. Rim Tank reacted once again like an explosion. He lurched and bucked like mad, spraying mouth foam onto the boards of the corral. Coolidge leaned over and pulled hard on the reins. *Is this animal going to land on top of me?* More slobber from Rim Tank's snorting mouth sprayed Coolidge's face with every leap and stomp of its hooves.

"Whoa, whoa, whoa," said Coolidge. Behind him he saw Wyatt's body hit the ground. Rim Tank crashed into the railing.

"Hang on to him, Coolidge!" he heard Cal yell. "Move him forward, move him forward!"

Coolidge had no control, but because he was trying not to get stepped on, he successfully pulled the horse away from Wyatt by accident. His arm felt like it had been ripped from his shoulder, but he held on to keep his balance, and Rim Tank rebounded from the railing to the middle of the corral and stood there shaking. His eyes were shining with anger, panic and despair. The saddle was still upright on his back, and Wyatt stood up and moved quickly toward Coolidge. Wyatt grabbed the reins from Coolidge. "You okay?" he asked.

"Are you okay?" said Coolidge.

"I'll live," said Wyatt. He breathed hard, then winced. *He's in pain.*

"Wyatt, check that cinch before Coolidge gets on," said Cal.

Coolidge looked in panic at his boss on the railing above him. *My shoulder hurts a lot. Will that work as an excuse?* One look at Cal's expression gave him the answer. *Why not wear football equipment? Some hip and shoulder pads, and even a cup would be pretty nice right now.* He looked back at the sweaty horse. *He's feeling what I'm feeling.* Coolidge felt sorry for him all of a sudden.

"I'll do it," Coolidge said. Wyatt rubbed his arm and hung onto the reins. Coolidge grabbed the saddle, reached down and gave the cinch a firm tug making Rim Tank dance nervously and turn his head as if to bite them both in the back. Wyatt jumped and jerked the reins downward to divert the horse's head. Rim Tank stomped his front hooves and swung his back end into the corral's railings away from Coolidge. *How am I ever going to get on this wild animal? Is this what they go through with every horse here?* Fear flowed in waves from his stomach to the ends of all his limbs weakening them. *I can't squeeze my hands together.*

"Get on the horse, now Coolidge, while he's up against the railing," said Cal. "You can bail onto the railing if you need to. Wyatt, keep the head next to the railing if you can."

The out of control feeling increased as Coolidge approached the saddle and realized that he was about to climb onto a horse without holding onto reins. He had been riding just long enough to come to depend on reins like a parachutist depends upon a pull cord. *Steering is the least of your problems right now.* Rim Tank had stopped prancing, but his leg muscles were twitching. "Whoa now, boy, whoa," said Wyatt into Rim Tank's ear. *Does that really do any good?* Coolidge put his left hand on the saddle horn and lifted his left boot tip to the stirrup applying a little weight. Rim Tank didn't flinch or move away, so Coolidge put more weight on saddle.

"You've got this, Cool," said Wyatt. "Take your time."

"Get on and ride that horse, Coolidge!" contradicted Cal. Coolidge noticed Earl looking down at him now from the top railing. *Must have climbed up there to get a better view with Cal.*

"Swing your leg over slowly, and hang on," Earl said.

Thinking it was better to get it over with, Coolidge swallowed dryly and somehow made his hands grab the horn. He put his full weight onto the saddle. Miraculously, Rim Tank stood still for this. *Maybe I'm okay.* Slowly Coolidge swung his right boot over the saddle and eased it between the horse and the tight railings. Gently he felt for the stirrup on that side and slipped just the toe of his boot into it. The last thing he wanted was for his feet to fall through the stirrup and get stuck. "Whoa now, boy, whoa, whoa, shh, shh," he said as much to himself as to the bomb ticking beneath him.

"Nice going, Cool," said Earl. "You're a natural."

"You've got it, Coolidge," said Wyatt patting Rim Tank on the neck. Suddenly the horse staggered forward brushing Coolidge's right leg hard into the railing. Coolidge lifted his leg instinctually to keep it from getting crushed, and just at that moment the powder keg exploded. The front of the saddle dipped downward abruptly pulling Coolidge forward onto the horn where his hands gripped frantically. Then Rim Tank raised his neck and front hooves off the ground, yanked the reins from Wyatt's hands and sent Coolidge backwards twisting like a high diver. His right leg, already out of the stirrup had nothing to stand up on, so his weight fell awkwardly onto his left foot in the other stirrup. The huge expanse of the bucking horse ripped his hands from the saddle horn and catapulted him over the back of the saddle and onto the hind quarters of the Appaloosa. Looking down, Coolidge saw the spots on Rim Tank's hide just as the next buck lifted him high in the air. Rim Tank moved forward when he felt Coolidge's weight launch from his hindquarters. He aimed and kicked his left rear leg at Coolidge's head.

The blow landed perfectly, of course, right on the back of Coolidge's skull. Like a cartoon cliché, Coolidge experienced a flash of bright light accompanied by clanging bells and weird bird calls. Time disappeared. He did not feel himself fall to the ground, but moments later, when the flashing cacophony in his head dissipated slightly, Coolidge realized he was still in danger. Rim Tank's feet were stomping next to and between his legs. Coolidge twisted away to escape the hooves and rolled under the bottom board out of the corral. Looking back through the dust, he saw that Earl had jumped down and was helping Wyatt regain control of the reins.

"Are you okay, Coolidge?" It was Cal standing over him.

"My head hurts," said Coolidge recognizing pain now that panic had subsided. *But I'm alive.* His entire right ear was numb. "I think he kicked me."

"Yep, he sure did. What a kick in the head!" said Cal laughing. "Stand up, Coolidge. We've got to make sure you're okay."

Coolidge got to his knees. He wasn't dizzy or anything, but his vision was a bit blurry. He stood up and leaned against Cal.

"Look at me," said Cal. Cal peered into Coolidge's eyes. "Are you dizzy or nauseated?"

"No," said Coolidge. "It just hurts." He stood back from Cal and wiped the tears on his face with his forearm.

"You're all right. Get a bag of ice from the granary and drink some water. We'll go to lunch, then Earl and I will take care of Rim Tank this afternoon. Wyatt, give the horse to Earl! Coolidge, you and Wyatt handle the rides this afternoon."

"Okay, Cal," said Coolidge rubbing his head and backing away from the corral.

"What a kick in the head!" said Cal again with enthusiasm, as he climbed back into the corral.

"Hold on, Cool. I'm coming with you," said Wyatt rolling himself out as Coolidge had done. He handed Coolidge back his hat and walked with him quietly to the granary.

Going to lunch, each lurch of Earl's steering wheel hurt Coolidge's head, but the packed afternoon horse rides were even worse. Wyatt, realizing Coolidge was off his game, took charge and led the rides, but Coolidge still had to follow, groggy and dispirited as he was. Coolidge refused to share the tip from the three o'clock tourist ride. "I wasn't much help, Wyatt. You keep it."

That afternoon, each time the horses returned to the stables to load up a new ride, Coolidge looked over at Rim Tank in the breaking corral. There wasn't much action to see, just Cal standing with him waiting for Earl to finish helping with the ride. At four o'clock, Wyatt asked how it was going and offered to switch with Earl, but Earl refused. The reputation of his Australian corral design was on the line. "We're making progress," he said, "but that horse is crazier than Wings." Wyatt laughed. Earl and Wyatt enjoyed making Wings references. Wings was the consistently smashed bartender at Benny's who winked and believed their fake ID's. That didn't mean they didn't mess with him. He was a notorious sucker for any sort of bullshit they slung his way.

"Well, okay, then. Maybe you should feed it some beer?" Wyatt replied.

"Or a No-Pest Strip," said Earl. From the looks of him, Earl had had a rough afternoon. His face was filthy and there was a distinctive limp to his walk as he headed back to Cal. Coolidge rubbed the knot on his head and turned his horse to follow the last ride of the afternoon. Wyatt was singing a cowboy song about blood on the saddle to the campers, but Coolidge thought he was screaming it out for Earl's benefit:

"Oh, there's blood on the saddle!

And blood on the ground!

Great big sploodles of blood all around!

There lies a cowboy

All covered in red

'Cause that darn horse just

Squashed in his head!

There's blood on the saddle,

And blood on the ground,

Great big sploodles of blood all around."

Wyatt decided to take the last ride around the lake, which was a relief for Coolidge because once the horses were on that long loop, they just went along on automatic pilot because there weren't any short cuts to the barn. Clomping along the edge of the road as it meandered its way past cottages and small parks was pleasant, and the campers always enjoyed getting out of the camp property, so they didn't need as much verbal bantering to keep them entertained.

It was a welcome mellow ride in the back for Coolidge. He needed the rest because when they got back to the stables at 5:00, he saw that Rim Tank was out of the corral and tied up by his bridle to a post next to the barn. Just the sight of his whitish grey coat covered with hundreds of black spots was enough to trigger the same fear in Coolidge as when he was launched and kicked by him that morning. He could feel the whole experience again in his stomach as he slid off his horse and helped Earl and Wyatt dismount the campers. He rubbed the huge swollen bruise on the side of his head. *Still hurts.* They watered each horse, and then put them all back into their stalls. Each time he passed near Rim Tank, Coolidge couldn't help but look into his changed eyes. They weren't nervously twitching any more, just empty now staring out into space. He didn't seem to even react to the other horses walking past him on their way to the barn for food. Rim Tank was just standing there, flies gathering around him, tail barely twitching.

"Coolidge!" Cal's voice reached him in the barn from outside. All the horses were inside now munching hay gratefully except for Rim Tank still out in the sun. "Get out here. There's a horse out here you need to ride!" Coolidge looked over the barn door and saw Cal sitting on the spool table tugging on a beer.

Coolidge unlatched the gate to the barn door and stepped back outside. The campers were all gone now, anxious to get to the lake for a swim before dinner. He noticed the water trough was almost empty. He picked up the hose by the barn wall and dropped the end into the trough. He was about to pull the handle on the faucet to start the water flowing when Cal said, "Stop fucking with the hose, Coolidge. You can do that later. Get on that horse tied up right there," he said gesturing to Rim Tank.

Immediately Coolidge remembered crawling away from Rim Tank's kicking feet, the desperation of that moment, the pain and fear. *What the hell?*

"It's okay. He won't buck. Get on," said Cal.

There was not one part of Coolidge's nervous system that believed him. He believed instead his past history with this horse. *Cal's an asshole.* All Coolidge wanted was to drink some cold water and lie down. Not repeat that morning's nightmare. He felt exhausted, like he had run ten miles through the ravine back home, only without the sense of accomplishment that usually accompanied his efforts. His head hurt when he looked anywhere other than straight ahead. *Will I need an ambulance when I get kicked in the head again? My mother is paralyzed and needs help getting in and out of a wheelchair. Am I next?*

There are corners in life, dead ends, dilemmas, that inevitably make you grow when you finally escape them, if you get a chance to escape them. But how one grows afterward is a fair question. Toward beauty and fulfillment? Or toward expansion of personal compromise, loneliness, and resentment? Coolidge knew the dead end he was in with Cal's frowning expectations. He knew protests were futile and he would ultimately get on Rim Tank standing there in the yard, and that he would hate it... probably...or maybe not anymore. He could no longer think beyond the pain in the back of his head. He obeyed Cal like a machine, no matter how he felt about him in his heart. *Whose legs are these, walking toward this horse? Whose foot is this slipping into this stirrup? Whose crotch is settling into the saddle? Whose hands desperately grip this worthless saddle horn? Whose body am I inside of?*

Rim Tank, broken now, just sat there, no more concerned about Coolidge on his back than about the flies sucking moisture from his nostrils and eyes. Coolidge stayed on him silently for a while, dizzy and staring straight ahead. Then he got off and trudged back to the barn to help the others finish the day's chores.

The Cabin on the Other Side of the Lake

For the remainder of July, Rim Tank became a reliable horse. He never bucked again, and he learned to lead eventually due to constant work by the peons pulling his head aside and kicking him onto alternative paths. He had a plodding walk and trot, but a very smooth and fast cantor. "We need to send him to Hillcrest before the pack trips start," said Cal to everyone at the next meeting. "We'll need an extra lead horse over there for August."

As much as Coolidge got used to riding Rim Tank, he was glad that Marvin hadn't brought any additional wild horses for them to break. Passing the breaking corral on the way to the outhouse each morning was enough to keep the painful memory of the whole experience alive for him, even if regular headaches weren't already doing the job. He didn't complain, though, or go to a doctor. There was work to do, and he could still breathe and walk. Each day was busy, packed in fact, and the others depended on him. There would be many stories to tell his school friends next fall when he started high school.

One story he wanted to tell but couldn't yet was about "getting a chick." Nearest he could count, Earl and Wyatt had hustled a dozen girls between them, and God knows how many Parker entertained over at Hillcrest. According to

Lenny, if he hadn't been sleeping out under the stars with chicks of his own all the time he would have to have "put up with Parker's squeaking mattress every night." What was bullshit and what was truth about these stories Coolidge could never tell, but he felt that if even a small percentage of them were true, then out of all the peons he was certainly the one who was inadequate and missing out.

"You can go midnight riding anytime you want, Coolidge," said Wyatt in the granary during the next meeting. They were waiting their turn to talk to the bosses and pulling on the top half of a Point Beer from the fridge. Earl opened the screen door and poured half his out onto the grass and said, "No one ever drinks the bottom half of a Point unless they were too drunk to know the difference because it tastes like crap." No one disagreed, but the rest of them tried to do it anyway because the beer was free.

"Just grab some twine and go for it. White Devil leads, and she has a nice round back," continued Wyatt. Coolidge thought about his advice. *But what bullshit should I use to get a girl to come back at night, mess around with me? Probably acting crazy won't work. Earl leads a tourist ride and the cutest girl on the ride comes back at night for sex. How does he do it? What's his secret?*

Earl, second only to Cal in mastering of use of bullshit to get what he wants, told intriguing stories about his conquests but was not exactly a forthcoming teacher. Wyatt could tell, though, that Coolidge wanted some coaching. "It's not that hard, Cool. Just be nice to them and ask them. They usually want you as much as you want them."

That can't be true. He didn't believe that girls felt the same inevitable arousal every time they saw a body bouncing up and down on a saddle. Did they almost faint from a rush of eye-blinding desire at the glimpse of an inadvertently exposed nipple or bit of underwear? *I doubt it. I'm supposed to say, "Hey, do you feel horny? Do you want to touch me as much as I want to touch you?" No way!*

But I can at least try to bullshit someone to come on a midnight ride. Why not? I can talk about how fun midnight riding is, how the shadows look so cool in the pasture under the moonlight, how it's so great I do it all the time, etc. Oh, and I could say there is no charge for it either. A free ride! Maybe, Lenny is right, that once a chick is on the horse behind you there's nothing they won't do later. Maybe I could just transition somehow from them hugging me on the horse to hugging me in the hay? These thoughts swirled, but he just didn't know anything for sure. Coolidge certainly wasn't interested in forcing himself onto anybody, but if the process of a midnight ride resulted in sex, who was he to say no? *Maybe it was a bit like using the breaking corral for horses: control the location, whittle away resistance slowly, insist on results. Slow and steady bullshit's the key, like slipping a blanket and a saddle on them for the first time. Huh! If I don't get kicked in the head again! With my luck...*

The chance to practice his theory came for Coolidge the next Saturday afternoon. Sign-ups for tourist rides had been moderate, and only one peon was needed for the sparsely attended rides going out. Just as Earl was about to take his turn and disappear down the trail with a family of five, a small but attractive teen-age girl appeared by herself from the road to camp.

"I've come for a ride," she said. "I live on the lake." That explained why she had cut through the camp instead of coming in a car. The dirt road through camp was the quickest way to walk to the stables from the private cottages on the lake.

"Hey, no problem," said Coolidge. "You're just in time. There's a ride going out right now. Hold on, Wyatt, one more!" he yelled. "What's your name?"

"Jo," the girl said.

"Okay," said Wyatt. "Always room for one more cow girl!"

"I'm not really a cow girl," Jo said when Coolidge brought out White Devil for her. "I've just seen your horses go by so often I wanted to give them a try. I've never ridden before." She smiled at him.

"Well, that's great! This is our gentlest horse, White Devil. She's so gentle we always put her at the end of the line. You'll get a great view of the ride from there. It's easy. Here put your foot right here. Now grab the horn and climb on. Up you go. Good! Let me adjust the stirrups for you. Hang onto the reins now – they are your brakes; pull back if you need to stop and give White Devil a little kick to go if she falls behind."

Coolidge checked the cinch carefully and adjusted the stirrups. The girl had short-ish dark hair and wore a white blouse that fell open a bit as she got on the horse. He noticed that her breasts were small and held tightly in place with a bra. She patted White Devil on the neck affectionately.

"I would never kick a horse. Isn't that mean?" Jo asked.

"Hey, Coolidge," yelled Wyatt from the front. "Looks like we're going to need you on this ride," he said with a grin. "Grab Rim Tank and ride in front of White Devil."

"That's Wyatt," said Coolidge to Jo. "Okay, Wyatt, I'm on it," and he jogged to the barn to bring out Rim Tank.

Soon the ride was winding its way through the pine trees and down the trail toward the lake.

"So, Wyatt," yelled Coolidge from the back. "Jo here lives on the lake!"

"Well, I'll be hornswoggled!" said Wyatt. "Is she a duck?" Jo laughed.

"No, well, I don't know. She doesn't look like a duck. Are you a duck? She lives in a cabin on the edge of the lake."

"Well, then, hi Jo! How about we ride to your house, eh? Do you want to?"

"Sure," said Jo. "I thought that is where you always go..."

"Oh no," said Coolidge. "Rides around the lake are tiring for the horses. Only special people get the round the lake ride."

"Well, there must be a lot of special people because I see them all the time," said Jo.

"Yeah, we go around pretty often. It's a great trail," admitted Wyatt.

"This is our third ride this summer, and we've never been around the lake!" the ten-year old boy with his parents and cousins ahead of Coolidge piped in.

"See, Jo," said Coolidge. "And you get to do it on your first ride!"

"So, let's yell out our names for everybody starting from the front and going backward. My name is Smelly Garbage," yelled Wyatt.

"It is *not*!" said the same boy who spoke earlier. He was riding Sam behind Wyatt.

"You're right, it's Wyatt," said Wyatt. "Who are you?"

"James," the boy said.

"Do you like it shaken or stirred?" asked Wyatt in a British accent.

"Huh?"

"Never mind, and who's behind you, James?"

"I'm Mark, his cousin. I'm a year older than James."

"Wow, I thought your name was Clark Kent!" said Wyatt.

"You did not!"

"Well that's the name I saw on the signup. If you're not Clark Kent, who is?"

"I'm Elizabeth," a younger girl - obviously Mark's sister - said next in line on Pratt.'

"Elizabeth, is that man behind you Clark Kent?"

"No, silly, that's my Uncle Louie."

"That's Louis Clark Kent to you, girl," said Louis.

"He wishes," said the next in line, obviously his wife. "I'm Carol."

"Nice to meet you Lois, I mean Carol," said Wyatt smiling. "You must have gone out with Earl before if this is your fourth ride."

"We get him every time. Always gives us a good ride."

"Except his jokes stink!" laughed Louis.

"Yeah, well, he learned all of them from me, so you're in for more suffering, I'm afraid," said Wyatt.

"Yeah, I know about pain on these rides, that's why I have a pillow on my butt!" said Louis.

"Louis, stop talking about your butt," said Carol.

"Yeah, Dad, no one cares about your butt and your stupid pillow!" said Elizabeth.

"Yeah, well, you guys are going to be jealous when your butts hurt like hell in an hour."

"And that's Coolidge riding Rim Tank," continued Wyatt.

"Yeehaw!" yelled Coolidge.

"And last but not least, we have Jo bringing up the rear on our cleanest horse, White Devil. Hi Jo! You're a big fan of ducks, I hear?"

"Um, not really."

"Well, I guess I better not egg you an about that one anymore, you might drown me in the lake," said Wyatt.

"You're right," said Louis. "Your jokes aren't any better than Earl's."

The ride continued like that with Wyatt keeping the family in front entertained with nonsense as the horses resigned themselves to the longest trail in their repertoire. This was Coolidge's chance to hustle Jo.

"So, Jo," Coolidge asked, "Do you live at the cabin all year-round?"

"No, no one does on the lake that I am aware of," said Jo. "Well, maybe the Carters, but we don't know them very well."

"I see," said Coolidge. "Do you like it up here?" *Be nice to them.*

"Beats Wauwatosa," said Jo.

"I can imagine," said Coolidge. He knew Wauwatosa was on the south side of Milwaukee. He didn't know much about it except that there weren't any private schools there and people talked with a heavy accent. His school was on the North side near the Milwaukee Golf Club that had a strict dress code for the course and fancy houses on half-acre or more plots. Earl's home had five acres he heard him say one time when he was talking about his parents' place near the club and his dad's famous law practice.

"I've been to Wauwatosa once," he lied. "Good bratwurst!"

"Oh yeah, where'd you go for brats?"

"Um, I don't remember. It was a while ago." *Damn!*

"I'm sick of brats. My parents cook them all the time. Clements on the grill. They're good, but three nights a week? I guess my mom wants a break from cooking up here."

"What's your mom's name?"

"Nastia Petrova," said Jo.

"Nastia, is that Polish?" Coolidge knew there were a lot of Polish people on the south side of Milwaukee.

"No, come on! Russian."

"Oh, right," said Coolidge. "Sorry. Who else is up at the cabin with you?"

"My dad, Alexander, and my little brother, Demetri. I'm here to get away from him for a while."

Wyatt was singing a song he was making up about laundry mats for some reason. Coolidge gave the hustle conversation a rest. *She's talking about herself – that's good, I guess, but what's next?* Wyatt started a trot and that shook things up a bit, although not Jo's chest very much, he noticed. *Do I really like her?* After the trot, the line of horses moved through an open gate in the fence onto the one-lane road around the lake. The horses could smell the water now and quickened their pace. Wyatt would usually stop at the public beach to water the horses. So far no cottagers had complained about the occasional horse apples they left behind in the sand, but he would skip the stop if someone were swimming there.

The beach was empty, and the horses all found a place along the shoreline to splash their way a foot or two into the cool water. They pulled slack on the reins from their rider's hands to allow their heads to drop. They drank long and hard. Some, like White Devil, were silent drinkers, almost dainty in the careful way they pulled the water into their mouths, and others, like Rim Tank and Little Brother underneath Louis, drank with loud rhythmic sucking sounds like they owned the lake and wanted everyone to know it. It's a different feeling being on a horse over water, even water just a few inches deep. It feels like the water could get you wet very easily even though it is still a long way below you. Sometimes horses did like to roll in the water to cool off, though, so Wyatt had everyone pull up on the reins and get back into line just as soon as they were done drinking. Little Brother was reluctant to leave the water – he was one sure to roll if given the chance – but Louis gave him a good kick in the ribs to get him going, and Coolidge was glad he put him on Little Brother.

Coolidge thought it might be good to wait until Jo said something next, but she was silently listening to Wyatt's banter with the family ahead until they rounded a bay at the far end of the lake.

"That's my house," she said, pointing at a white cabin with blue trim. It had a feminine touch, but it was not much bigger than the cabin the peons slept in back at the stables. It had a small covered porch, though, and a shed attached lakeside.

"Nice place," said Coolidge. *Kinda small.*

As if on cue, the front door opened to the cabin and a small boy in shorts and a Green Bay Packer t-shirt peered out. "Mom! Here come the horses!" he shouted.

"That's my little brother," said Jo. A thin dark-haired woman in an apron appeared behind the boy and waved. They stepped onto the grass in the yard and a heavy-set man in a sleeveless t-shirt, presumably Alexander, Jo's father, then appeared in the blue doorway as the horses passed by.

"Hi Daddy!" said Jo. The man gave a wave and a huge smile. "You look good up there! They stuck you at the end, huh?"

"Yeah, Daddy. This is White Devil!"

"Well he looks like a nice horse," he said from the porch putting his arm around his wife.

"It's a girl, a mare, Daddy, not a he," said Jo. Looking back, Coolidge imagined he saw a loving eye roll on Alexander's face, but he wasn't sure.

"I see. Well, have a great ride. Call if you want us to pick you up."

"That's okay, I'll walk," said Jo over her shoulder.

"Daddy, did Jo say she's riding the devil?" asked the little boy as his parents went back inside. He stared at his sister and moved out closer to the road for a longer view as the ride disappeared around the bend.

"Well, did you ever imagine seeing us go by every day that you would one day be riding by your own place?" said Coolidge. *I've got to say something...*

"Uh, yes, that's why I walked over to the stables," said Jo.

"Yeah, I guess so," laughed Coolidge. *I suck at this.*

Coolidge couldn't think of what to say next, so he let Wyatt's joking around take over for a while.

"Did you hear the one about Ann Rose?" said Wyatt loud enough for most people on the lake to hear him. "She sat on a pin. Ann Rose. Get the point? Ann sure did!"

There was the sound of groaning from James, Mark, and Elizabeth.

"I don't want you to needle me about that," continued Wyatt.

Sounds of fake barfing from Louis.

"I love that joke, especially the way it threads itself together like that," pressed Wyatt.

"We take people out riding at all times of the day, you know," said Coolidge turning back to Jo. She was grimacing, but from pain or amusement, Coolidge wasn't sure.

"Oh, yeah?" she said, turning her attention to him. She looked pretty on the horse. *How old is she?*

"Yes, like after the campers go to bed we can take people out for rides in the moonlight. It's pretty cool." *Be nice...*

"Can you see where you are going okay?"

"Oh, sure. We do it all the time. Moonlight helps. White devil is the best for nighttime riding. She sees great and is easy to catch in the pasture."

"Oh."

"If you wanted to, I could take you for one, a midnight ride, that is..."

"That's pretty late..."

Was this a no?

"Yeah, well think about it, and come on over if you're game." *Is that how Earl would have said that?*

"Okay," she said shyly and looked back over her shoulder toward her cabin that had reappeared again through the trees across the water.

They were almost around the whole lake now and were reentering the camp property on the other side. Soon they would swing by the abandoned train cars and the back pasture before returning to the barn.

"If you didn't bring enough money to pay for the ride, don't worry," shouted Wyatt. "We got a train to rob coming up. You ready to rob a train, James? How about you, Mark? I know Elizabeth has robbed a few in her day, haven't you, Elizabeth?"

"We did this last time!" said James. Coolidge recognized his tone. It was similar to the tone of regular camp riders who called you out on your bullshit, but still deeply wanted you to bullshit again anyway. James loved cantering around the train cars and shooting his hand like it was a gun. In fact, Coolidge suspected this part was probably the main reason he and Mark talked the adults in their life into coming back so many times. When Coolidge noticed Louis really getting into it more than the kids, though, whooping it up and shouting bang-bang while Carol rode silently but gracefully in front of him smiling, he wondered if maybe it was the other way around.

"Horses! Horses!" shouted Wyatt after the robbery was over. He asked everyone to join him in the shouting as the ride neared the barn. This was more than just fun for the riders. The cry warned the horse boys back at the stables to be ready on deck for them. Once the ride was in the barnyard, it was very important to get the riders off the horses as soon as possible before the line broke up too much and horses headed off on their own to the water trough or to the barn door.

"So, Jo, how was your ride?" asked Coolidge, quickly tying up Rim Tank on the railing and helping her off White Devil.

"It was fun. I love White Devil!" said Jo.

"Good!" said Coolidge. *Now or never.* "So, what do you think? Want to come back tonight for another ride? We can both ride her again, maybe mess around on the rope swing in the barn."

"Uh, I don't know, Coolidge. Can I call you?"

"Yeah, sure," said Coolidge, but he felt this had gone off script somehow. *Do chicks call up Wyatt and Earl before coming over? I've heard them both talk to girls on the phone before, so maybe this is okay.* "I mean, great! I will look forward to your call. You know the number?"

"It's the one in the phone book, right?"

"Yes. Well, okay then..."

"Do you want my money?"

"No. The ride's free..."

"It was...?" Jo asked, surprised.

"No, I mean tonight's is free. Of course! I mean, yes. $7.50. Thanks..." Coolidge stood awkwardly as Jo gave him a scrunched up five-dollar bill from her pocket and counted out quarters for the rest. *Did she raid a piggy bank for this?*

"Thanks!" said Coolidge. He put the money in his own pocket and turned to help Wyatt secure the other horses. By the time everyone else had climbed down complaining of saddle sores (except for smug Louis) and Elizabeth and Carol had fed sun-heated carrots from the car to each of the horses, Jo had quietly disappeared down the road back to her cottage. *She's never going to call.*

She did, though, after the supper ride was over and Coolidge and Wyatt were cleaning the barn while Earl was taking the last tourist ride of the evening. There was a cute girl in the group, and Wyatt lost the coin toss.

"Coolidge, phone call for you!" screamed Cal from the granary.

"Go get 'em, Cool!" said Wyatt as Coolidge put down his push broom and jumped out of the barn door by the manure spreader.

"Hello," said Coolidge catching his breath and picking the black receiver off the floor of the granary where Cal had left it.

"Hi, Coolidge. This is Jo calling back," said the voice meekly.

"Oh, hi. I'm glad you did. How are you?"

"I'm fine, but I can't come over."

"Oh, okay."

"My dad doesn't want me to walk over there at night."

"Huh, well, I could come pick you up...?"

"You drive?"

"No, I mean on White Devil. I could come on White Devil, and we could ride from your place..."

"Just a minute." He heard her palm scrunch over the receiver and the sounds of a muted conversation with lots of pauses in the background.

"My dad says okay, but I have to be back by 11:00."

So much for spending the night in the hay. "Okay, then, see you when it gets dark."

White Devil wasn't happy to stay tied up on the yard railing after Wyatt brought the last ride in, and the peons released the other horses through the corral gate and carried the saddles and bridles into the tack room. Even with her saddle off, she tossed her head and neighed relentlessly for her herd running freely in the pasture and munching fresh hay in the mangers, until Coolidge quieted her down with a special quarter-bucket of oats. "You better oat that horse if you're going to work her extra tonight, Coolidge," was all Cal had to say earlier about his evening plans.

Wyatt and Earl were going to Benny's with Cal after dinner to torture Wings with bullshit, so the Impala was rumbling and waiting for everyone to grab clean clothes for the shower and a quick meal at camp. Wings had started to irrationally and disproportionally object to picking up the dice the boys accidentally dropped over the bar during enthusiastic games of Liar's Dice at Benny's, so Wyatt had loaded his pocket with little granite pebbles. The plan was to toss a few onto the concrete floor underneath the bar glass washing station when Wings wasn't looking, and then stare coolly under the dice cup as if nothing happened. With a few beers in them, and surely a lot of beers in Wings, the entertainment promised to be significant. "He'll get pissed and kick us out after two times," said Wyatt. "Nah, he's good for at least a dozen pebble tosses before he catches on and loses it completely," countered Earl. Coolidge thought White Devil looked lonely tied up to the railing as they drove into camp to eat and get clean.

High clouds outlined in silver whisked past the moon when Coolidge returned and swung himself onto White Devil's comfortably round back. Her sweat and hair would dirty his clean jeans quickly tonight, but that's the price one had to pay to go double bareback. At first the matronly horse planted her feet and refused to head toward the trail from the barn. It was pasture time, after all, and her pink eyes glistened with longing glances backward for the comforts of freedom, but several sharp jabs from Coolidge's boots persuaded her reluctantly to cooperate. He trotted her down the shortest trail to Jo's side of the lake. *This better be worth it. It's a lot like work.*

When they arrived, it was clear this was the evening's big event for the whole family, not just Jo. As he approached the tiny brightly lit cabin, he saw a small face quickly disappear behind the rustle of a white window curtain. Demitri. *What's he want?* The light from the front door then cut brightly across the lawn, and Jo stepped out wearing blue jeans, a t-shirt, and white sneakers.

"My dad wants you to come in," she said.

"Uh, okay," said Coolidge, sliding off the back of the horse. He wrapped the reins of the bridle securely around the trunk of a small birch tree, ran his fingers through his hair, and followed Jo into the cozy warmth of a tiny kitchen. There was a small table beyond, a couch, and a stand-alone rabbit-eared TV console blaring in black and white. The cabin smelled like the remains of dinner, sauerkraut, maybe, and definitely bratwursts. Jo's mother was at the kitchen sink washing dishes. She grabbed a dishtowel. Her father was getting up from the couch, and Coolidge noticed spying little eyes peering down at him from the loft. *What did I get myself into?*

"You must be Mrs. Petrova," Coolidge said extending his hand to the woman drying her hands.

"Yes, and you're Coolidge, I hear. I saw you today on the ride. Welcome, would you like something to eat?" she said warmly.

"Oh, no thank you. I don't think my horse would have the patience for that, but it does smell great!" *Is Jo going to help me out here?*

Alexander rose to his full sturdy height and extended his hand toward Coolidge. "Coolidge, good to meet you. I'm Alexander, Jo's father."

"Good to meet you, sir. Are the Packers on?" Coolidge asked.

"No, preseason doesn't start for a few weeks, unfortunately. About the best we can get up here are Jackie Gleason reruns and Walt Disney. So, I hear you have come to take my daughter on a date." He cleared his throat.

"Um, yes," said Coolidge. "It's just a ride," he said. He looked at Jo who looked at him and then at her dad, smiling.

"Well, I guess she only has one chance to say that her first date in life was someone who picked her up on a horse!" He laughed.

"A date!" her brother squealed from the loft, "Jo's going on a date!" Jo shot Demitri a deadly glance, but he started down the ladder instead of disappearing. Apparently he was brave enough now to get a closer look at his older sister's big date. *Get me out of here!*

"Well we're lucky it's a nice moonlit night and White Devil is a very gentle horse," said Coolidge noticing Jo's mother smiling kindly at him. *It's easy to be nice to her, at least.*

Must be pretty good to spend your vacation days all togeth-er in a little cabin with nothing to do but get bored, eat de-licious meals and swim in the lake. Easier than working fif-teen-hour days, that's for sure. The smell of the cabin remind-ed him of going on ski vacations in Colorado with his family when he was Jo's brother's age. He loved staying in the rustic ski lodge near Indianhead Mountain and eating grapefruit in the morning before hitting the slopes with his mother. His dad was usually off fly-fishing by himself, though. Perry pre-ferred trout streams to ski slopes. His mother fell a lot on the slopes, and sometimes couldn't handle the wind and cold.

He looked again at Jo's family, and another memory sud-denly cut through the tension and gave him pause. It was a few years ago, when his mother first came back from the Mayo Clinic with a diagnosis and a bottle of injectable vita-min B-12. He had to help her with that and with getting off the toilet, and one day she had finally managed to climb back on top of the covers of her bed for a rest. She was looking with a sad expression at the toe of her right foot. "Can you make it move, Mom?" he had asked. "No!" she cried with surprising and scary desperation. Thinking of his long endurance runs in the ravine he said, "Come on. You can move it, Mom! Honest. Work at it! You can do it, just concentrate real, real hard..."

"Okay, Jo, you can go," said her dad looking seriously at Coolidge. "But be sure you are back here at 11:00, or we'll have to send the posse after you!" He smiled to himself and sat back down on the couch.

Jo headed quietly for the door and Coolidge followed her out. "Thanks, enjoy your show..." Coolidge said, but Alexander was already ignoring him. The mom, still smiling, held the squirrelly brother back with one arm and gently closed the door behind them. Before they had even walked to the horse, he saw Demitri again peering out, the window curtains framing his face like the habit of a nun.

"You ready?" said Coolidge after untying White Devil and pulling the reins back over her head. "I'll get up first, then you use my foot as a stirrup to hop on behind me."

"Okay," said Jo gamely.

Coolidge swung on and scooted forward over White Devil's nearly nonexistent withers. *It's a good thing she's so round, or my nuts would be crushed.* He stuck out his left foot and reached for Jo's arm. She hopped up without a moment's hesitation. *Is she in a hurry to get away from her nosey brother? I sure am.* Her hands rested gently on his waist, and the tips of her sneakers poked the calves of his boots.

Coolidge decided to head for the trail in the woods near the train rather than risk a problem with cars or walkers on the road around the lake. He could feel the extra weight affecting White Devil's gait. She exhaled heavily but plodded ahead. For a moment Coolidge felt guilty for making her do this when she should be resting, especially when this "date" was probably heading nowhere. *Hell, I need some sleep too. I've been working since before dawn this morning. My head hurts, and my butt is really sore.* Well, he would give White Devil some extra oats again tonight and try to rest her for a couple of rides tomorrow when he was on duty with Lenny. It was Sunday, after all, a pretty light day, in the morning at least.

"So, do you guys have a boat?" asked Coolidge. *I've got to talk about something.* Jo's tits were either too small to reach his back, or she was holding herself away on purpose. *What a disaster.*

"Just a canoe. My dad likes to fish for perch, so we use it for that," said Jo.

"Perch are fun to fish for," said Coolidge. "They can fight like crazy."

"If they're big enough. Crappies are the best, though."

"Yeah, they're flat enough to tug hard on the line," agreed Coolidge. He thought about his grade school summers as a camper before his parent's financial decline. He remembered a canoe trip to the Boundary Waters where he caught a lot of Northern Pike. "Are there any northerns in this lake?" he asked.

"No, just bass. It's easier to catch the perch, though."

"Yeah, I hear you," said Coolidge. "Bass are tough." *I miss fishing.*

The air turned cooler when they entered the forest. Staying on the horse was tricky without a saddle, even more so in the darker forest where branches were harder to see in the shaded moonlight. A few steps in and White Devil walked too near a branch that shoved the riders off to the side, but Coolidge managed to grab the branch in time and pull them back upright. The action tightened Jo's grip and brought her closer to Coolidge's back, and she stayed there until they were out of the forest. *Hmm, maybe it's time for a trot.*

"You ready to trot around the train?" he asked.

"I guess so..." said Jo.

Coolidge gave White Devil a little kick. The trail around the train was devoid of obstacles so it was perfect for faster riding. Jo hung on tightly to Coolidge and both laughed at their struggle to stay balanced as White Devil rounded the train and slowed back down to a walk in front of the engine.

"That was challenging!" said Coolidge.

"Yeah, I'm glad we didn't fall off," laughed Jo.

"Want to get off and go into the boxcar?" asked Coolidge. Earl had told him that one time Wyatt had gotten a CIT in the boxcar while on a midnight ride.

"Oh, I think we better head back, don't you?" Jo replied.

"Yeah, okay," said Coolidge. *What a waste of time.* He turned White Devil around.

I'm beat.

"So, you say you are from Milwaukee?" Jo asked after a while.

"Yes," said Coolidge, but he wasn't sure he wanted her to know the specifics. Wyatt and Earl always said that the best part of being at the stables is that no one really knows who you are and where you come from.

"Where in Milwaukee?"

"Oh, north side mostly. I move around," Coolidge said.

"Where do you go to school?" Jo persisted.

"Harrison," Coolidge said. It was another lie. Harrison was the big public high school near his house. He didn't want her to know he went to a fancy private school on an academic scholarship because his dad was going bankrupt. Truth didn't really fit in with the night's game plan. *I guess it doesn't matter – I'm failing anyway.* Still, keeping his real self distant from what he was doing and saying seemed the correct and safest path. How could he talk to Lenny, Wyatt and Earl about how he bullshitted this chick on a midnight ride if he really just told her the truth? Wouldn't that be betraying the peon code? Besides, why would she even be interested in him if she did know the truth? *What do I have going for me, really? I suck compared to Earl and Wyatt.*

"Oh," said Jo. "Never heard of it."

"It's just a big public school, nothing special. I live for my summers," said Coolidge, thinking about Cal, but then he thought of the plays he was in at his real school in Milwaukee and how good he was at memorizing lines and standing up in front of an audience of his classmates and their parents. That theater life, and studying for three hours every night in the university library to avoid going home, seemed like a lost world to him now.

"Do you like to ride horses?" Jo asked quietly.

"It's all right, I guess. Beats working at a car wash, or a Kentucky Fried Chicken!" replied Coolidge.

"I wouldn't know. I've never had a job. My parents probably wouldn't let me. I'm just a freshman in high school, or I will be next year."

We're the same age. Better not tell her that. Cal had made it clear at the meetings that they all had to act like they were older than they actually were for PR reasons. *But I want to tell her. No. Not good bullshit.* A sudden sadness hit Coolidge hard. It turned quickly to frustration. The heat from the horse was making his crotch sweat, and the feel of Jo's chest on his back suddenly wasn't the turn-on he thought it would be.

White Devil really didn't want to head away from the direction of the barn again to go back to Jo's cabin, and Coolidge had to kick her hard to get her to move. It wasn't easy to do that and not kick Jo too. "Giddy-up, yah!" he said. No response.

"Why are you hurting her?" she asked, a little bit upset.

"It's okay. She just wants to go back to the barn. Once she gets going, it will be fine," Coolidge said really digging in with his boot heels until White Devil finally gave up her hope to go home and started walking again. Jo said nothing in response, but he noticed her scooting back away from him a bit and her grip lightening on his sides. *She doesn't understand horses at all. Does she even realize how much effort we're putting into this?*

Coolidge was out of bullshit and Jo had nothing to say either. A great horned owl hooted in the woods at them and a whippoorwill whooped its obnoxious and insistent cry when they finally reached the family cabin. The light was still on in the kitchen, but no one was looking out the curtains. *I hope that little shit of a brother's in bed.*

Jo slipped down off the horse. "Thanks. Don't get off. It's okay. And thank you, Devil," she said looking White Devil in the eye and giving her a kiss and a quick hug. She glanced at Coolidge briefly and walked to the door. There she stopped for a moment, and making a decision, turned with a little smile to wave goodbye, but the light from the kitchen only illuminated Coolidge's back as he trotted away.

Damn, this sweaty horse - I need another shower.

Bad PR

The next morning Wyatt and Earl woke up early enough to go to breakfast at camp. Coolidge was happy about that – he had expected to have to walk while they slept in on their day off, but instead they all climbed into the Impala. Earl unlatched the roof and ran the little motor that folded it into a space behind the back seat.

"I think Sarah will be up for a little quarry action today," said Earl, turning the key.

"Well, let's see what her friend is like first," said Wyatt, obviously not as enthusiastic about spending his day off with counselors, or maybe he was just still waking up.

"Right," said Earl, and the wind outside overtook the conversation.

Earl's driving speed always accelerated and then declined proportionally to the distance they were from camp center. Going toward camp, the first quarter mile was fair game for a full-throated demonstration of V-8 Chevy power, the next quarter mile was for fast skids in the sand and bump-jumping between the pine trees, and the final half mile was for combing hair and slowing down for a PR-respectable ten-mile an hour approach to the dining hall and other camp buildings. Today's thrilling ride was no different, and Earl backed the purring Impala gracefully into a small open parking space near the bathhouse.

It never mattered what was served for breakfast, the general survival strategy for the peons was to eat as much as possible in the short time allotted. Today the menu was pancakes and sausages, and the dining hall was nearly empty since many of the campers had left on Saturday. The next week's arrivals wouldn't show up until after lunch when Cal, fresh from sleeping in, would meet them, bullshit the parents, and sign up as many campers as he could for rides. "Let's go check her out," said Earl to Wyatt stepping out of the car.

Coolidge was happy to drift alone to a small table with a few stay-over campers who had light appetites and were easy to entertain with lies about the horses and other nonsensical drivel designed to make them think he was insane. *Should I stuff on pancakes or sausages?* The sausages won out for being deliciously greasy. "You eat like a horse, and you smell like one too!" a little camper said to him. Coolidge pretended to cry to make her laugh.

After breakfast, Coolidge found Wyatt and Earl outside hanging around the Philadelphia-style camp bell with counselors and kitchen staff who also had a rare day off. It looked like Sarah was interested in Earl's plan for a swim judging by her smiles and the way her, it turned out, very attractive friend in shorts and a swimming top was chatting it up with Wyatt.

"Well, Marie's only here for the day. She has to get back to Shorewood, but we were just going to hang out by the lake and get a tan, so sure!" said Sarah, obviously happy with Earl's attention. Coolidge flushed a bit seeing her and remembered how she looked in the shower room washing Cal's back.

"Okay, that's cool. We need to go get our stuff. Meet you back here in half an hour?" asked Wyatt.

"Sounds like a plan, Baby Cakes," said Sarah, letting go of Earl's arm. Marie smiled at Wyatt. She looked like she might be in college, or a high school senior.

"Hey Coolidge, bring the car around would you?" said Earl tossing Coolidge the keys.

"Uh...sure..." said Coolidge, surprised. He caught the keys on the second grab down by his knees. *He wants me to drive?* He walked back to the Impala. *I've got this. Turn the key, start the engine, drop the gearshift to D, step on the gas, steer.*

He opened Earl's door and climbed into the car seat. He was taller than Earl, so he could reach the pedals no problem. He gave the wheel a tentative turn back and forth and looked out over the big red hood to plan his route – *around the circle and stop on the driveway by the bell.* He could see Wyatt and Earl still laughing with the girls. Sarah had her arm hooked into Earl's again like she was about to promenade him at a hoedown or something. Coolidge looked back at the controls of the Impala and tried not to let his nervousness show. *The top is down. Campers are looking at me.*

The engine started on the first crank and Coolidge released the key and dropped the car into drive. Looking up he touched his foot to the gas. As expected the car shot forward. He steered it onto the dirt circle and headed clockwise toward the dining room. *Wow, I'm driving!* He put more pressure on the gas pedal to keep going. The car sped up.

Too fast! Coolidge managed to steer okay at first but completely forgot about using the brakes. The front end slid in the sand. "Crunch!" The bumper hit the tree by the kitchen hard, and Coolidge's chest hit the horn rim on the steering wheel. Braaaaaaa! *Shit! I crashed Earl's car. Everyone is looking at me. How do I get this horn to stop!*

Earl came running immediately. "Get in the back, now!" he said to Coolidge, jiggling with the steering wheel until the sound finally stopped. Coolidge climbed into the back. *I want to hide.*

"Sorry!" he said.

"Don't you know how to use brakes?" said Earl. "You can't go that fast around a curve!" He started the car and backed away from the tree. The bark was missing in the spot where the bumper had struck, but otherwise the tree was fine. The bumper was bent, though. Wyatt jumped in the passenger seat, and he and Earl waved and smiled at the gathering crowd of campers as if it were no big deal. They drove away slowly.

"Goddammit," said Wyatt. "That will be all over camp in about five minutes!"

"Definitely bad PR," said Earl. "We're going to need to tell Cal."

"Your foot slipped off the brake, if anyone asks," said Earl, passing the camp buildings now and accelerating back to the barn. Coolidge noticed Earl wasn't going as fast as usual this time. Coolidge felt terrible. *Did I ruin his car?*

"It looks like nothing worse than a bumper bend. The shop can straighten that out for almost nothing, Earl. Good thing you weren't going any faster, Coolidge," said Wyatt.

Cal had harsher words to say about the incident when they got back and woke him up.

"You did what?" Coolidge heard him yell at Earl inside the cabin while Wyatt examined the front of the car. The bumper looked more than a little bent to Coolidge. The sound of the horn was still ringing in his ear, and his collarbone was bruised from hitting the steering wheel. Coolidge was amazed at the damage to the car considering how slowly he was really going. *I'm glad I wasn't going as fast as Earl.*

"Wyatt, Coolidge, get your asses in here!" said Cal. *Cal's pissed. I've ruined their day off.* Just at that moment Coolidge heard Hank's Harley coming around the barn with Lenny on the back. *Oh, great, an audience.* Plus he had to work. He and Lenny would need to get the horses in soon for the morning rides. Maybe Lenny would get it going without him. *I'm going to owe him.* He stepped into the cabin behind Wyatt.

"This is a fuck-up, you two," started Cal. "Yes, you and Earl," he said to Wyatt. "No one drives anyone else's cars in there except the person who owns them. Son of a bitch! You also know better than to let Coolidge drive. He could have run a camper over! Now I've got to explain this to Father Able. What am I going to say, you are too lazy to drive your own cars?" Cal spat on the cabin floor without taking his eyes off of them.

"You're right, Cal. Sorry. I wasn't thinking," said Earl.

"Yeah, we were focused on some chicks. It was a fuck-up, for sure," said Wyatt.

"Turn around," he said to Earl who knew what was coming. Cal punched him hard in the right hamstring.

"Yeeow!" said Earl under his breath and did a little limping dance. He looked briefly at Coolidge.

Cal turned Wyatt around by the shoulders and punched him equally as hard in the same place. "You should have known better, Wyatt."

"Oomph," said Wyatt, also limping.

"Coolidge, flex your arm up," Cal said pulling his own fist up under his neck to show him. Coolidge did what he was told, and looking at Earl and Wyatt, took the punch in his triceps. *Oh my God!* It felt like he had been shot. The pain flashed up his arm through his shoulder and into his jaw. It stopped his breath cold.

"Now get out of here, you fucking peons, so I can wake up more peacefully," said Cal. "Tell Hank I will be out in a minute."

"Yep," said Earl grabbing his swimsuit and a towel from a nail quickly before leaving, Wyatt did the same and followed Coolidge out the door. "Maybe we'll see you at the quarry later..." said Wyatt to Cal as he closed the screen gently behind him. *Is he still limping?* Coolidge couldn't tell.

Outside, Coolidge looked around right away for Lenny, but he wasn't nearby. *Must be in the barn already.* Hank was leaning on his Harley rolling a cigarette with American Spirit tobacco. "Hey boys," he said.

"Hey Hank," said Earl.

"What's with the bumper?" said Hank. *Shit, he noticed. Is he going to punch me too?*

"Oh, Coolidge had a little confrontation with a white pine."

"Tsk, tsk," Hank said lighting up. "Coolidge, Lenny is taking a dump if you're looking for him."

"Okay, thanks," said Coolidge. He was glad he didn't ask him anything more about the car accident. He was feeling bad enough about it already, especially for getting Earl and Wyatt in trouble. All of a sudden he noticed burning in his throat, sausage coming up, so he walked past the cloud of smoke surrounding Hank to chug some cold water from the granary. He leaned on the side of the refrigerator rubbing his triceps. *I'm tired. Late night last night. My arm hurts. It's going to be another long day...*

True to form, the Sunday tourist rides were slow in the morning and then, fortunately for Coolidge and Lenny, remained slow in the afternoon, probably due to the hundred plus degree heat and stifling humidity. Everyone liked to stay near the water and go swimming on days like this. With just two peons working, the light load was an unexpected blessing. One would nap, answer the phone, and greet drop-in customers while the other rode what few riders showed up. Coolidge was able to give White Devil a pass on all the rides that day. Her white hair was still stuck to the inside seams of his pants from the night before. *What a waste of time.* She still had to stay tied up in the stall, but at least she was in the shade with plenty to eat.

Around two-thirty that afternoon while Lenny was taking his turn leading a ride for two newlyweds from Chicago traveling in a minivan around the Midwest on their honeymoon, a white VW convertible pulled in. A beautiful girl who looked to be about seventeen parked it crisply and hopped out, hair bouncing everywhere. Coolidge, trying to wake up from a nap as he went to greet her, could not believe his eyes. She was wearing the shortest pair of denim shorts he had ever seen and a flimsy white blouse tied loosely beneath her clearly visible and freely moving breasts.

"Can I help you?" swallowed Coolidge as he approached her. *This is the most beautiful chick I have ever seen.*

"Yeah, Lenny said he'd be here," the girl said looking around.

"Oh, he's out on a ride."

"Yeah, he told me last night he might be riding when I showed up. Said I could wait for him, maybe somewhere inside?" she asked looking up at the already blazing sun. "Maybe somewhere cool where I could lie down? We were up pretty late last night..."

"Uh, sure thing," said Coolidge. "You can wait in our cabin over there, I guess. Need something to drink?"

"Got a soda?" she asked, suddenly brightening.

"I think I could find an orange? That okay?"

"Sure thing, handsome," she said smiling. "I'm Lucinda."

"Coolidge."

"Oh, yeah, Lenny was telling me about you. You're the youngest, right?"

Coolidge led the way to the cabin, and opened the screen door for her. As she stepped into the shady cabin ahead of him, he smelled on her a mixture of perspiration and Sea and Ski suntan lotion. "Make yourself at home," he said, and went back outside to the granary for the orange soda. It belonged to Wyatt, but he didn't think he would mind considering the circumstances.

"Here you go," he said coming back into the cabin and handing it to her. She was sitting on the side of Cal's bed.

"Thanks," said Lucinda. Coolidge watched as she placed her full lips around the frosty bottle and took a slow but deep swig. "That's perfect. I hope you don't mind if I am here until he gets back? He said the rides don't last more than an hour?"

"I think he'll be here in twenty minutes," said Coolidge looking at the alarm clock on Cal's nightstand. He noticed Lucinda's nipples poking against her white blouse. "I was just taking a nap..."

"Oh, by all means, rest. Don't let me stop you," Lucinda said, smiling and taking another gulp of soda. She crossed her tanned legs under her on the bed. Coolidge climbed up on his bunk and looked down. *Gorgeous. How did Lenny pull this one off?*

"So," he said after a few minutes had gone by. She had finished the soda and was lying back on Cal's bed. Her lips were a little orange now and her hair spread out behind her on the army blanket. "How long have you known Lenny?"

"Oh, I met him the other night. We went riding."

"Yeah, he's a good rider."

"Well, I was horny and he was available," she said in a matter of fact tone.

What? Then her calm dissipated, and she seemed agitated all of a sudden.

"Oh," said Coolidge. *Lucinda, her name is Lucinda...*

She got up from the bed and moved over to the door to look out. The daylight outside illuminated her frowning face and the pink tips of her breasts were completely visible now through the thin white fabric. Coolidge's breathing slowed to nearly nothing, and he lost control of the muscles in his jaw. *She said she got horny with Lenny. Could I ask her to climb into this bed with me?* Every inch of Coolidge's skin could imagine exactly what that would feel like. He looked down at her. *I want her. She probably knows it, too.*

"You know, I don't really know why I am back here right now," she continued, speaking as much to herself as to Coolidge. "Men are all pigs, you know? All they ever want is to get in your pants." *Um...*

Coolidge had no idea what to say. He kept looking at her chest as she was looking out the door. Considering that she had described fairly accurately exactly what was on his mind at that moment, he didn't think it would be honest of him to disagree with her. Yet a deeper part of him really wanted for that not to be true. *She seems very smart and nice, actually, and she's here to see Lenny. That's cool. But she just wanted him because she was horny? Was what she was saying bullshit?*

The moment lingered. She stuck the soda bottle in her back pocket, which stretched the already too short fabric even more revealingly. Her frown was gone, but she looked sad now instead. Coolidge stared at her and said nothing.

"Horses, horses!" The shouting came from the trail signaling the ride was coming in a bit early. *Did Lenny come back sooner because he expected her?* Coolidge saw her smile when she heard his voice. *Wow, I guess I'm taking the next ride, for sure, unless she wants a horse ride too.* Lucinda was already outside walking toward the barn by the time he got his boots back on.

Consequences

Of course, Lenny got no work done the next hour while Coolidge took a ride of tourists around the lake. It was a group of boy scouts from a local Boy Scout camp, and they were all hotdogs. Coolidge decided to trot them for the first fifteen minutes – that way they couldn't complain that they "never got to go fast." Trotting was a relatively safe strategy for hotdogs, and the bouncing wore out their butts enough that they were content to meander mellowly about the trails in the cooler part of the pine forest for the rest of the ride.

When he returned, the VW was gone, and Lenny, smiling, looked like he had a reason finally to smoke a cigarette. He noticed hay in his blond hair, and it didn't take Sherlock Holmes to figure out where he had spent the last hour.

"Lucinda's nice," Coolidge said to him when the boy scouts had loaded themselves back into the jeeps and sped off with their uniformed and overweight leaders.

"Yeah, she's okay for an occasional tumble. Kind of a bitch, though, when it comes right down to it. Demanding," was all Lenny had to say to that. Coolidge thought of his date with Jo the night before compared to Lenny's success and the mature beauty of Lucinda's body. A wave of frustration and sadness hit him again, and his mind flashed on the accident with the Impala that morning. He remembered

248

with a shudder the blaring of the stuck horn. It was a nightmare sound, unstoppable. Everyone heard it. He never wanted to go back into the camp again. *Laughing stock. Was it his
fate to screw up everything?*

Remembering Lucinda's body, Coolidge was compelled
to make a few trips to the fly-infested Executive Palace that
hot afternoon, but the feeling of worthlessness and shame
only deepened whenever he succumbed to the urge.

Hank and Cal didn't return in time for dinner, so Lenny
and Coolidge had to walk the mile into camp to eat. They
left the horses saddled in the barn because there was a seven
o'clock ride and an eight o'clock signed up. The plan was for
Coolidge to take the last ride so Lenny could get the barn
clean and go back to Hillcrest before Coolidge returned, but
Hank and Cal had different plan.

"Lenny, keep Rim Tank back on the last two rides," said
Cal looking at the sign-up on the clipboard in the granary.
"He's your ride back to Hillcrest tonight. You're going to
need him there next week for the pack trips."

"I've got to ride him to Hillcrest tonight?" said Lenny
amazed. All the relaxed perkiness he had gained from the afternoon in the hay with Lucinda seemed to drain completely
out of him. It was at least a two-hour ordeal tacked onto the
end of a long day's work.

"Yeah, it's a great time to ride. Cooler air, moonlight.
You're going to love it, and we need that horse for next
week!" added Hank getting on his bike. "I'll have a beer for
you when you get there, Lenny. Later, Cal," he said kicking
the Harley to life.

"Later," said Cal, heading into the cabin.

"Shit, Coolidge, this sucks!" said Lenny kicking the barn door when Cal was out of earshot. "Sunday's are supposed to be easy days. This really blows."

"Yeah, that's a bitch," said Coolidge. He wasn't completely buying it, though. From what he figured, Lenny led half the rides he did every day and with fewer horses. *Hillcrest is a piece of cake compared to Crane. What's he complaining about? It's beautiful to ride at night on your own across the fields. No people to deal with.* "I'll take the last two rides for you, if that helps," he offered.

"Okay. Thanks, Cool, but let's get most of the damn barn cleaned now before the next ride gets here," said Lenny. Coolidge knew somehow that he would be doing most of the work on the barn considering all the cigarette breaks Lenny enjoyed, but he let it go. Lenny was the only one at the stables who was technically his equal, and Coolidge wanted to have a connection with someone as strong as Wyatt's was with Earl. There was so much bluster and bullshit with Lenny, though, about stuff he seemed to know more about than Coolidge did, the stuff of being older, high school stuff, girls, and even stuff about how to do the stables thing in a fun way. *I don't really like Lenny. Am I supposed to? Probably. Better try harder. Still, the cigarettes and his fake laughter...it's a life of lies. He's good at it, but it's bullshit.*

Together they put the horses needed for the next ride outside on the railing so they could start cleaning the stalls. Any horses that didn't go on the next ride would go back into one side of the barn only. That way they could get half the barn cleaned early. They worked quickly. They watered the horses one at a time, checked their saddles, and looped the reins over the railing posts near the trailhead. They left Rim Tank in the near barn with some extra oats and started cleaning the far stalls. To his surprise, Lenny worked quietly and efficiently, but Coolidge noticed him shake his blond curls every once in a while, and spit. *Probably going to miss another night with Lucinda, or does he even like her? He's lazy, I guess. Too many cigarettes?* Coolidge yawned and shoveled the day's manure into the spreader.

The last two rides of the night had been reserved by an organization for the deaf running week-long retreats for students from various high schools around the Milwaukee area. There were two hearing adults along for each ride, but they didn't know horses very well, so, unfortunately for Lenny, two peons were needed for each of the evening rides. Coolidge tried to shorten each one by giving extensive instructions that were translated by sign language to the deaf teens before he led the rides out, but still it was a long two hours for everyone. Even Rim Tank was needed as a lead horse for the last ride because many riders from the first ride signed with emphatic gestures that they wanted to go out again. The counselors were happy to pay the extra fee, but they had to draw straws – in this case literally pieces of straw – to decide who would go.

Watching the kids cheer or be disappointed, it surprised Coolidge a bit that the silent ride had been so enjoyed by the first group that so many of the deaf kids wanted to repeat the experience. He liked the rides too, actually. From the first moment on Rim Tank leading the special group, relief from not having to verbally entertain them allowed him to feel the whole experience in a different way. *I don't have to act crazy for these guys.* He appreciated the quiet sounds of the horses trailing after him and how it really felt to ride Rim Tank who, though broken now, was still figuring things out himself. He sensed Rim Tank's moods and questions intensely as he rode him. *Rim Tank's body is my body too right now.* He listened to the birds' evening chirps for once, and how the roar of cars and trucks on the highway faded interestingly as he led the ride deeper into the woods. *Wow, Rim Tank is so heavy he really does clomp, even in dirt.*

On the last bit of the last ride, he obeyed an impulse and led the group on a short trail he usually skipped that loops through an open field next to the outer pasture. As they came out of the woods a herd of fifteen or so white-tailed deer perked up nervously in the grass. Incredibly, they waited there staring at the horses until every rider could see them. When one of the deer finally decided to bolt, they all bounded away and leaped magnificently and effortlessly over the pasture fence. Their tails bobbed in the evening light like little surrender flags. *That was amazingly beautiful.* The riders oohed excitedly and turned and signed with each other about what they had just witnessed. Coolidge decided not to freak out about how they dangerously held the reins in their teeth to do so. He gave Rim Tank a little kick and led the riders carefully and gently back to the barn.

"That was an amazing ride. I'm so glad we came here. Thank you so much," the head of the group said smiling. She tipped Coolidge and Lenny twenty dollars, and the kids all signed their appreciation to the horses and to them before reluctantly climbing back into the vans. It was the biggest tip of the summer for Coolidge.

After the last horse was released into the pasture and Coolidge and Lenny had done fast work on the far stalls, it was dark outside. Only Rim Tank was left tied to the railing in the barnyard, and he wasn't happy about it. The moon, still nearly full, was low on the horizon over the granary. Lenny would have plenty of light to find the trail in Capp's field beyond the highway that leads to the road to Hillcrest. After seeing the deer on the last ride, Coolidge was envious of the beautiful adventure ahead of Lenny. *I would like to be out there alone tonight, no talking, moving as one with Rim Tank, finding my own way through fields and forests and listening to the frogs, cicadas, and owls.* Lenny was walking to the granary to get his jacket for the ride. "Hey Lenny," he said, but then he realized that Hank would probably not be willing to drive him back afterward. "Never mind." *Sleep is good too, I guess.* He gave Rim Tank a small bucket of oats and waited with him, feeling his loneliness and anxiety.

Even though it was dark and cool, Wyatt and Earl hadn't returned from their quarry date yet. *Must be getting Sarah and her friend somewhere in camp, or maybe they're all drinking at Benny's.* When Rim Tank was finished with his oats, he gave him a reassuring pat on the neck. *Do I love or hate this crazy-ass polka-dotted horse? He tried to kill me. Why am I so sorry to see him go away?* "Easy, boy," he said. Now that the oats were gone, Rim Tank just couldn't stay still. Coolidge knew why Rim Tank was agitated – everyone else was freely running about in the corral, and he was still in his saddle, tied up alone in the yard. Lenny exited the granary with a cigarette and an old wine jug full of cold water from the fridge. The screen door slammed behind him making Rim Tank jump a little bit. "It's okay, easy boy," said Coolidge.

"What were you trying to say to me, Coolidge?" Lenny asked, exhaling smoke and crushing the cigarette on the bottom on his boot before putting on his jacket.

"Nothing. Just that you might need a stick to get him started, but once he's away from the other horses, he should lead okay," he said to Lenny. *I should be doing this ride – I've ridden this horse a lot more than Lenny has.*

Lenny looked at Coolidge and took a long drink from the bottle. "I know that," he said, handing the empty jug back to Coolidge and climbing on. Rim Tank lurched toward the corral, and Lenny pulled back hard on the reins, stopping him abruptly. "Whoa there, asshole!" he said.

He's going to need a stick, unfortunately. Coolidge found him a stout one under the pine tree by the cabin. "Here you go, Lenny. Have a good ride."

"All right, thanks," he said, "See you later, Coolidge."

"Yeah, have a good one," said Coolidge. "Say hi to Lucinda for me."

Lenny pulled Rim Tank's head away from the corral and kicked him hard in the ribs. No go. "Use the stick," said Coolidge.

"Get moving, you worthless horse!" said Lenny. He struck him hard twice on the rear, and Rim Tank finally pranced around the barn toward the stable's entrance.

Seeing him go made Coolidge feel empty and exhausted. He waited until he heard Rim Tank's hooves clomp across the highway during a pause in the traffic. *He's gone.* He looked up at the moon and turned with a sigh to go into the cabin.

"Barn's clean and Lenny's on his way to Hillcrest," Coolidge said in the cabin as he handed Cal the money from the last ride, minus the tip in his back pocket. Cal was busy looking over the mail again, his ledger and checkbook open.

"Okay, I'm going for a shower in a few minutes, Coolidge, if you need a ride," he said without looking up. Coolidge noticed a light blue envelope from Sam on Cal's lap – another love letter for the collection Cal kept stacked neatly next to his bed. Coolidge missed Sam too. *She was nice. Will she come back at the end of the summer?*

"Yeah, that would be great. Thanks," said Coolidge, and he reached under the bunk into his duffel bag for a change of clothes.

The traffic noise from the highway was a constant, especially on a Sunday night when many weekenders headed back to the city. Coolidge had learned to tune it out so well that the tire screech, as long and drawn out as it was, never registered in his exhausted consciousness. Cal noticed it immediately, though. He looked up from his books. A moth fluttered around the light bulb near his head. "When's the resultant crash?" he asked with a laugh and a snort. The screech finally stopped. He looked back down not really caring that Coolidge didn't say anything.

What's he talking about? But Cal didn't seem to be expecting an answer, so Coolidge went back to rolling clean socks, underwear, a white work shirt and his last pair of clean jeans into his bath towel for the shower. *I hope Cal is ready soon. I could climb in bed right now if I weren't so filthy. And a breakfast ride tomorrow.* He lay back on the bottom bunk and waited with an arm draped across his eyes to block the light.

"I killed him! I killed him!" screamed the hysterical voice from somewhere near the barn. Both Cal and Coolidge bolted upright on their beds.

"I killed him! I killed him! I killed him!" It was Lenny's voice, now obviously headed for the cabin.

Cal instantly put on one of his boots, and pushed Coolidge aside to get to his other one. Just as he was tugging that boot on, Lenny tore open the screen door and cried out desperately, "I killed him! I'm sorry! Accident! Accident!" His sweaty face was scraped and full of dirt, and his shirt was torn partially off his shoulder. His legs didn't seem to get the message to stop running. He ran from one side of the cabin to the other.

"What the fuck happened, Lenny?" said Cal. He caught Lenny and looked him squarely in the face.

"There's been an accident! Come quick! Oh my God, I killed him!" Lenny said and twisted away to run back out the door.

"Stop!" yelled Cal tearing out of the cabin after him. "Go call the sheriff. Lenny! The sheriff. Call him. The number is by the phone! Tell them what happened and where we are. Go do that right now, Lenny. Call the sheriff. Tell him! Coolidge, let's go!" He grabbed a flashlight from the door of his Mustang and ran toward the barn.

Coolidge could see across the corral that there were lots of headlights stopped along the highway. Cal ducked under the railing and took the shortcut through the barn to the dirt driveway on the other side. Coolidge followed right on his heels.

At the highway, there was a man waving his hands to stop the traffic approaching from Fieldsburg. Already there was a long line-up of cars and trucks with drivers getting out to have a better look. Coming the other way, traffic was also stopped. Rim Tank was blocking that side of the road. He was on his back, thrashing and bleeding all over on the highway. His saddle was shoved down around his broken hind legs. Blood spewed like a fire hose from his nose, and his mouth heaved, the bit and bridle still firmly in place with the leather reins trailing. In front of him was glass everywhere and a blue Volkswagen van with its front end smashed in.

Cal ran immediately to the van. Coolidge followed him. "Keep everyone away from that horse, Coolidge!" Cal yelled. "Are you okay, sir?" he said through the broken windshield of the van.

"No, my legs are stuck!" a man's voice responded clearly. Coolidge saw that none of the gathering crowd dared to approach the writhing horse. Rim Tank had flipped to his side and was now trying to push himself up onto his front feet with his broken back legs. He rose and fell kicking himself forward away from the van and toward the far ditch. The blood pool was enormous. *Lenny is right – Rim Tank's dying for sure.* He looked back at the balding middle-aged man in the van. There was a lot of blood on his face where he had obviously hit the windshield. *Was he going to die too?*

"Does anybody have a crowbar, or a jack handle?" Cal yelled over his shoulder. He grabbed the door handle and forced it open. Coolidge smelled gas coming from the van.

"I do," somebody yelled.

Just then, Lenny ran up to Cal. "They're on their way." And as if on cue, sirens could be heard coming from town.

"No, no crowbar. Wait for the medics," the man in the van said to Cal. Cal looked down and saw that the man's knees were crushed between the seat and the metal dash of the van. "The gas tank's away from the engine, so there's no danger of fire, I don't think. Oh, God that hurts!"

"Okay, hang in there. We'll get you out. I hear them coming," said Cal.

Lenny got up into Cal's face. "I couldn't hold him on the trail. I tried. He was nuts. He bucked me off and bolted back to the corral! Oh my God, I killed him!" screamed Lenny.

"Lenny, shut up!" said Cal looking at the man in the van. Lenny stopped but turned to stare at Rim Tank. Rim Tank's body was now fully in the ditch, but somehow he had thrashed himself around so that his head was still on the road. Those spooky eyes had the same look in them Coolidge remembered from the breaking corral. *Fear is fear, no matter what its cause.* Someone in the crowd snapped a photo. *Oh, PR. The camps will find out. The stables is doomed.*

The man in the van looked at Cal and Coolidge. Blood was oozing from the cuts on his face. "I was passing that other car and the horse came out of nowhere," he said quietly but intensely. "Nothing I could do." *How can he even form a sentence when his legs are crushed like that?* Coolidge looked away and saw the flashing red lights coming up the shoulder toward them.

"Sir, are you the only one in the van?" the officer said approaching, flashlight in hand. He sniffed and shined the beam at Rim Tank in the ditch and the bloody glass on the road.

"Yes," the man said.

"Okay, the medics are right behind me. Any other cars involved?"

"I was passing somebody, but I think I'm the only one who hit the horse."

The officer walked through the pool of blood to the Rim Tank in the ditch. "Whose animal is this?"

Cal replied, "It's ours, sir. From the stables here."

"Well you might want to look at it, make a decision. It's in a lot of pain." Cal nodded and stood by the officer. *The blood smells metallic. Poor Rim Tank!* Lenny was sitting on the road with his head in his hands, pulling on his stringy hair.

The medics arrived and worked on the trapped man. They put a cuff on his arm and yanked on the van's metal firewall pressing against his knees. Other officers arrived and waved their arms. Radios squawked. A lane was cleared on the stable-side shoulder away from Rim Tank. Cars started up again and took turns going by. Everyone rolled down their window and had a good long look at the blood, the smashed van, and the still lurching horse. Heads shook.

As they worked on the driver, Cal and the first officer conferred with intense gestures away from the van. Then Cal turned to Lenny and said, "Lenny, get up. Go get a soda out of the fridge and stay in the granary. Officer Bunterman here is going to need a statement later. Go. Now! Coolidge, get over here."

Coolidge went to Cal and the officer. Cal pointed at the stables. "Coolidge, go with Lenny. In the cabin under my bed is my 30-06. Grab it and the box of ammo. Bring it to me. Now! The rifle. Don't forget the ammo! It's a blue box."

Coolidge ran with Lenny to the officer directing traffic and got his attention. "I killed him, Cool," Lenny said. The officer stopped the traffic and let them cross in front of the headlights.

"I know, Lenny, but it was not really your fault. Rim Tank just wasn't ready yet for that." He left Lenny in the driveway and tore back through the barn to the cabin. There was a lot of dust in the air.

"What's going on, Cool?" asked Wyatt, jumping out of the Impala. He followed Coolidge into the cabin. He and Earl must have just come back on the dirt road from camp. They looked clean and their hair was wet.

"Rim Tank got hit. Bad accident. Cal's out there, wants his gun," said Coolidge, breathless. Coolidge dove under the bed and grabbed Cal's rifle bag and the box of ammo. Winchester was printed across the leather. He ran back toward the driveway ahead of Wyatt and Earl. "Come on!" he yelled over his shoulder as he ducked under the railing and into Lenny again. Lenny was trying to light a cigarette in the barn. *Smoking? Now?*

"What happened to you, Lenny?" asked Wyatt stopping when he saw the blood and Lenny's shaking hand.

"I've got to go!" said Coolidge. Earl followed him.

When they made it back to the highway, Coolidge waved the rifle in the air, and the officer stopped the traffic again to let them through.

"Holy shit, this is bad," said Earl when he saw the accident scene. The crushed man was on a stretcher now heading to an ambulance. He was still talking. "My wife's number's in my wallet," he said calmly to the paramedics.

Coolidge ran up to Cal and handed him the Winchester and the box of ammo. Cal grabbed them and in a flash had the weapon out of its leather. He set the ammo box on the road and ripped it open, spilling it on the highway. He grabbed a handful of bullets, popped open the single action chamber and slid one home. Coolidge walked away from him and over to Rim Tank who was still heaving in the ditch. *Put him out of his misery.*

"Thank you, officer," Cal said. "Coolidge, get away. Get back over here," he shouted indicating behind the van with the tip of his rifle, but Coolidge kept looking at Rim Tank and didn't obey.

Cal moved next to Coolidge above Rim Tank in the ditch. "That's a direct-order," he said firmly looking over at the crowd.

Coolidge heard him clearly but didn't do what Cal said, or even look at him. *I am not taking orders from you anymore. That's it. This should never have happened. I am going to see this through my own way.*

Maybe it was the crowd witnessing this scene with horrified expressions on their faces, and the police lights glinting off broken glass, and the cartridges spilled emphatically on the asphalt that gave Coolidge the courage to stand there. In any case, the gruesome seriousness of that beautiful Wisconsin summer night turned horribly tragic was a part of him now. *Shoot me too, Cal, asshole. Am I in your way? Too bad. I'm seeing this through, now. I'm done with you.*

Coolidge looked at the people behind him, normal everyday folks who probably spent that weekend with family fishing on a beautiful lake. He needed to fully feel what the consequences of the misjudgments really would be for his summer family now, for Cal, for Lenny, and for the stables, and so he needed to witness utterly and completely, in all its gruesome details, the rawness of Rim Tank's final moments.

Perhaps it was the memory of the tragedy of his mother back home who would never again move on her own that rendered Coolidge unable to move at that moment. In the face of deeply knowing in his heart this beautiful animal's nature and the inevitability of its unnecessary death, could he ever trust anyone again but himself? *No. I don't know why, but I've got to be with Rim Tank now no matter how sad or scared I am or what might happen to me.*

Coolidge may not have known all the deep reasons for his need to stand strong at that moment, but he did know one thing for sure: *I am done with bullshit forever.*

"Coolidge, goddamn it. What is the matter with you? Get off this road!" yelled Cal, shoving him aside and releasing the safety.

Heedless of the rifle, Coolidge shoved Cal back hard and planted his boots firmly on the bloody tarmac. The crowd gasped. "My name is Michael," he spat at Cal. He turned again to look at Rim Tank still breathing in the ditch. *I love you, Rim Tank, and I'm so sorry.*

Michael Bentley stood on the highway with his hands on his hips, crying. He stared resolutely into his best friend's

desperate and watery eyes until the crack of Cal's rifle separated them forever.

Acknowledgments

First and foremost many thanks to Kate Mulligan, my spouse, finest editor and champion of children. Many thanks also to my friend, James Coley, for his inspiration, comments and unwavering encouragement. Thanks also to my sensitive and wise colleagues, Clay Blankenship and Kyla Sweet, for their support and invaluable feedback on my early drafts.

Reading Group Guide

Chapter One: Dumped Off

Under what circumstances does Michael arrive at the stables?

Does Perry have his best interests in mind? Why or why not?

Discuss Michael's first impression of Cal.

Chapter Two: Peon Punch

What is the historic attitude toward females at the stables?

How does Cal feel about working at the stables?

Why did Cal punch Michael? How did it make Michael feel?

Chapter Three: Going To Town

What does Coolidge like about his trip to town with Cal?

Is Cal trustworthy?

Chapter Four: Horseshit And Father Figures

Discuss Tim Reinke and Marvin as roll models for the boys at the stables. Good or bad?

Why do you think Marvin feels the need to use vulgar language around the horse boys? What is his level of respect for women?

How does Coolidge's relationship with Wyatt change after cleaning out the back of Marvin's truck?

How is the pecking order of the peons similar to the pecking order of the horses? Or is it?

Chapter Five: Bullshit And Fences

Discuss the fence-touching scene. Was it child abuse or a right of passage? Who had the power in that situation? Why didn't Coolidge just quit right then?

What does Coolidge learn about bullshitting in this chapter? How is it the same, or different from acting on a stage?

Discuss the attitude toward beer and underage drinking at the stables. Is that abusive behavior?

Chapter Six: Getting The Business

Discuss the legality of the stables' business structure and the old boy network. Why do you think it survived successfully for so many years?

Are horses too dangerous for teenagers to safely work with unsupervised? Why or why not?

Discuss the role of bullshitting and maintaining good PR at the stables.

Is punching as a punishment abusive in these circumstances? Why or why not? At what point is corporal punishment abuse?

Chapter Seven: Horses And Cliffs

Everyone works hard at the stables, and the work is technical and complicated. Is that why the older boys and bosses seem to love it so much? Or do they?

What did Coolidge like and dislike about the quarry and what he was forced to do there? Again, was this abuse, or a nudge toward growing up?

Chapter Eight: Splitting Up Is Hard To Do

Why did Wyatt and Earl go along with the "breaking in" of the first year peons' new boots? How does abuse help to perpetuate a dysfunctional social structure? Are the horse boys a gang of sorts?

Why didn't Coolidge go to an adult or the police to complain? Should he have?

What does Coolidge learn about Wyatt and Earl on the ride to Hillcrest? What is their attitude toward women?

The executive shower – a good experience for Coolidge? Or a bad one? What does he learn about Cal there?

Chapter Nine: The Meeting

Like almost everything at the stables, the meetings have a particular structure. Is it a good one for the organization, or a bad one? Explain.

What does Coolidge learn about himself and beer at the meeting?

What do we know now that they didn't know in the late sixties about teenage drinking and the brain?

Chapter Ten: Effort And Betrayal:

What does Coolidge figure out to do to be entertaining on his rides? Was it degrading for him, or a good acting experience?

Discuss the flies and the general filth of the physical environment at the stables.

Discuss the sex life of the horses in comparison to the sex life of the boys at the stables. Are they equally animalistic?

How is Little Brother like Cal?

Chapter Eleven: Getting Chicks And Other Objects

Discuss Coolidge's work ethic. Is he a good fit for the stables in this respect? Did it help him mature to work there?

The peons lie to the campers to entertain them. Was that okay in your opinion? Under what circumstances, if ever?

Discuss the dating habits of Earl and Wyatt. Could their attitudes toward women have been more respectful? How?

How did Wyatt and Earl influence Coolidge in his attitude towards women? Lenny?

Why do you think it was so hard for Coolidge to talk to anybody about his developing feelings as a sexual person?

Why did Lenny feel the need to exaggerate his accomplishments so much?

Chapter Twelve: Rodeo

The stables boys fit into the rowdy crowd at the rodeo no problem. Was it a healthy environment for them? Why or why not?

Is bullshit funny? If so, under what circumstances?

Are rodeos abusive of animals? Why or why not?

Pot laws were very strict back then. Why do you suppose the bosses and horse boys were willing to take the chance to smoke it upon occasion?

Chapter Thirteen: Midnight Construction

How does bullshitting get them out of trouble with the owner of the oak trees?

Again, why did Coolidge go along with everything when he knew stealing was wrong? Did he have a choice? If so, what could he have done?

Chapter Fourteen: The Corral

What do we learn about Cal in this chapter? About Earl and Wyatt?

How did Rim Tank change? Was it for the better? Why or why not?

Was getting kicked in the head a positive or negative experience for Coolidge? How about getting on Rim Tank after he was broken?

How are Coolidge and Rim Tank the same at the end of the chapter?

Chapter Fifteen: The Cabin On The Other Side Of The Lake

How does the summer vacation life of Jo's family compare to the one Coolidge was living? Was he jealous of them at all? If not, should he have been?

Why do you suppose Coolidge hated Jo's little brother so much?

How did the attitude toward women that he developed at the stables ruin his date? Why was he "unsuccessful"? Was he scared of Jo's intelligence and common sense?

Chapter Sixteen: Bad PR

Why did Earl ask Coolidge to fetch his car?

What effect did the crash have on Coolidge's self esteem?

Discuss Coolidge's conversation with Lucinda. Is she right about men when she says that all they want is sex? Why does she seem to like Lenny, do you think? Is he as indifferent to her as he pretends to be?

Chapter Seventeen: Consequences

What was the main cause of the accident? Was anyone to blame for it? Why or why not?

Coolidge's relationship with Rim Tank deepens and ends in this chapter. Why did Coolidge feel connected to Rim Tank?

Is Rim Tank a symbol? If so, what does he represent?

Why does Coolidge shove Cal and disobey his direct-order in order to stare into Rim Tank's eyes at the end of the book? Was this a good decision? Why or why not?

Is the ending hopeful or depressing? Explain.

About the Author

J.T. Blossom is a middle and high school English, humanities and art teacher who has spent his career helping young people discover their passions and be true to themselves despite ever increasing social pressures to the contrary. A lover of the great outdoors, Mr. Blossom is humbled by the power of nature and the enormity of the problem of environmental abuse. He holds a BA in English from Carleton College and a Master of Arts in Teaching from Colorado College. He lives in California and Hawaii where he uses a bike for transportation whenever possible.